Do You Think Your Mother Would Like Me

T. A. GRANT

Kingdom Glory Publishing

This is a work of fiction. Names, characters, organizations, places, events and incidents are either products of the author's imagination or are used fictitiously.

Printed in the United States

Published by: Kingdom Glory Publishing. You can contact by phone: 754.400.0704; or by email: tgrant@anovelescape.com; or on our website: anovelescape.com

ISBN-13: 978-0-9824343-4-5
ISBN-10: 0-9824343-4-0

Cover design by Trevauhn Grant, KGPublishing
Images used in the design of the cover are copyright of iStockphoto.com, Inc., Or its affiliates.

Amazon, the Amazon logo, are trademarks of Amazon.com, Inc., Or its affiliates.
Facebook, the Facebook logo, are trademarks of Facebook.com, Inc., Or its affiliates.
Twitter, the Twitter logo, are trademarks of Twitter.com, Inc., Or its affiliates.
Instagram, the Instagram logo, are trademarks of Instagram.com, Inc., Or its affiliates.

Dedication

To the woman who opened the doors of her heart to a complete stranger. To her vulnerability which inspired and floored me in the same breath. Thanks for leaving me speechless. I needed that wake up call.

Thank You

anovelescape.com

Sign up on my website for email updates on upcoming books, free short stories, and chapters from the editor's cutting room floor.

Also follow me on

Facebook.com/anovelescape

Twitter.com/tvauhn

Instagram.com/tvauhn

Do You Think Your Mother Would Like Me

Say Sorry

o n e

ALL AT ONCE, a haze of light, a throbbing pain, and confusion swirled in her head. The feeling of hot bile churned in her stomach attempting to erupt like a volcano. "Oh my head. Crap! Why is it so bright in here?" words were difficult at this time in the morning. "Left those damn things open." Rays of sunshine beamed through an unmasked window antagonizing the after-effects of one too many Vodka Red Bulls. Through the haze, came a sound. Something familiar that her liquor induced mind could not quite process. *Shine bright.....Shine bright....beautiful like diamonds in the sky.* If anything could wake her from the dead, it would be the sound of her iPhone's ring tone blasting a Rihanna track. Slowly the haze gave way and reality started to set in. Yeah, reality, with an entire host of upchuck attempting to trespass its threshold.

She slowly placed one palm against the bed, slightly lifting her head. She turned her face towards the direction of the vibrating melody attempting not to shift her body out of fear of eruption. One slight movement could turn the entire contents of last night into projectile, molten, wet and slimy vomit. "Oh man, I think I might have over did it just a little," she whispered to herself. Her Red Leather Gucci Soho bag was laying by her waist, which thankfully made it easy to reach in and pull out her life line. Without even looking to see who was calling, she clumsily swiped the screen and answered, "Hello."

"You need to come get Josh," the voice over the phone said, rather emphatically. "You need to come get Josh, he's gonna be late for school again."

"Ma," she replied. "Can't you just drop him for me? I had a late night at work."

"You know what, I am tired of always taking care of your crap. You're always having late nights and plus my car is in the shop. I gotta take the bus today. So you need to get your no good hide out the bed and take this boy to school. He's about to be late so hurry it up."

"Ok Ma," she muttered.

"Sylvia," her mother said and paused. "Sylvia," she said again and paused, her silence demanded acknowledgment. She only called her Sylvia when she was really upset. In every other mood, Sylvie was the name of choice. Sylvia still could not help but feel as if she was alway upset at her; always disappointed.

"Yes," Sylvia answered with a sigh, knowing that tone in her mom's voice all too well. Knowing some smart jab to the face was on its way.

"Please don't come over here dressed like a whore; god knows Josh don't need to see you like that, or whatever state you're in," and with that the phone went blank.

Mom always knew how to push her to the edge of loosing it. And even though Sylvia expected it, she'd always hoped it wouldn't come. The comments which were more than just words. She'd almost hoped that some supernatural maternal instinct would kick in and suddenly transform her loveless mother into just an inch better than what she was. But no, 31 years has been long enough for miracles. "Who the hell is she to judge anyways," toxic thoughts roamed through her head. *I so hate her sometimes.* Always acting like she knows me. The least she could do is make up for all the crap she put me through as a kid. Whatever, I don't need her handouts. Sylvia's anger brought back memories of a life long ago.

Sylvia was mom's mistake. She had Sylvia in her teenage years. Her high school sweet heart and Sylvia's dad got mom pregnant on prom night. When he found out she was pregnant, the phone calls stopped, mom's sweetheart turned sour and he ran off to college never looking back. Mom would always warn Sylvia about men who make huge promises. Sylvia always figured that her dad was the very reason for this. Maybe he was a big dreamer or maybe he knew mom was materialistic and used it to get into bed with her. "Don't you ever let a man get between your legs with promises of a big house in the Hamptons. You better work hard and make your own way," Mom would say. Back then, a gold necklace would have had Mom melting. A man could have bought her soul with diamond earrings. Imagine how bitter she became when the gold turned out to be gold plated and the diamond was a cubic zirconia. The last they heard of the dead beat, he was a car sales man in some undisclosed part of the country. He had a great job as an accountant, but then he got caught embezzling money. "Don't bite the hand of the one who feeds you," Mom would say. Another quote from her library of wise words to live by. Some of the stuff she would come up with seemed to have been birthed from the pain and bitterness of years gone by. "Never trust a man who blinks with one eye." Really, who comes up with this stuff. The wise words of mom, Sylvia was sure, came from some backwater superstition of her childhood in Colombia, add a dash of the Holy Catholic church and voila. How did Bernie, Mom's husband, put up with her all these years. He must have been some saint of a patient man or just simply as crazy as Mom. Well whatever he was, he was patient or crazy enough to marry her in the middle of all her ridiculousness.

Either way, Sylvia was a mistake and a failure and Mom saw her in no greater light. She was hard on Sylvia. Maybe Sylvia was an embodiment of Mom's younger self; an embodiment of her shattered dreams. Maybe Sylvia's life was a mirrored image of Mom's dreams and the vanity of it all; doey-eyed, naive, and desirous of sparkling things. Maybe if Sylvia had fallen for the big house on the hill top, Mom would have thought different of her. All it took were few snorts of coke, vodka, and a date rape drug and she was pregnant; mirroring Mom's own teenage pregnancy with Sylvia. The combination had her so doped up, the doctors had to juice her a few times with those electric paddles to bring her back. At least those guys felt bad enough to call the Paramedics once they saw her nose bleeding. And it was under these circumstances Josh came to be. Joshua Bradley, the miracle boy was conceived under a little less than ordinary circumstances. You could not make this stuff up if you tried. The fact that he survived pregnancy with Sylvia is a miracle all in itself.

She pushed against the soft sheets and left the phone where it laid. She slowly lifted her groggy and sopping body leaving a palm and body print in the memory foam. Her legs were not fully functional but she was able to somewhat stand. "Here we go," she said to herself, finally coming to terms with what she had to do. One step after the next finally got her to the restroom of her small one bedroom apartment. She slumped face first over the toilet and allowed the juices to flow. The porcelain had become her salvation from the tormentuous demon in her stomach. Once she felt as though she had sufficiently relieved herself, Sylvia made it over to the kitchen and took the opportunity to make some coffee. "This is definitely a black coffee morning. I need to get going." Her strength slowly returned as the sick feeling drained away. Her legs still quivered, from more than just side effects, but dancing five hours with small breaks here and there. After the third hour, her legs really hated her. At the end of the night, she could barely push the gas pedal without her legs shaking uncontrollably. "I'm really getting too old for this," she said to herself hoping her legs would work after only a few hours of sleep.

Sylvia made her way back to the bedroom and caught a glimpse of herself in a full body mirror, which was leaning adjacent to her closet. "Ow, I'm already starting to bruise," she said out loud scrunching her nose at the reddening palm print on her derriere. She ran her fingers through her tangled dark brown hair. The curls, which took her the better part of an hour to style, were all but gone leaving a tangled mess in the wake. Sylvia's hair was thick and reached down to her breasts. As she got ready for a shower, she could feel the huge hand sized welt on her left butt cheek beginning to get sore. "That jerk," she said under her breath. "Had to make him pay for it." He knew the rules. Many of them did: no slapping or groping or sticking or licking or biting or anything freaky unless your dancer agrees to it; and he chose not to obey them. Sylvia was doing that grinding thing she does, which usually drives them wild, but Gerald got a bit too excited and landed a hot one on her backside. "Now, Gerald," Sylvia was sure that was not his real name, but he said she should call him that. And who would give themselves a fake name like Gerald. Considering the circumstances a hot 5 feet 4 inches latina grinding her 41 inch butt on his minuscule rod, he should have been prompted to choose a much sexier name. Sebastian would have been a far better choice, Sylvia thought. But all the man could come up with was Gerry. I guess I can understand why he felt the need to slap me like that, she thought. He lacks originality and his prude of a wife probably doesn't allow for such behaviors. "You know you shouldn't have done that. If you want me to continue, you're going to have to show me that you're very sorry. Gerald say you're sorry," Sylvia had said holding out her hand expectantly. Gerry laughed and showered her with twenty dollar bills. Then Sylvia turned and poked her butt at him, "Gerry, say you're sorry." She reproved him with sass, turning an otherwise bad situation to her advantage. Sylvia was always good at that. Actually, Sylvia was quite exceptional, and as a result, turned bad situations into money opportunities. She looked over at the large Gucci bag laying on the bed to see the cash had already spilled out. There had to be at least two grand in there, she thought. The glee filled her chest, which made the rotten feeling in her stomach worth it. "Thank you Gerald," she said unable to stifle a broad grin.

The others girls said that he was a Mayor or something, which wasn't strange. The only people who came to these parties were men and women of high esteem. Those who were far too popular, who had to maintain an appearance of virtue in the public eye, secretly enjoyed all the pleasures Miami had to offer. Of course, it all took place in an environment where they knew their identity would remain unknown. There were even quiet rooms, where these people could go if they had to take a call from someone they didn't want knowing about the strippers. The traditional strip club would simply not do. Hence, Max Dinaro, the owner of the Royal Playhouse, threw these private parties for his high end clients. Clients, for whom money was no object.

Some twenty minutes later Sylvia pulls up at Mom's house in a shiny new Mercedes. She beeps the horn, jumped out and leans up against the side of her brand new luxury car. Late but always fashionable. Mom bolts out the front door, attempting to not be surprised, "took you long enough." She steps past Sylvia and heads for the bus stop.

"Ma," Sylvia calls after her. "Ma wait!"

Josh, not far behind, could see Sylvia attempting to catch up to the energetic 5 feet 4 inches, 44 year old woman, Latina spice.

"Ma wait," she repeated. Finally caught her by the hand, pulled her, and slowed her pace. "I'll just take you to work."

"Don't bother," Mom was playing hard to get as always when it came to Sylvia.

"Ma, c'mon, please just let me drop you to work. You don't need to take the bus. Don't you have to be at work by eight. You might as well come with me. You're gonna be late." Sylvia tugged, still holding fast to Mom's hand.

Mom stopped. Sylvia could see the disappointment in her eyes, the fact that the car looked brand new and was expensive disgusted her. "I don't want to ride in that thing." She pulled her arm quickly, freeing herself, and made her way across the street. This time Sylvia did not pursue her.

Standing at the side of the street Sylvia pleaded, not caring what any passerby might have thought, "why can't you just be happy for me, just this once?" A lump developed in her throat, making it difficult to get the words out, "Would it hurt you to just, to just…" Her words trailed off, not finding the courage to finish what she started.

"To just what?" Mom replied over the sound of the passing cars and the large city bus lumbering down the street. "To just what Sylvia? What did you have to do to get that car?" Mom started to speak again, but her words were drowned out by the bus grinding to a halt. Sylvia stood on the other side of that two lane street and watched Mom climb into the large city bus.

Josh, on the other hand, seemed very happy to see the car. That thing was a beauty. All black with red leather seats. She had changed the front grille to black which gave the car a mean Night Rider look. It was sitting idle in the driveway purring like a Persian kitten. The car took up a cool, calm, and collected posture, as it sat lazily in Mom's driveway. Sylvia saw Josh eying the car. She thought, *don't let's pretty exterior fool you.* Because under that hood was a monster cat waiting to be unleashed and Sylvia was in one of those moods. The car was much like her, pretty and ferocious.

Josh was still standing at the porch admiring the beast from a far when she called to him, "hey Josh let's go." The tone in her voice drew his attention away from the car and to her eyes. Her eyes were sunken from lack of sleep and sad as if she had been mourning for days. "Jump in, let's get to school." She pulled out of the drive way slowly and started down the street. "Why can't she just be happy for me. I've always wanted this car and now I finally have it and she had to just go and kill the entire experience. I can't stand her." Her level of anger was directly proportioned to the weight of lead in her foot. "I can't wait to just get out of here. I hate this place, this city," speed steadily increasing.

"Sylvia," Josh called out loud enough to break her train of thought and to remind her he was still sitting in the back seat. She realized the speed she was going, pressed the brake and quickly slowed the pace of the car. That car moved so effortlessly, it almost seemed out of place to drive it slow. Sylvia quickly looked through all her mirrors and breathed a sigh of relief that no cops had caught sight of her blazing down the busy street.

"You know I am still your mother right," she commented.

"Yeah, so?" Josh replied.

"Usually, good little boys call their mothers, mom or mommy or something like that."

"You'd be surprised, good little boys are hard to find," he had a smirk plastered across his face. Sylvia, through the rear view mirror, realized he was wearing a blue and grey jacket. It was embroidered with a basketball insignia. There was the word Trojan on the top arch, a replica of the Trojan warrior's helmet in the middle, and the word basketball on the bottom arch. She didn't know he played basketball and she felt guilty for not knowing such pertinent information. Sylvia obviously had not gone to any of his games, which might have actually been a big deal to him.

"Well you are my good little boy and I think you should call me mom," she insisted. Though after seeing the basketball jacket, she did not feel deserving of the title.

"Well Sylvie," he drawled, "if you get me to school on time then I might consider it," he looked down at his watch and it was already 7:35. "Oh well, too bad, it's already 5 minutes too late for that."

"Ok Mr Smarty Pants, we will continue this another time," they finally pulled into the school drop of area. "Have a great day today."

"Yeah," he slowly opened the door but felt a bit disappointed that no one was there to greet him at the drop off. There was no one to show off his mom's hot new ride to.

"Baby," Sylvia said, she paused for a moment and softy said, "I'll pick you up by four ok?"

"Don't bother, I'm going to Chad's after school and I can walk back to grandma from there," he replied. "Sylvie, I'm late, I really have to go." With that he stepped out of the car and ran into the building. The door closed behind him.

Teacher's Note

t w o

HE WALKED THROUGH the door and waited until it was shut before looking back. He peered through a shatter proof window, the wires that ran through them obscured his vision. He could still see the black Mercedes-Benz parked to the side. Sylvia was still sitting inside and for a full 30 seconds she did not move. Her head was against the steering wheel. He could not help but be a bit worried for her. And though he did not want to be near her, he pitied her tortured existence. Finally he saw her reach for her bag and pull out what looked like her cell phone. She placed it to her ear and with her other arm turned the steering wheel and drove off. Josh let out a big sigh, turned and headed off towards his first period class. On the way, he stopped by his locker, quickly put in his combination, flung the door open and shoved his school bag inside. He pulled out his English book, closed the locker door and sped off to class. The entrance to the class was towards the back of the room. If he was quiet enough, he could easily sneak in without the Ms. Anders noticing. His assigned seat was towards the back but all the way at the other end of the classroom. He peeked into the window and saw that the teacher's back was turned. So he slowly open the door and tried his best the tippy toe across the hard concrete floor. Just as he was halfway across the classroom, Brian noticed him, raised his hand and said, "Ms. Anders, I have a question." Josh's eyes brightened almost popping out of his head. He should not have be surprised that Brian would do something so brazen to give him away. Josh's surprise quickly turned to anger. He turned his face towards Brian and shot a fierce look. Ms. Anders, without turning her head said, "yes Brian what is it."

"Ahhh... actually never mind Ms. Anders, I believe I found the answer to my problem," he said sarcastically. By that time Josh had found his seat.

"So good of you to join us Mr. Bradley," she said again without turning her head. "I'm so glad you made it into class today, albeit a little late. But you know what they say, better late than never."

"I am very sorry Ms. Anders, my mom," he barely stumbled out the words before Ms. Anders cut him off.

"No worries Mr. Bradley, we will certainly speak about this incident and your mom after class," she said, without a trace of sarcasm. The comment made the class go "Oohhh."

Josh again looked over to Brian who was staring straight ahead with a stupid grin on his face. "What a jerk," Josh said under his breath.

The bell rang and he stayed seated as the other kids stood up and walked out of the classroom. Once they were all gone, he stepped towards Ms. Anders' desk. She was obviously very young. The rumor was she was about 23 years old and had recently broken up with her boyfriend. With thick flowing brown hair and cheek bones that made her look like a Victoria Secret model had lost her way and somehow ended up at this school; and those legs. It is probably not lawful for a teacher to be this hot. The boys in the class could not stop staring every time she wore a skirt. "Miss Anders, that was a great lesson today by the way. I thought the one last week Wednesday was truly enlightening but today's lesson beats them all," Josh said without a blink and in his most cheery voice. Miss Anders now moving back in her chair folded her arms and looked at him with an unimpressed smirk. Not a word nor sound came from her, but only a singular penetrating look. "And about this morning, I assure you that this small mishap will never happen again. I mean, I was only about 5 minutes late."

"As a matter of fact, you were 10 minutes late for the third time this month. Another tardy and it will have an unexcused absence.," Ms. Anders said in as stern a voice as a Victoria Secret model could manage. "I would like to meet your parents Mr Bradley," she said again. She reached into her desk drawer and pulled out a letter. "Please give this letter to your parents and we will have to setup a meeting for all of us to sit down and talk. Plus, I didn't get a chance to meet them at the parent teachers conference."

"That sounds really good Ms. Anders, but really, a note?" Josh said in a tone which suggested that she had gone way too far.

"What? I have to make it look realistic," Ms. Anders said, she got up from her chair and moved closer to Josh. The classroom was finally empty and they were alone. "I wouldn't want anyone thinking that I'm giving you preferential treatment, now would I?" Ms Anders said in a sarcastically implied tone. She grabbed his belt buckle and pulled him towards a supply closet. Her heels made her only a few inches short of Josh's six feet two inches basketball frame. "I missed you," she said softly and kissed him. Josh's hands studied her slender body, traveling down the low of her back. His arms where trained and strong. He knew what she would like. He grabbed her by the waist and lifted. The two figures, still attached by the lips, and her head bowed to meet his. But there came a sound, setting off alarms in their minds. He lowered her back to the ground. "Call me," she said softly. Josh was left speechless like many other times before. She liked the rush. The feeling of almost being caught, but he didn't.

"I would be more than happy to pass this note along to my mother. But see the thing is my mother can be a very busy woman," Josh said, speaking loudly and attempting to sound as mature and educated as he could. He peeked through cracks in the closet door, but the other students where still standing outside.

"Then what about your father," she replied. "Your girlfriend will be one lucky girl," she added in a whisper. Whenever she said that, it always left him confused. One thing was for certain, she did not consider herself his girlfriend.

"Well, I would have to send out a search party to locate that dead beat," he said so matter-of-fact that Ms Anders could not help but smile in amusement. "What are you talking about!" Josh replied in like whisper.

"Well, try your best Mr. Bradley. Please see what you can do in getting your mom to meet with me," Ms Anders said before sitting back in her chair.

"I'll try Ms. Anders," he reluctantly agreed. With that he smiled, picked up his English book and walked towards the exit of the classroom.

As he reached the door, he slowed his pace and looked back to find her brown eyes meeting his. He quickly looked ahead as though he was caught doing something he should not have done and stepped out the class.

"I'll try Ms. Anders," Brian standing outside the door said in a condescending voice. "I am very sorry Ms. Anders," he continued mocking him. "I love you Ms. Anders, I want to have your babies Ms. Anders."

"Dude, you're such a jerk. Really...why do you have to be such a jerk?" Josh said briefly looking at Brian before walking away.

"Oh please, you know you want to have her babies. She is by far the hottest teacher in this entire school, and she asked you to stay after class." The thought had entered Josh's mind many times throughout the class period, but it would be quickly dismissed, because what is the possibility anyway? That look, the time their eyes met. No, that was probably nothing.

"Yeah, all because you wanted to be a jerk and raise your hand just to get me in trouble. Now I have a note from the teacher to my mom." Brian took a few quick steps attempting to catch up to Josh's pace.

"Your mom is pretty hot too, what I wouldn't give to have your mom and Ms Anders," Brian replied, licking his lips.

"Seriously, you're sick. You need some serious help," Josh said shaking his head attempting to rid himself of the thoughts.

"Hey, I was just helping a brother out," Brian said raising an eyebrow and throwing one arm around Josh's shoulder.

"Yeah, that's what you said about Denise," Josh replied in a tone of disbelief.

"Well I can't help that she liked me better. I mean I am the cute one. Or at least that's what I've heard," he said with a self assured look on his face. Brian was cocky but it was not just talk. He did catch the eye of many of the girls in their class. He had the reputation of a big time flirt and he was equally disliked because of that. Irrespective, his short blonde hair and blue eyes would always make some other girl lose her speech mid-sentence.

"Please, someone send for the bomb squad, Bryan's head is about to explode," Josh said while rolling his eyes. "You're full it."

It did not help that as soon as they got to the lockers Britney and Ren were staring at him. "I'll be right back, my adoring fans await," he nudged Josh with his elbow before stepping over to the two girls.

Josh opened his locker and exchanged his English book for math. He opened his school bag and pulled out a calculator, some pencils, and his notebook before closing the locker again. As soon as the door to the locker closed, there were Brian's blue eyes staring right at him. "Rena wants you bad, and I mean really bad," Brian said with a bright look on his face. "Bro this is your time to shine." Josh turned the combination lock on his locker and walked away without a word. "Bro really?" Brian stood there with his palms open and arms out. "Oh come on, you can't seriously be going to class at a time like this."

"See you later Brian, I'm going to be late," Josh said as he walked towards his next class.

Rubber Ball

t h r e e

THE LUNCHROOM WAS noisy, loud, and bustling. There were kids everywhere picking up trays getting their food, sitting down, having loud conversations, laughing, and jeering. All this social interaction was far too tiring for him. Josh found a seat in the corner of the lunchroom to sit by himself. This was one of those days that he did not want to be bothered. Of course, not wanting to be bothered was like most days. The events from this morning with his mom picking him up and with Ms. Anders giving him a talk and with Brian being a jerk had already worn him out for the day. The troubles of mere mortals, he sometimes felt were far beneath him and he had no time to deal with these insignificant things. "Mexican pizza, I guess it's Thursday," he said to himself.

"Are you talking to yourself," Rena stood there in front of the table where Josh was seated. His eyes slowly crept up to meet hers. The freckles on her cheek gave her this unique type of beauty. She had light brunette

17

hair, which today was in a bun. She wore a green t-shirt with what seemed like a few pixels on it. Gamer girl possibly? No, undercover gamer girl. No matter, she looked good in her fitted jeans and high top sneakers. He hadn't realized how cute she was. She was a sophomore and he a junior so they had not shared many classes, but he had seen her around.

"Sometimes I need someone intelligent to talk to," he said with a somewhat serious look on his face.

"Well I have come to your rescue," she said without a hitch.

"Well please, have a seat kind lady. To what do I owe the pleasure of your company," again sounding as proper as he possibly could, not sure why, he wasn't talking to Ms. Anders. This was maybe a trend he did with girls he was attracted to or maybe he was just intimidated.

A smile adorned her face, "I was just in the neighborhood and I figured I'd stop by." That smile made Josh nervous. It was that smile that broke his defensive wall. There might be room for at least one more social interaction before implosion. "I am having a party on Saturday night and I wanted to extend a personal invitation. Can you make it?" Josh stared at her for a few seconds without saying a word. "Really, is our basketball star so busy he can't come out on a Saturday night. It's my birthday you have to come. I'm having a DJ and lots of food. You know what maybe this was a mistake, forget it Mr Bradley," her monologue was so quick that Josh barely had time to come up with proper responses. He wanted to flirt, but the words just wouldn't come.

"No, wait," he said with alarm. He could hear her breathe in. "Please don't go, I mean I want to go, but I don't know if my mom would allow it." Rena's attention turned back to him as she slowly released the breath she had been holding. It was a suitable lie to stop the downward spiral of this conversation.

"Well if you don't come on Saturday, you will have to make it up to me," she said quite sternly attempting to regain her composure. You could tell she was a little embarrassed but it was too late for that now. "And don't forget to bring a gift," she smiled, pulled a piece of paper from her pocket and quickly placed it on his lunch tray. "Here is your official invitation, it has my address and phone number on it. Let's just say it is the only one of its kind. So don't lose it," and with that she walked away.

"That was a bit awkward," Josh said to himself but he was still happy for it.

As luck would have it, Brian and Chad came prancing through the doors just in time to see her heading away from Josh's table. They looked at each other with stupid grins on their faces and hurried over to Josh. They threw themselves down in the chairs facing him and began the interrogation process, "Bro, what just happened? I want to know everything," Brian emphasized.

"Dude everything," Chad backed him up.

"It was nothing really," Josh said rather unimpressed.

"Are you kidding me," Brian replied.

"He's lying. Look at that face, he is lying," Chad said.

"Bro, I can't believe you would actually hold out on us. I thought we were friends. I thought we were best buds. After this I just don't know," Brian said in his regular sarcastic tone.

"We were never friends," Josh replied.

"Ouch," Brian said loudly.

"Come on bro, what's the big secret," Chad again reinforced.

"Since you have to know, she invited me to the party on Saturday and that's it," Josh said it with a sigh in his voice as though it was no big deal.

Chad's eyes wandered down to the lunch tray and saw the piece of paper. "Oh hello, what's this," with the sound of interest in his voice.

Josh remembered the piece of paper quickly grabbed it and pulled it from their sight, then slowly pushed it into his pocket. "It's nothing and if you would please excuse me I would like to finish my Mexican pizza," he said with an attitude.

Brian looked him in the face, "you're such a jerk."

"Look who's talking," Josh said. "I'm sure you received the same invitation."

"Anyways, are you still coming over after practice?" Chad questioned. All three of them played for their school's basketball team, of which Brian was their star player and captain. Josh and Chad knew never to utter his average points per game, lest a single number tip the scale and cause his already bulbous head to explode. "I just picked up Call of Duty Black Ops yesterday, and that freaking game is amazing. You have to check it out. It even came with a special edition controller. Of course I had to spend a little extra on that but it is totally worth it. So what will it be man are you coming over or what."

"I'll sure be there," Brian throwing in his two cents.

"At this point, anything I can do to keep me out that house," Josh replied. "Will your folks be home?"

"My dad is out of town and my mom will be working late, so no worries. We have the house all to ourselves," Chad said with a devious smile.

"Well then it is settled, gentlemen we will reconvene after school at Chad's place," Brian announced. "And may the games be ever in your favor." He always had some Hunger Games quote to finish off his conversations. The two looked at him with disbelief.

"You're such a nerd," Chad said and Josh nodded.

They pulled up to Chad's house in the drop-top Ford Mustang. Chad's brother, who was a freshman at the University of Miami, had just received this hot new ride as a graduation present. Chad was only a sophomore though so he still had a few more years before his parents would agree for him to have a car. Their home was beautiful. It had a large circular driveway with a small fountain in the middle. The driveway was nicely paved in terra-cotta stone. Once they got out the car there was a single walkway leading up to the door. The doors were by far one of the most beautiful things Josh had ever seen. Who would've thought anyone would actually spend money, real money on a set of double doors. They were tall probably 9 feet, with semi-opaque glass. This was not the first time Josh and Brian had been to Chad's house, but it amazed them every single time. The house was right on the inter-coastal and had a curb appeal among the best in that section of Coral Gables. Though the home was amazing it seemed like Chad's parents were never home to enjoy it. It was always Chad and his brother Mike. Once you walked through the grand doors you could see all the way through to the inter-coastal. Or at least to the less-than-modest boat that was docked out back. Chad's dad was a boating fanatic. One of the reasons he bought this house to begin with. From the foyer were stairways on either side leading to the second floor. Chad's brother went off to the left, while Chad led the boys to the right stairwell. There was a game room on the second floor, which had a loft style feel to it. There was a large brown leather sofa facing what must have been a 70' inch flat screen television.

"Holy…you've got to be kidding me," Brian said, eyes bright and mouth open.

"Guys you have to check this out," Chad said while picking up the remote and flipping on the TV. "My dad just got Playboy channel."

"Are you kidding, my mom would never allow my dad to get something like that," Brian said with excitement in his voice.

"Guys, really I'm not up for watching smut on TV," Josh said with a tired sigh.

"Are you kidding, I want to see," Brian said while turning his attention to the television.

Josh shook his head as naked figures started to emerge onto the television. "I can't believe this."

"You're acting like such a fag right now," Brian said in a mocking voice.

"Hey, you've got to check this out," Chad motioned towards a computer sitting to the left of the leathers chairs.

"Where's your kitchen, I want something to eat?" Josh questioned, wanting to escape what he knew was about to come.

"Dude, you're acting so gay right now. The kitchen is downstairs, come join the real men when you're done," Chad said. Josh paused and turned his attention to the TV, wanting to prove that he was no fag nor was he some squeamish kid who didn't know what sex looked like. Check this out, Chad led the boys to his bedroom and awoke his computer for its slumber. "There are some crazy stuff online, check this out. I usually just do a Google search," Chad continued with his demonstration. "Sexy, girls, whip," he said, speaking and pausing as he typed the words into the search engine. "Then I go as far down into the search as I can. And sometimes I'll come up with some crazy stuff. I'm sure half these things are illegal." Chad continued, skipping all the way to page 46 in the Google search engine. He pulled up a site with naked women in all sorts of insufferable positions. They were being tortured and whipped.

"Wow," Brian said, ecstatic at their find. "How did you know where to look for all this stuff?" Brian spoke like a child amazed at a brand new discovery.

"Ahh," Chad struggled to explain the origin of his knowledge. "Well," he paused again. "I caught my dad looking up this stuff. And it's pretty easy to track if you're not careful. I mean, all I had to do was check the history and cookies and that was it." It was obvious that he was embarrassed at the prospect that his father enjoyed porn. After all, Chad's parents had been married for some time now. It ludicrous to Josh that someone with a beautiful woman at his side would subject himself to the frustration of another woman on a screen. Why, when you have the real thing next to you and sleeping in your bed, Josh thought.

"Yeah, my dad's got a whole box full of crap under his bed. He's very proud of his collection. He has them all neatly stacked away. There's stuff in their from the 80's. Girl's back then clearly didn't believe in shaving. I saw some bush as big as the amazon." The boys laughed as

Brian attempted to act out what the Amazonian rain forest would look like growing from his crotch.

Chad went from site to site, not bothering to pause, but he skimmed and stopped only at images which he said looked interesting and what Josh thought to be gruesome.

Josh leaned away from the screen feeling disgusted, but just then caught something. "Guys," Josh said in a disbelieving tone. Chad was slowly scrolling through another site and Josh thought he saw a familiar face.

"What, you're going to run away now fag," Brian said but both boys laughed.

"Wait, scroll back up," Josh said in alarm.

"What?" Brian said.

"What is it?" Chad questioned. Both boys looked at Josh before looking back at the screen.

"Holy…," Brian was speechless.

"Is that your mom?" Chad questioned. "Well let's find out." Chad was about to click on the thumbnail leading to the video, but Josh reached over his shoulder and pressed Alt+F4 on the keyboard closing the entire window. "Hey, what are you doing. Don't you want to find out."

"No I don't," Josh said firmly.

"Well, hell I do," Brian said. "Pull it up again."

Josh pushed Brian to one side by the shoulder. Brian looked surprised. Josh had always been the calm level headed one of the group. "What the hell do you think you're doing," Josh's anger rose hot. His eyes were wild and mad, something no one had ever witnessed in him before. He turned shook his head, attempting to subdue the true nature of his feelings and he made his way down the stairs. "That's B.S. Why the hell would you want to see that again," he said. His anger was like a caged animal, clawing at the bars, wanting to get out. The shock of what he had just seen and the possibility of it swelled within him. He knew what his mother did for a living. He knew how she had come by that shiny new Mercedes and the vast amounts of cash she carried around in her purse, but did she go this far? Had she gone this deep; kinky sex on a low grade porn website? He did not want to believe, but Sylvia's track record did not leave much hope.

"Alright, alright fine we won't look," Brian said, his voice shaky from being pushed so suddenly.

"Alright, come back, I swear we won't look" Chad continued. Josh made his way into the kitchen opened the fridge and found a soda. Josh slammed the door to the refrigerator. His mind began to race, random thoughts rushing in and out of his head. It all seemed like a terrible coincidence. His mother kneeling naked on a bare concrete floor. Her hands and feet bound with a black rubber ball in her mouth. "I can't believe this," Josh said and slammed the soda down on the counter, denting the can. Brian and Chad walked into the kitchen.

"Hey, look bro, it's screwed up, don't even sweat it," Brian said. "No one has to know, alright."

"Yeah, this stays between us," Chad confirmed.

Plans

f o u r

"LADIES AND GENTLEMEN, may I have your attention please," the voice over the speaker was recognized by everyone, causing all the heads in the room to rise almost simultaneously. There were a few whispers behind where Marcus was seated. It was certainly a beautiful day. A day everyone was hoping would not be devastated by heartbreak and crying.

"What is he doing here?" one voice said, attempting not to bring too much attention to the fact that he was talking while the CEO, Bobby Royal was standing right there at the front of the room with a mic in his hand and a fake smile on his face. The 30 something year old was the fairly new CEO after his father was far too old to continue running Royal Financial.

"I don't know," another voice replied. "I hope no one else is getting axed." The anxiety level rose ten fold in only a matter of seconds. You could cut the tension in the room with a knife. Eyes widened as they saw him. Some started to sit up straight others shifted in their seats attempting to make it seem as though they were doing something important. It would seem that many of them stopped breathing for a few moments before catching their breath again. It was only a few weeks ago that the branch manager Mike Rolando got sacked. Nerves were to be expected, especially when Bobby was around sporting that ridiculously expensive suit. He did not seem like the cocky type, but he sure did like to dress well. He was definitely type A though. Totally anal which made him ruthless. The board of trustees and investors all agreed that he was fit to run the company. But no one hardly saw him, unless it was a big event like firing the branch manager. What Mike did, placed the entire company under heavy scrutiny by the government. The IRS started doing investigations and it did not take long before Mike was found funneling money into off shore accounts in addition to messing with interest rates.

"I've never seen him this many times in a month, hell in a year. What the heck is going on," a third voice whispered.

"Yeah what now?" the first voice questioned. "Was there someone else involved in the scandal."

"No need to be alarmed," he said with a smile and a drawl in his voice which left an uneasy feeling in everyone's gut. "I am simply here to announce some amazing news," emphasis on news. "One of your very own has shown exemplary performance during his time here at Royal Financial and has been selected as the new branch manager. So everyone please raise your glasses for Marcus Warren, our new branch manager." Marcus was already sitting at the front of the room. The anxiety in the room changed instantly to confusion. Marcus was one of the newest members to the team. Apart from Becky, Brandon, and Justin, who had left the company and returned, Marcus was only hired about eight months ago. How could he possibly be the new branch manager. There were murmurs swirling around in the room. "I know, I know, you guys are so excited to finally have a new branch manager, in only what, two weeks? And I want to personally thank you for your patience in this selection process. But we believe that Marcus has what it takes to run the Atlanta office of Royal financial. Well Marcus, is there anything you would like to say?" Bobby literally shoved the mic in his hand and took one step away.

"Well, ahh, thank you so much Mr. Royal for this amazing opportunity," he turned to Bobby gave him a slight nod then turned his attention back to the rest of the room. "It is indeed an honor to be branch manager here at Royal financial. I promise you that I will do my absolute best not to let anyone here down. I know that I've been here only a mere eight or nine months, but I believe this and my previous experience at other financial institutions has prepared me for this position." His voice started to rise, as he felt his wind coming. "And..."

"Well thank you Marcus for that arousing speech," Bobby stepped forward again and took the mic from this hand before he could even start the next sentence. "Everyone please put your hands together for your new branch manager Marcus Warren," there were more murmurs throughout the room mixed with a few people clapping. "Marcus will begin his new position in the coming month, as he will be going through training with us in New York to become more familiarized with his position." Bobby dropped to the microphone from his mouth and whispered, "and you better not screw this up." He placed the microphone to his mouth one more time, "thank you everyone, have a great rest of your day." And with that Bobby put the microphone back in its stand and walked out the room leaving him standing there looking into the wide eyes of his other coworkers.

"Well, I'm glad we got that out of the way," he awkwardly said while attempting to put a smile on his face. And with that he walked over to his desk sat down and continued working. The sheer shock and surprise of what just transpired left the room quiet for a few minutes. But the murmurs would not stop. What sounded like curiosity and surprise was becoming jealous anger.

"Who do you think he slept with to get that position?" Some of them weren't even trying to hide the the fact that they were talking badly behind his back. Hell he was still in the room, "this is pure bull. Who are they kidding." A female voice spoke, "this is so not fair to any of us."

It was not long before he got frustrated, picked up his things and left the office. As soon as he was outside the building, he picked up his phone and called his best friend. The other voice on the line answered, "did it work?"

"I suppose it did," his smile shining through the phone. "I don't think the other people in the office are too happy with me, but don't hate the player in the game."

"Yo, we have to celebrate. Tonight Uncle Louie's, we are going to drink our brains out," his friend insisted.

"Simon, you are one crazy piece of you know what. How did you know something like that would work," Marcus replied.

"Trust me, all those big shots have something to hide and we're just here to reap the benefits. Alright I'll see you tonight, I got some fine honeys at the crib who need some attention if you know what I mean," the phone went dead before Marcus could even say goodbye. He was right, Bobby did have something to hide. During the time he'd visited the Atlanta office, he'd consistently been having sex with the office manager. Marcus walked in on the two in the mail room one afternoon. Simon had advised Marcus to follow Bobby closely. Marcus finally found out where he had disappeared to and caught the whole thing on his iPhone's camera. Now it wouldn't have been so bad if he were single. But too bad for Bobby, because he is married with kids and is worth some 25 million dollars. And that was before his promotion to CEO some 9 months ago. So it was either give Marcus a promotion to Branch Manager or face a messy divorce. Thankfully, a messy divorce was not in Bobby's best interest. Their plan had worked and Marcus was on his way to a new tax bracket. It was time to celebrate.

Marcus wasted no time in calling his parents and letting them in on the amazing news. How he secured the position was not that important to their conversation, but he was excited to update them on the latest development in his world. His parents, especially his mother, were happy to hear that he'd got a promotion and he was slowly moving up. He was probably more happy to tell them than they were happy to hear it. They had hinted at him taking over the family business if this finance thing didn't work out, but producing and selling wine was far from what he wanted to do for the rest of his life.

"But baby you're a free spirit, you shouldn't be couped up in a lousy office," Martha, Marcus' mother said in her best attempt at dissuading him. They were the proud owners of Warren Vineyards, the producers of award-winning dry, semi sweet, and sparkling wines. The vineyard was the love child of his parents. And they sincerely wanted the business to stay in the family, something that Marcus had considered. But the whole idea of simply taking over from his parents did not appeal to him. He wanted to test himself. He wanted to see if he could really go out on his own and make something of himself. He supposed some of his thirst for adventure was a result of his sister.

She was determined to go her own route, never looking back. She was the wild child who was there when the Warrens were attempting to first get the vineyard going. Of course, like any other business, aka love child, they require time and attention. All the time spent with the business was time away from an attention hungry little girl. Emilia resented the vineyard for that reason. For her, it was the thing which stole her parents and consequently her childhood. Emilia was quite adamant about leaving the vineyard to never return. Mom and dad probably felt guilty and agreed to allow her to go to any school she wanted, which they had no problems paying for. Emilia moved to the city and attended UCLA and studied to become a veterinarian.

Uncle Louie's was one of those bars that had been around for over 20 years. It was a staple in the community and in that city. About seven years ago the owner died and his son took over. And from that moment the bar took on new life. It went from being your neighborhood hole in the wall, fantastic place to hang out to a upscale venue for all the bigwigs in town. Not really the type of place you want to be if you're trying to lay low for a while, but if you are trying to meet the right people, it was the perfect place.

Simon was already at Uncle Louie's when Marcus arrived. Simon probably saw him step out of the cab, because he met him at the door with two bottles of Corona Light in tow, "here you go Buddy. We're on our way up," Simon said with a huge smile on his face and swinging one of his huge muscle-bound arms around his neck. Marcus took the drink and they clinked their bottles together.

"Cheers!"

"Come on, I have two friends I'd like you to meet." There were two tall blonde girls standing at the bar staring in their direction. They were both in extreme high heels, short black dresses and they both had cocktails in their hands, "you know I like em in pairs." Simon nudged him in the side with his free hand.

It was only 7PM and the bar was bustling with local patrons. Young business men and women on their way from work stopped by to unwind from their busy day. The bar had the feel of an old Irish pub, modernized to fit the busy metropolitan. Lots of wood and bronze-colored metals. Wine glasses hung from the ceiling behind the bartender, flanked by floor to ceiling bottles of wine. All of which were back lit for effect. Marcus took in the scene and his attention drew to the television as breaking news flashed around the screen in catchy bold letters.

Marcus shook his head in sad disbelief. The missing girl was beautiful; she had long blonde hair, piercing blue eyes, and thin pink lips. Wouldn't be surprised if her stage name was Barbie because she could sure pass as one, Marcus thought.

"All right big Baller, I see how you roll," Marcus said enthusiastically as his attention returned to Simon and the ladies he entertained. He was so giddy from the excitement he could barely contain himself. Both men started to walk over to the ladies, but Simon dropped his head to whisper something in Marcus's ear.

"You know what bro, I've been thinking of a little getaway vacation celebration. I got this new investment property down on Miami Beach and I don't have a renter for it yet. I'm thinking we should go take a little trip to Miami and have ourselves a good old time. Now what do you say to that," he spoke with an air of confidence which bordered on arrogance. Any spectators, seated at any location in the bar could clearly tell that Simon was a little more into himself than the normal man should be. He made such big to-do about the simplest things. He was the type who would laugh for days about crazy talking bird videos on YouTube. Based on personality alone, no one would take him seriously. But Simon did have a knack for real estate and a truly special gift for negotiations. One could easily say that Beethoven was born to play the piano and write music. In the same way, Simon was born to sell and buy real estate. He always seemed to know a good property when he saw one. Something natural that could not have been taught. Some say he got lucky choosing the right properties during the market crash some years back. Of course, he attributed it to a gut feeling. Or it could be that he just hid his true knowledge and outsmarted them all.

"Man, you are crazy. Of course I'm down," Marcus laughed, ecstatic at the idea. Marcus paused for a second, "Next week Bobby is trying to get me to New York to do this ridiculous company training, so I can only stay for the weekend."

"Don't sweat it, we can leave tomorrow and party all weekend," Simon said again with an assured confidence in his voice.

"Alright let's do it," Marcus replied with little hesitation. Marcus always wondered how Simon is able to just pick up and go. When did he find time to work when he was always playing. Marcus could almost hear his friend say the words, life is easy when play is your work and work is your play, in that smug voice he used when attempting to sound intellectual. Simon and Marcus grew up together in Sonoma Valley, California. Their parents knew each other and were very close. And despite their varied personalities, Marcus the more quiet computer nerd and Simon the adventurer, they got along quite fine. Simon was an only child and Marcus, though he had a sister, was the only boy; it was safe to say they were like brothers and they felt as such. They helped each other in tough times, they fought each other, they got in trouble together, everything a good brother could be Simon was it. Marcus trusted the word of his brother over any girl and only dated the ones who had Simon's blessings. They did not attend the same University. Simon went to UCLA and Marcus at Georgia Tech University, but Simon moved to Atlanta after graduation. He'd visited Marcus and liked the city. Now Marcus was about to step into his new role as Branch Manager at an investment firm, while Simon was a Real Estate Broker and Investor at Keller Williams Realty.

The next morning Marcus felt rays of sun shine beaming through the window of their high rise apartment. Marcus awoke to a headache and a foot jabbing him in the side. He looked over to his right and saw the source of his discomfort who just happened to be the joy of his night. Was that Becky or Julie, who knows? His surroundings seemed familiar but not quite his, this was Simon's apartment. Nice, he really knows how to live, the thoughts ran through his mind. I'll be in Miami today. The sun, beaches, and beautiful ladies were a welcomed change before being dragged to New York for company training. And last night, what happened last night? He looked over to his left where there was a glass table with some white powder. Wild parties were a norm with Simon, a little blow was to be expected. The woman whose foot was firmly planted in his side began to stir. He tried to move quickly but the after-effects of last night's late night was like a ball and chain on his arms and legs. His movements stirred another feeling in the lower part of his stomach and nature could not be denied. So he rolled out of bed, made his way to his feet and as quickly as he could headed for the restroom.

"Is that you Marcus," Simon's voice echoed from the living room. It was now apparent that he was in the kitchen doing something. He was not known for his cooking, so breakfast was out of the question.

"Yeah," Marcus tiredly replied. His voice sounded like a creaky old door.

"Bro, come to the kitchen to get some coffee, we got to get going," Simon spoke as though absolutely nothing happened last night. This was sort of a normal routine for him, the way he started and ended every single day. Moments later he walked into the room and pulled the sheets off the naked woman laying there and firmly said, "wake up! Get your stuff and go. Come on, wake up. Get your stuff and leave now." Marcus quite stunned by the remarks peeked out from the bathroom into the face of the girl now sitting up. She was cute, more cute than he remembered. She looks young, more young than he remembered. He wondered, 21 years old maybe. Whatever the age was, she was far too young to be living this type of lifestyle. But nowadays what is too young? The girl hazily tried to gather her things. Marcus saw a few articles of clothing littered throughout the room and proceeded to help her get it together.

"Can I get you a glass of water," he asked.

"Yeah, that would be nice," the girl replied.

"All right stay here I'll be right back," Marcus stepped out of the room and went to the kitchen. The other girl that was with them last night was already at the kitchen table having a cup of coffee. Marcus grabbed two mugs, filled them with coffee and a bottle water from the refrigerator door. Simon was never out of bottled water. He quickly returned to the room with water and coffee. "I wasn't sure which one would be better. How are you feeling?"

"I'll be fine. I'll just go," she said with a sad made up smile.

"Please let me walk you downstairs and get you a cab," Marcus pleaded. Once she was finally dressed they went out the room together and about 10 minutes later he returned alone. By the time he was back in the room the other woman had already left, he probably missed her on the elevator.

"Alright bro, we've got a flight leaving out of ATL 2 PM. You better get home and get ready for this. This is going to be on another level," Simon said as soon as he walked through the door.

"Let's do it!"

Like Mother

f i v e

"MA," SYLVIA LOOKED sheepishly over to her passenger seat where she could see the gray starting to slowly litter her mother's hair. Her mother, Sophia Ramirez, was beautiful. But it would seem with every passing year, that beauty was fading a lot quicker than she had seen in women her age. She was a tough woman, able to take the world's burden on her shoulders. But even the strongest beasts of burden eventually get tired. Sophia was certainly tiring.

"Why did you come? I didn't even call you," Mom said in a tone which sounded more than a little displeased.

"Well if you didn't want me to come then why did you get in the car?" Sylvia rebutted.

"Don't you dare talk to me like that. I raised you all by myself, with no help from your worthless father. So don't you ever dare think I need your help," Mom said.

"Ma really? Why do we have to go through this every single time I see you," Sylvia said with anger bubbling inside.

"If my car wasn't in the shop, I wouldn't be sitting here right now.

"The fact is ma, your car is in the shop and because I came by, you don't have to walk nor take the bus home. Can't you just be grateful for that?"

"I'll be grateful when you don't come and pick me up in a slut mobile. You're putting that sweet boy of yours in, in, in…" her voice stuttered with anger.

"In what ma, in with what," Sylvia's voice climbed.

"You're a disgrace," Mom finished with a final blow. Sylvia rolled eyes, dismissing her mother's words. She knew her mother to be a bitter woman, but that did not stop her words from stinging. She placed the car in reverse and started pulling out of the parking lot of the Bank of America where Mom worked.

"Too bad I didn't have a mom to teach me how not to be a disgrace," Sylvia muttered under her breath, actually hoping her mother didn't hear it. There were already too many hurtful words. Under any other circumstance, if it were anyone else, Sylvia would not have stood for it. But her mother reminded her of Josh. Her little Josh, who at first she couldn't have cared less about; though she wanted to. Looking back now, she felt as though she did not have the capacity to love anything or anyone back then. She felt incapable of giving love and also unable to receive it. She had made so many mistakes and Josh bore the brunt of it. He was practically an orphan. Sylvia didn't even know who his father was. That truth held her tongue; instead she would take the lashes her Mom dished out. The truth held her still, because kicking this seething cesspool of bitterness, aka Sophia Ramirez, out of her car might actually endanger the safe haven she'd created for Josh. The reality was Sophia, mother of Sylvia Garnet, was more of a mother to Josh than she had been. She was always out doing her thing, making that money, financially supporting Josh, by fattening the pocket of this aging, greedy, insufferable woman. Sylvia's knuckles went white as her grip on the steering wheel tightened. She understood that Josh and Sophia, and everyone else had full right to hate her. After all she was a no good slut, a whore, a body for hire.

"Ma, I know you hate me and that's fine. So I'll figure out a way to take Josh full time," Sylvia calm resolve took over.

"I don't hate you," Sophia snapped back. Hate might have been too strong a word. After all, a good Catholic woman like Sophia doesn't hate. How dare she even consider Sophia, her mother, of all women, with such harsh discontent. "I just hate the demon in you."

"Mom, I haven't heard the words 'I love you' in God knows how long," Sylvia's voice pleaded. First time for everything she thought to herself. This was never a subject these two were prone to discuss.

"Oh stop, what difference does it make anyways," Mom again snapped. Her face was in a pout as she looked out the passenger side window.

"What do you mean what difference does it make? You're my mom. You are my mother, doesn't that mean anything?" Sylvia replied, voice cracking. The jumbled thoughts irritated her tear ducks, causing them to burn.

"What difference does it make when all you do is go and find love in some other man's bed," Sophia said in a softer voice. "I never intended for you to turn out this way. Even though your father left me, I had you all for myself. You were mine. You were always mine. Mine to protect and to keep safe. I prayed to God that you wouldn't fall into the same crap I fell into when I was your age. But you just ended up in worse," Sophia said then sighed. "He needs you Sylvia. That boy, Josh, really needs you. Not your money and not a new toy or video or computer. He needs his mother."

"I've been trying my best to provide for him," Sylvia's words felt inadequate. At this point, she was like a horse running on heart. No physical strength to go on, there was only pride. "He doesn't even want me around."

"He is your son, you're not allowed to give up on your son," Sophia said, the words catching in her throat. Sylvia noticed the profound revelation in Sophia's eyes. She had given up on Sylvia. The night she got the call from the Miami-Dade Police Department was probably one of the worst nights in Sophia's life. The MDPD had called and asked if she knew this 5 feet 2 inches female with black hair. Sophia knew her daughter to be the rebellious thrill seeker, much like she had been, so she expected this call. Sophia never imagined that Sylvia would have ended up in the hospital. At the time Sophia worked nights at Walmart so she would be able to drop Sylvia to school and pick her up. But Sylvia had gotten mixed up with the wrong crowd and was now failing high school. Sophia was so angry. Sophia worked so many hours to provide, thinking that Sylvia would be a good girl and do what she's supposed to. The call from the MDPD sent Sophia rushing to the hospital. Her heart was in her mouth as she saw her 15 year old girl, hooked up to tubes. The doctors told her that Sylvia's heart had stopped and they had to use a defibrillator multiple times to get it going again. Sophia thought that maybe this would be the wake up call

Sylvia needed. She thought this would get Sylvia on the straight and narrow. She had hoped and thought for certain that this was a sign from God for her daughter to be the good girl she was meant to be, but to her surprise, Sylvia was pregnant. Sylvia, the immature, fun seeking, back talking, angry, and rebellious child of hers was bringing another human being into the world. Another mouth to feed, Sophia had thought. Here comes another person to take care of. To make matters worse, Sylvia started hanging with the same crowd that got her into this mess to begin with and Sophia was left to pick up the pieces. But she was tired of picking up the pieces. She was tired of always being the old lady everyone took for granted. Tired of shouldering the burdens. And now she had allowed her spoiled rotten daughter to run over her and take advantage of her love. If she wanted to go wreck her life, Sophia would stand aside and let her. Sophia had given up and she knew that she was in no position to say otherwise. "He needs you, be there for him," Sophia said and again turned her head towards the window feeling the conviction of her own choices.

Family

s i x

THE LOCK TO the front door turned quickly with familiar hands. The door swung open and in came a healthy dose of pure Latina sass, attitude written across her face. She hung her purse on the prescribed hook, meant for exactly that purpose. She placed her shoes on the shoe rack, meant exactly for that purpose. She took to the kitchen, opened a drawer from the island and pulled out a box of cigarettes. Without a word she took off through the back door and into the backyard. Josh, sitting at the dining room table with his books out shot a look over to Bernie who was sitting in one of the two armchairs. "Oh boy, this looks like trouble," Bernie said with a small grin on his face. You did not have to be psychic to see that there was trouble in paradise. Bernie knew, the cigarettes meant that they are only witnessing the aftermath. Plus the door was still open. It was certainly not a common practice for her to leave the front door open or any door for that matter. The humidity of Miami was more than enough to turn a seasoned adventurer into a A/C loving hermit. So there would be no doors open lest you be assaulted by heat, sweat, and those pesky little flies. Plus Grandma would not have her cooling bill skyrocket because some undisciplined, ungrateful, good for nothing, man in her house left the door wide open. That woman might be short, but she sure knows how to fight. It was probably remembering this that Bernie got up and headed towards the door, "I got it." Josh chuckled a little. They knew without speaking to each other exactly what the other was thinking. He reached the door just in time to see Sylvia walking up the steps of the front porch. "Oh, hey Sylvia." She seemed a lot less in a hurry than Sophia who just barged through the door.

"Hey Bernie, good to see you," she replied with a smile, seeming genuinely happy to see him.

"So I take it you and the old lady had a little run in huh?" Bernie banged the nail right on the noggin. Sophia and Sylvia fighting was nothing out of the ordinary.

"Nothing a few cigarettes won't fix," Sylvia replied again, the smile slowly draining from her face. She casually stepped through the door as though all was well with the world. "Hey Josh," looking in Josh's direction.

"Sylvia…" Josh replied.

An obvious sigh escaped her nostrils and a shake of the head before she sat at the table where he was seated. "How was your day," attempting to make conversation.

"A standard day in the life of a budding high school kid," he quite bluntly replied.

"Meaning, buzz off mom I don't want to talk about it?" Sylvia said with a question in her voice. Hoping her response would break the ice and get her son talking.

"Meaning, buzz of Sylvia I don't want to talk about it; mainly because there is nothing to talk about," he assured her sarcastically. He really didn't want to talk to her. Hard to be a mother I do not need, he thought. The back door opened with authority. The pressure caused the air to shift drawing attention to the sassy attitude which came stepping in. All the heads in the room turned, as though a debutante had just made her fashionably late arrival.

"You're still here," Grandma said without batting an eye.

In order to keep herself from completely flying off the handle, Sylvia turned her attention back to Josh. "I guess she only had one cigarette," she joked. He smiled. He certainly tried not to smile. But it was funny; a little inside joke everyone had on Grandma. Everyone else in the room knew of Grandma's grumpy habits. Smoking was not something she did on a regular basis. It was simply something she picked up when she felt as if she lost control; which would usually be as a result of Sylvia. Grumpy is the sort of thing you would associate with old people, living alone, in a nursing home with no one to talk to. *But Sophia was far too young to be grumpy*, Josh thought. But what else could there be. *It's got to be menopause or something*, Josh tried to think of all the conditions a female might battle as they got older. Sophia couldn't be lonely, she had Bernie and Josh and if she ever got bored and wanted a good fight she had Sylvia. But you know what they say, it is not the age it is the mileage. She had been through a lot, or at least that is what Bernie said. For a while Josh didn't think any different, but lately he'd been thinking Sophia was just making excuses for herself. I had a tough past, so I'm totally allowed to blow up on whoever I want, be as grumpy as I want, and kick Sylvia around as many times as I want.

"Sophia, how was your day?" Bernie sitting from his arm chair attempted to break the tension in the room. "I picked up some food from La Granja." He angled his head in the direction of some already opened foam food cartons sitting on the kitchen island. Grandma didn't respond. She just stood there and looked at him with that diva-esque sass on her face. Bernie's face looked as if he suddenly remembered something, he sprung from his chair, darted over to the kitchen and started fumbling around with plates and the food. Sylvia looked at Josh attempting to hide a grin. Grandma took her seat in the other arm chair. She was finally at home; her sanctuary, where no one else mattered. All this commotion had totally distracted Josh from his homework. Plus, he had certainly not expected Sylvia to be at the house.

"I thought you were going to Chad's," Sylvia seemed to remember. *She probably wanted to chastise me for lying,* Josh thought. *So yes I did go to Chad and you know what I found out mom, that you're, you are. Josh didn't want to think of what his mom was.* He found it hard to admit. But was it the truth or had she changed? Maybe this new 'try hard' is her way of changing. Or maybe he wanted her to change and she'd been the same as before. He shook his head and looked down at his paper.

"I did go to Chad's, but I asked Bernie to come get me," Josh replied.

"Why, did something happen?" Sylvia asked. *There she goes, trying too hard again,* Josh thought. He really did not want to get into any discussion with his mom. Especially that his relatively good friends were trying to get him to watch hot steamy porn at their house and they accidentally stumbled across pictures of his mom naked with a rubber ball in her mouth. It did not seem like good dinning table discussion, especially with Grandma seated in her favorite chair attempting to calm down from something or someone who had upset her.

"No Sylvia and I'd rather not get into any further discussions about my day," Josh said in defiance. He felt indignant towards Sylvia. He was giving her what she gave him for so many years. It was exactly what she deserved. She neglected him. She chose her parties and clubs over him. She chose a lifestyle that didn't include him.

"Alright, alright," Sylvia replied; relentless in her pursuit. "Then you'll be happy to hear that you won't have to put up with your old lady this weekend. I have to work."

"No surprise," Josh spoke low, but he knew she heard it. He could see her eyes contort as though some annoying flying had flown right for them. He was actually very pleased. He'd hurt her and he wanted to hurt her. He wanted to hurt her like she had hurt him.

Sylvia let out a heavy sigh which seemed to have caught her by surprise, "You could at least act like you wanted to hang out with your own mother." *Not when I could be hanging with Rena*, Josh thought.

"Josh, what's this?" grandma said seated in her chair. Josh hoped that he would have been in his room when grandma found the teacher's note. He had placed it on the table next to her chair for her to find. Sylvia, walking into the house, had ruined his plans. She got up and walked over to the tabled and dropped the note on the table. Sylvia picked it up and started to read it under her breath:

To the parents of Joshua Bradley,

Your son has had a really great start to the school year. I can tell from the quality of work that he has turned in so far that he will do great. Unfortunately, his tardiness is becoming an issue. This morning makes his third day marked as tardy in my class, one more will be an unexcused absence. I would like to meet with both parents to see what can be done. I would hate for such a special young man to fall through the cracks over something like tardiness.

"It's all your fault," grandma spouted.

"Josh, I am so sorry," Sylvia said in response.

"Now I have to go and meet with his teacher, I don't have time for this," Grandma's anger renewed.

"Hey, you're as much to blame for this," Sylvia turned her attention to her mother.

"Guy's, why are you making a big deal over this?" Josh said, obviously distressed over the brewing battle between his grandmother and the woman who birthed him.

"Your mother refuses to take responsibility for what she'd done," Grandma replied.

"How have I not taken responsibility. Ma please, don't do this now. Let's just try to figure out this problem," Sylvia said, her voice getting louder.

"You know what, forget this," Josh said, slamming his books shut and quickly picking them up. "I'll go finish my homework in my room." Sylvia and grandma were still at it. They were too focused to realize that the center of the conversation had left. Josh heard Bernie's voice as he pulled grandma outside again for another cigarette.

"Josh," a voice came from the other side of Josh's room door. "Hey, I'll call her and straighten everything out okay." There was a pause which hoped for a response. "Josh, I'm sorry okay, about everything," her voice trailed off as she attempted to compose herself. He could hear Sylvia's footsteps, leaving the alcove where his room was located, into the living room, the front door opened, then closed. Josh opened his room door, peeping out, he could smell the odor of another cigarette and hear the amazing sound of that Mercedes Benz engine as it revved up and backed out of the drive way. He closed the door, returning to the dimly lit room where his books where on his computer desk. He looked at his books then fell in bed, finally relieved of some of the pressure. The books will have to wait, he thought. He picked up the remote and started to surf through the channels. Grandma had basic cable, so there was little chance of running into anything he shouldn't see. Not that it mattered, he had a computer in the room. And if all else failed, he had Chad and Brian who would make sure all innocence was siphoned out of him. Computers were something Grandma never really bothered with, except at work. Working on a computer for eight hours everyday, didn't sound so bad, but Grandma made it sound like a pain.

"Nothing on TV. I should have stayed at Chad's. Certainly better than here," Josh said out loud to himself. "Whatever," *no good mulling over regrets now,* he thought. He remembered the piece of paper Rena gave him which he still had in his school bag. He reached over to the side of his bed and picked up his bag, searching anxiously for the piece of paper. "Wait no, it's in my pocket," he reached into his pocket and pulled it out. "Stupid!" He placed the piece of paper on his night stand next to the land line phone and stared at it. He wondered if it would be right to call Rena when he and Elizabeth had this thing going on; thing or fling or whatever. Actually he didn't know what he and Elizabeth had. It certainly wasn't a relationship. Relationships, somewhere along the line, included love or at least open to the possibility; not just random hookups. Love was certainly not a possibility with Elizabeth, which she explained to him as a sort of terms of an agreement. If she allowed herself to love, it would make the whole thing sloppy: the sad goodbyes, the jealousy, the desire for more of each other, which includes but is not limited to: dating, marriage, and the like. Having a sloppy thing will only aid in getting caught, which would mean jail time for her. But the thing that he and Elizabeth had was just a thing, not love. It was a swirl of unidentifiable emotions culminating in sexual relations to simply quell the burning desires in each others bodies. In other words, the thing between them was purely physical. But it felt wrong to call Rena, because if he had to be honest with himself, there was still a thing between he and Elizabeth. He took a deep breath, because he knew what he'd have to do. The thing between he and Elizabeth would have to stop. I'll just have to see what happens with Rena first, he thought, shying away from making an immediate decision.

     "Come on, don't be a wimp, just do it," he said, picking up the phone. He placed the handset to his ear and realized his hand was shaking. "You're such a wimp. Just do it." He dialed the number without hesitation. The first time he fat fingered the buttons and ended up dialing the wrong number. The person who picked up the line did not make it any easier on his nerves.

     After asking for Rena, the husky voiced man over the line simply said,"wrong number and hung up the line."

"Girl you better not be screwing with me," he again said to himself out loud attempting to encourage his flailing heart. He dialed again, being careful this time to dial each number accurately.

"Hello," a sweet cute little voice answered.

"Hi, is Rena home," he replied.

"Rena," the voice screamed. "There is a boy on the phone." The cute little voice came back on the line, "are you Rena's boyfriend? What's your name?"

Finally Ren picked up the line and returned the scream with an equally loud bellow, "hang up the phone." The other line went dead and the two of them were alone. "Hi," she sighed exhausted from obviously having to run to get the phone before the other person, probably young sibling, grilled Josh like a thick piece of steak.

"Hey!" Josh replied.

"Sorry that was my little sister. She can be so annoying sometimes." She sighed again, "I was hoping you would call."

"Really?" Josh sounded a little surprised but caught himself. It was unfortunately too late to reign back the excitement that had already gone over the phone. Rena giggled as he attempted to solidify his voice again, "yeah, I was hoping it wasn't too early. I actually dialed the wrong number at first."

"Really," Rena said, Josh could hear her smiling through the phone.

"Yeah, now that was embarrassing," he said as he chuckled.

"So…are you coming to the party?"

"Well…," he replied, drawing out the word.

"Oh come on, don't tell me you're going to go through all this trouble just to call and tell me no," Rena said.

"Well...," Josh continued.

"Joshua Bradley, the boy with the two first names, you better come to my party or you can trash my phone number right now," she sternly demanded.

"Okay...," he said.

"Okay what?"

"Okay!" he exclaimed.

"Okay, you'll be there?"

"Okay, yes, I'll be there," he finally said, teasing her with anticipation.

"Joshua Bradley, don't be a jerk, okay. Just don't, I've known two many jerks," she sighed a sigh of relief. "Thank you."

"My pleasure," he replied. Their conversation went deep into the night. For hours they spoke about everything. Their favorite things to do on the weekends, their favorite color, what they want to do outside of high school, the teachers they liked and hated the most, they even spoke about their favorite ice cream. When they finally got around to speaking about their family, Rena's family sounded great. They did stuff together on the weekends. They played games and went fishing, they even watched movies together; something Josh had only experienced with his friends. They had spoken for hours, but Josh still felt very nervous when it was his turn to talk about his family. He did not want to lie to Rena so he took a chance and opened the doors to her. And she was warm. She did not say much in response, she simply listened and acknowledged his feelings. He liked her way more than he did before.

After the call had ended, he found himself smiling and chuckling to himself. He felt good. There is something there, he reassured himself.

There was something that could last a long time; greater than what he had with Elizabeth. Though he did not want to let go of Elizabeth and he wished there could be more between them, he felt that the end was near. Rena might just be the bringer of that end.

Miami

s e v e n

"**B**RO, THIS PLACE is amazing," Marcus stood by the east wall which was floor-to-ceiling glass. The condo felt airy, almost as if you were walking into a celestial palace high in the sky. There was a beautiful open concept to the floor plan. The marble floor was like a painters rendition of a white wood finish. Though the floors and walls had an off white color, the kitchen was rich, with dark woods, granite counters, and stainless steel appliances. This place felt brand new. From the east window Marcus could see all the cruise ships. He could see little figures roaming on the ground below. "What floor are we on again?" He shouted to Simon, who was roaming around in what looked like the master bedroom. The apartment had two large bedrooms with two and a half bathrooms. It did not seem as if anyone had lived in it. "Was there someone living here before," again he shouted but had no answer. "Where the hell is this guy?" Marcus looked over to his right but the door to the bedroom was closed. He peeped through the door and could see Simon pacing the floor with his cell phone glued to his right ear.

"Yeah get your boys to come through, only high rollers, it's going to be amazing," Simon sounded excited. Come through, what does that mean, Marcus questioned to himself. Simon turned on his heel and caught his long time friend staring right at him. Marcus excused himself from the room.

"This place is great isn't it," Simon's voice came up behind him.

"Yeah," he said catching his breath.

"Everything Okay?" Simon asked, .

"Yeah, I'm probably a bit taken aback by this ridiculous view," Marcus said, a little embarrassed trying to save face.

"Anyways, we got some business to do, people to meet before the party tonight," Simon said.

"I didn't realize you were planning a whole party, I just thought we were going to show up in Miami have some fun and leave. But it looks like…" before Marcus could finish Simon cut him off mid sentence.

"Come on bro, get with the program. You're my main man right now, I'm going to need your help with some numbers. I'll explain later. Right now we have a meeting, so let's get going." This whole party thing should not have been a surprise for Marcus, he knew Simon was very impulsive. The whole trip to Miami was very impulsive or so he thought. Was Simon planning a party all along? *But how did he know I would be free, I only became free yesterday afternoon,* Marcus contemplated.

"He's always in his head. Always lost in thought," he could hear his mother say.

His sister would always make fun, "Mom, Marcus is lost in translation again."

"Marcus," Simon said suddenly. "Are you sure you're ok?"

"Yeah, yeah, let's go," he said. Both men left the apartment and drove about 20 minutes from the waterway to what seemed like the middle of the city. Marcus had only been to Miami a few times and he had never truly explored it like Simon had. He always stayed in hotels by the beach, never truly venturing out. Marcus felt secure in the things he knew best. He hated feeling like a fish out of water. They arrived in front a building, "The Royal Playhouse? We're going to a strip club," with a sound of disbelieve in his voice.

"Alright my little horny toad, don't get too excited. We're here for business," Simon attempted to quell Marcus' excitement. Both men got out the car and Simon led the way to the side entrance of the building. He's definitely been here before, Marcus thought. They got to a back office area of the building. There were pictures on the walls of beautiful ladies all smiling. A large LED TV hung from the wall. It displayed a live image of what was happening on the main stage in the club. Apart from that, the walls were a dark purple which stifled whatever artificial light was in the office. Simon was greeted by a relatively short and stocky Spanish gentleman. He wore a blue paisley silk shirt with a pair of white slacks, which by the looks of it both were very expensive. The jewelry was entirely too much, Marcus thought. Nothing wrong with jewelry but too much of it is like a cake with too much icing. The huge dollar sign chain around his neck, gold watch and bracelets, and a few rings on his pinky and wedding finger made him look like a miniature Spanish Mr T from the A-Team.

"Hola mi amigo," the stocky gentleman said as he slinked over to Simon with hand extended. He gave a slight nod to Marcus, a gesture that set off a feeling of disgust in Marcus' gut.

"Dinero," Simon said, with a air of excitement. The same excitement one would have when greeting an old friend. "This is my good friend Marcus, Marcus this is Big Money Max Dinero," Marcus returned the nod attempting not to overdo it. "Dinero is the brains and brawn behind this fine establishment." There was something about him that Marcus knew would take some getting use to. Of course, Marcus was always quite agreeable, which made him liked by many, except for maybe those at his office. But he would have time to win their hearts, he hoped.

"Ha, Papi, don't lie, there is nothing fine about it," he said in a heavy Spanish accent.

"Dinero's got some of the finest ladies in the city working out of this club. That's how he makes the money. There are girls who travel on the weekends, from all over the state, just to come and work here. I don't know how he does it," Simon said, putting one arm around Max's shoulder. A smile, the size of an ocean liner, plastered Max's face. Of course, this is how Simon would begin all his business negotiations. He would simply get them drunk on praise and in their inebriated state he could siphon off them whatever he wanted. Marcus could not help but gawk in astonishment, knowing that he could never do what Simon does.

"Gentlemen, please come," Max led the way out to the main area of the club. There were a few very happy patrons getting lap dances. Towards the back of the club were stairs leading up to a balcony area which overlooked the entire club. Max led the way up the stairs past a velvet rope and into what was labeled as VIP Lounge. The area was much larger than it seemed from below. It was equipped with its own bar, though there were no bartenders at the time. There were a few booths with polls in the middle. There were other dining tables, in case you got hungry, Marcus assumed. Max signaled to one of the tables and all three men sat.

"Max, how is business, you look like you're doing just fine," Simon said. Marcus sat there like a fly on the wall, except he felt as though he was intruding on some private conversation he had no business being in. *You don't need to say a word,* he assured himself, as though something was putting pressure on him to speak.

"Everything is good, mi amigo. But you know me, all about my money," Max replied with a serious look on his face.

"Word has it you're trying to expand. Any chance you've looked at my neck of the woods?" Simon said.

"What you got up there in ATL," Max replied, his accent had Marcus questioning whether he spoke English or had he reverted to Spanish. And in case it was Spanish, when did Simon learn?

"Atlanta is an amazing city. It's quickly growing. Soon it will be the next Miami, L. A., or even New York. You know what that means? It is prime for expansion," Simon spoke in a quiet voice, almost as if he was letting Max in on some kind of top secret plan from the government.

"Yeah, but what does that mean for me. Amigo, I am good here in Miami. You can call me king of the dirty south," Max retorted in a friendly joking manner.

"It's time to take your kingdom to another level Max. The price is right. Real estate costs are lower than most other big cities. So there is no better time to buy than now. Plus, I would much rather call you Emperor Dinero." Simon replied. Marcus listened as Simon spoke. He sounded so confident and so relentless, how could anyone help but listen. I don't know if I can be that confident, Marcus thought to himself; eyes stuck on Simon almost in awe of what he was doing. "You want more money, well imagine another club in Atlanta making as much or even more than this one. There are a lot of young business men who can't wait to throw their money and show off to all their friends. Your profits could double."

"I know Miami, Simon, Atlanta, I'm not too sure about. If we're talking open land, I would have to build. Otherwise I would have to renovate some other building," Max said, eye brows furrowed. Marcus knew that even though Max was attempting to come up with new excuses as to why he should not do it, Simon had him thinking.

"I didn't say there wouldn't be work involved. There is even a healthy amount of risk, but the risky investments are often the ones that bring in the most money. Ask my boy Marcus over here," Simon gave Marcus a nod as he spoke.

"Well what do you have to show me. Don't tell me you're going to come in here with empty hands and nothing to show," Max replied. But it was obvious to even Marcus that Simon had him. That was easy, Marcus thought. Simon had his iPad in hand and with an entire slide show ready to wow Max's pants off.

"I'm having a small get together tonight, have your girls come through and see if they won't be more than satisfied," Simon's eyes narrowed. Max was no push over, but money was certainly his language.

"Everyone has a weakness," Simon's words from a conversation long ago echoed in Marcus' ear. Max's weakness was so obvious. He hung it around his neck for all the world to see, it just took the right person to exploit. Marcus until now did not realize that at the center of the dollar sign was the his alias: Max Dinero. *Wonder what his real name is*, Marcus thought to himself.

"Marcus," Simon said, snapping Marcus back to the world of the living. Simon looked at him with that look which said it was time to go. Apparently both men had discussed further business proposals, but Marcus' mind was long gone. Day dreaming was a particular skill he was quite good at, unlike negotiating or selling stuff. It was almost as if he was too honest to sell. Others could easily see his discomfort if he had to sell something he truly did not believe in. Not that the thing was bad, but if said thing had no worth to him, he could not bring himself to offer it to others. All three men made their way back down the stairs, this time heading for what seemed like the front doors. Simon walked next to Max as they approached the entrance. "So Max, be sure to take a look at the buildings I sent to your email. Each one is located in an area where you're sure to be noticed, yet discreet enough for your guests. Max this is a great opportunity; I'm really looking forward to doing business with you." They got to the door, Simon and Marcus gave Max a firm hand shake. Marcus went for the door but was surprised as someone pulled it open from the outside.

"I hope you have a great time Mikey, I'll see you again soon," a woman said bidding farewell to the bouncer standing outside the door. The woman came bursting through the door and was halted by Marcus' statuesque figure. "Oh my god, you scared me," she said placing a hand over her mouth in surprise. She had beautiful dark brown hair and a smile that could melt the heart of the most hardened of men. Marcus stared at her transfixed and for some reason could not break his gaze. "Excuse me," she said staring back at him. She side stepped Marcus and made eye contact with Simon. She continued through the building.

"Hey, hey, earth to Marcus. Earth to Marcus," Simon said waving his hand in front of Marcus' face.

"Wow," Marcus said, the hypnotism finally lifting.

"I wasn't kidding when I said Max has the best women," Simon said, Marcus agreed with a nod. When they had both made it back to the car, Simon turned to Marcus and said, "Hey, I have something important to ask you." Simon paused, waiting for Marcus' acknowledgment.

"Yeah, what is it," Marcus replied.

"I ran into Max a few years back while in college. I attended a networking event he threw. He had friends who were looking for both residential and commercial real estate in California so we kept in contact. He has more than once referred clients which had amazing turnaround and that kick-started my career. Not once has he ever asked for anything in return. He's brought to me a small problem which I believe you'd be able to help with. See the thing is, he has these side businesses, which at first weren't really pulling in that much cash, but they're now exploding. The problem is, he's having some problems making that cash disappear, if you know what I mean," Simon's words faltered as he tried to explain his plight. Marcus looked at him, skepticism written all over his face. He knew that whoever was trying to make money disappear was most likely doing something illegal or just trying to evade paying taxes or both.

"Simon," Marcus said, but he was interrupted by his friend.

"Hey, I know what you're going to say and I know what I'm asking you to do, but I owe this guy my success and I hate to say it, but you kinda owe me too. Anyways, just think about it. Don't answer now, but I would really like to find a few solutions for this guy," Simon said and smiled. "Well, mi amigo, are you ready to have some fun?"

"Yes sir, let's do it," Marcus replied trying to sound cheery, but he wondered what his friend was attempting to get him into. What kind of business was Max running that he didn't want the government to know about? Marcus started to suspect that there was a different reason for Simon inviting him to Miami.

Surprise

e i g h t

"HEY MIKEY," SYLVIA approached the front doors to the Royal Playhouse Gentleman's Club and saw her number one favorite bouncer. He was dressed in the same full black outfit bouncers tend to wear. Black was often used to camouflage unsightly curves, but there was certainly nowhere for Mikey to cover up those guns. His curves were huge but seeing them made Sylvia feel safe. His presence gave her a confidence boost. Plus, he was always nice to her. He never made her feel less than a woman, even though he had seen her, more than once, in her birthday suit. He was married of course, but Sylvia knew for certain that marriage did not stop men from looking and from wanting. If ever there was an exception though, it was Mikey.

"Hey Syl," Mikey said and threw his large arms around her. His great mass swallowed her whole. Sylvia was certainly not a petite woman, but next to Mikey she might as well be a child. "Hey, so I'm going on a little vacation."

"Vacation?" Sylvia replied in a inquisitive tone. "In all the years I've known you Mikey, I don't think I've ever heard you say you're going on vacation. Is everything alright? Are you feeling ok?" she said sarcastically.

"Sylvia, I've taken vacations before," Mikey said attempting to quell the notion of his undying devotion to the Royal Playhouse.

"Yeah, okay. Well, when you live in Florida going to Disney for two days doesn't count. So where are you going and how long is this vacation of yours," Sylvia said in a tone that expected his answer to be two days at Busch Gardens, another one of Florida's theme parks.

"Brenda had always wanted to go Dubai, so we're finally going," Mikey said.

"OMG," Sylvia said excitedly, emphasizing each letter. "That sounds amazing," Sylvia felt herself get warm. She had heard about the man made islands and had seen stunning pictures of seven star hotels and snow in the desert.

"Yeah, we'll be gone for a few weeks and we'll eventually make our way over to Puerto Rico to see Brenda's parents. We'll be there for a while, I think," Mikey smiled as he spoke.

"Good for you Mikey, you really deserve it," Sylvia said. "I'll miss you while you're gone." The words escaped her mouth before she truly realized that she would really miss him. She shuttered at the thought of knowing Mikey would not be around to protect her. To keep her safe. She felt so secure in his presence that she could totally unveil herself without the least bit of apprehension or fears of being judged by him. They hugged again. Sylvia attempted to ingrain the memory of him and the strength and confidence he'd given her and hoped that it would last when he was gone. "I hope you have a great time Mikey, I'll see you again soon," Sylvia reached for her phone, pulled the door and while looking down was startled to see a pair of white sneakers just beyond the threshold. Her heart leaped, wanting to escape through her mouth. "Oh my god, you scared me," Sylvia said reactively to the figure which stood motionless. She was so close she could smell his cologne. He smelled good. She allowed her eyes to travel up from his white Nikes to his fitted and intentional tattered jeans. He had strong legs, she thought. He'd definitely been a regular at the gym. Her eyes, as though on autopilot, navigated their way to his hands. His hands, looked strong but delicate. She could tell the only abuse to those hands came as a result of lifting heavy metal objects and not as a result of some arbitrary hard labor daily activity. He probably worked on the 25th floor of some office building. Maybe a doctor or business man. Her eyes continued in route to his arms and chest which were masterfully chiseled from the finest Italian marble. Oh my, Sylvia thought. Butterflies fluttered around in her stomach. Her eyes finally met his. He wore a pair of black horn rimmed glasses. Definitely a tech guy, she thought. He had this childlike face which made him look adorable, but certainly not a man she would normally be interested in. "Excuse me," Sylvia said to the statue who had not even acknowledged her presence. Sylvia laughed at herself for even allowing her mind's eye to take such a fantastic journey only to be turned off by his boyish countenance at the end of the road. They were so sincere, she thought. His eyes were so sincere, so innocent. A woman like her would probably corrupt a guy like him.

But there was another guy standing next to him. He had the same build, just a bit taller, blonde, blue eyes, with a 5 o'clock shadow which made him look sinister. But a sexy kind of sinister, she thought. Sylvia's eyes flirted with the blonde blue eyed demon, who seemed to have shared similar sentiments. She kept walking, knowing that she had left two very beautiful men dazed and hopeless. The thoughts washed over her with bliss.

୫

Sylvia could hear Max's booming Spanish accent coming from his office. She opened the door, stepped in and took a seat in a comfy arm-chair. "Hey, let me call you back," Max quickly ended the conversation and hung up the phone. "Sylvia, mi amor. Como esta usted hermoso la senora." He's in a frighteningly good mood, Sylvia thought. She did not respond to his flattery but simply dismissed it. Flattery was a deeply embedded doctrine for Max. He believed in the art. It's just too bad he was no good at it. He made it too obvious.

"Max, for the last time, you cannot sleep with my friend. Hell, Karen is like a full foot taller you. I'm sure some of the other girls in here would happily suck you off if you only asked nicely. Just make sure you're asking nicely with a 100 dólar bill tied around that pequeño pecker of yours," Sylvia giggled at her own remark and Max held up his hands in defense.

"No mi amor, I called you over because I have surprise for you," Max said attempting an innocent smile.

"Surprise? Really?" Sylvia said attempting to hide the bright sparkle in her voice. She loved surprises, but thought it best not to show Max, though he probably already knew.

"Now, don't go spouting off to the other girls, I don't want a bunch of jealous Latinas eating my ear off," Max spoke with his eyes, which bulged when he said the word eating.

"Okay, okay, what is it," Sylvia said, unable to stifle her enthusiasm. Max opened a drawer from his desk and pulled out a small velvet box; the kind that said wedding bells and flower girls. He walked around and sat on the front of his desk. He presented Sylvia with the velvet box. "Ahhh, what is this?" Sylvia said in a tone that already offered rejection. Sylvia had been proposed to multiple times over the years by so many men. Another proposal would certainly not come as a surprise to her. Max was not husband material.

"Open it," Max said with excitement. "Go ahead!" Sylvia opened the box and found a key inside.

"Ahhh, what's this," she said again in the same tone she had prior.

"It's a key," Max replied still sounding excited.

"Yeah but a key to what," Sylvia groaned sounding more and more disappointed with her gift. So far, it was not the surprise she foresaw. Safe to say she was itching for something with Prada or Fendi written on it. Not some dumb key. It wasn't even a car key. Plus, she had just bought a car.

Max picked up a brochure from his desk and handed it to her. "A key to here," Max replied still smiling. Sylvia felt confused, dazed, and shocked all at the same time and apparently all those emotions showed on her face, because Max let out a loud obnoxious cackle. "It's a new apartment Sylvia."

"What?" Sylvia whispered in disbelief.

"I just got this place and now you have the keys," Max sounded quite pleased with himself. His surprise was, for lack of a better word, surprising. It left Sylvia speechless.

"You bought me a condo?" she said, still in disbelief. At this point her heart was racing. Exhilaration bubbled in her stomach and she could barely stifle a scream.

Max let out another loud cackle. "Bought you a condo? Why the hell would I do that?"

"What?" Sylvia shook her head as though attempting to clear away a cob web of confusion.

"First off, I'm paying rent on this place and no, the apartment is mine, you just have the keys to it. But so do I. So don't get it twisted." Max laughed again, "Ha, bought you a condo." He said it as though Sylvia was some child who said something cute but stupid. Sylvia's heart sank like a roller coaster in its downward plummet. The exhilaration she had felt moments before made the disappointment far more difficult to handle.

"I don't want it," having to choke back tears, Sylvia was barely able to utter the words.

"What?"

"I don't want your condo or apartment or whatever" Sylvia said, finding a stronger voice a midst the slowly kindling anger inside her.

"You don't have to live there," Max replied again sounding as though Sylvia said something stupid. "But our good friend Gerald," he said, his eyes emphasizing the name. It was obvious Max did not believe Gerry was his real name either. "Would much like to see more of you," he continued. This conversation had been nothing but confusion for Sylvia, Max must have seen this because he proceeded to jog Sylvia's memory.

"You know Gerald, his mark is probably still imprinted on your backside." She hadn't expected to see him again so soon. And in what capacity did Gerry want to see her in again. "So be at the condo tonight at 9:30. There's a bar in the lobby, you can meet Gerry there and I expect you to show him a good time."

"What the hell are you talking about Max. I'm a stripper, not a prostitute," Sylvia's anger was red hot. "I told you, I'm not going to be your call girl."

The smile drained from Max's face, his features became ridged and hard. "You will do whatever I tell you to do," he said emphasizing each word.

"What the hell is that supposed to mean?" Sylvia said, her brows furrowed and the corner of her mouth began to twitch.

"You think you can make it in this city without me? I know all the other strip club owners. I would make sure that you're black balled from here to Atlanta. Plus, you'd never make as much money anywhere else as you do here."

"Max you don't own me," Sylvia said weakly; more weakly than she expected from herself. She doubled up and attempted another go. "Do you think stripping is the only thing I can do? I can do far more than you know." Sylvia said sounding more confident, though she knew he wouldn't fall for that pitiable excuse of a poker face.

"What else can you do Sylvia, what else?" Max slammed his fist against the desk, the impact caused Sylvia to jump. His anger eclipsed hers. Max stood up, prompting Sylvia to get to her feet; face to face, mono o mono. Though, Sylvia did not feel that she was on a level playing field or battle field. The odds were more like a lion versus a fox. Sylvia could smell the stink of the lion's cigar and cognac on his breath. He grabbed her butt and growled in a low guttural tone, "this is mine."

Sylvia pulled away, pushing the chair behind her. The metal on the chair made a loud scrape against the concrete floor, "don't touch me!"

"You need to go and get ready for tonight. Don't be late," Max said before returning to the other side of his desk where he took a seat and picked up the phone. Sylvia, still clutching the velvet box, every impulse screamed, throw the damned thing at his face and yet she dropped it into the depths of her tote, feebly wishing to never see it again. She knew she could not deny Max's threats. A 32 year old with a sub-par high school education and a PhD in shaking her butt, believe it or not, might not be the first choice for a decent six figure job. Sylvia felt boxed in on all sides. What had her life turned into? "And Sylvia," Max said without looking at her. "There's a party this weekend, I expect you to be there."

Boxed In

n i n e

S HE LEFT MAX'S office feeling dazed. She clutched the catalog to this new apartment, saw the address, and realized that it was on Brikell Ave; the location of many beautiful apartment buildings; apartments which had her wishing she had a million dollars. Then she would wish for a second million to upkeep and a third million for spending money. She had made a good living working as a high end exotic dancer, but was not close to the million dollar mark. In her early 20s when she was young and every guy wanted her firm parts rubbed all over them, money seemed to flow in and back out of her hands. The 20s flew by and she had nothing to show for it. The big 'three O' had sneaked up on Sylvia like a stranger in the night. In one moment she was graduating high school, happy to be rid of the gossip and whining cheerleaders with cruel intentions. Sleeping with their boyfriends might have had something to do with that. Those white girls were so plain compared to her Latina curves, which was the new flavor at the time. Now

Sylvia was quickly barreling towards 40, at least in her own mind. The hopes of millions seemed almost impossible at this point. She had never witnessed a 40 year old millionaire stripper. Maybe she would be the first. Maybe she would be the mother of the girls, the one who would orchestrate the parties. Yeah, I don't think so, Sylvia thought to herself. She wasn't much of a mother. She had no maternal instinct to speak of. No maternal instinct. The thought replayed in her mind like the repeat you get from a scratched CD. She had not been a great mother to Josh. Hell, she hadn't been a mother at all. When she started stripping, she'd told herself that it was all for Josh. Back then, it seemed like a noble enough cause. "I'm doing this for him," she'd argued with Sofia before leaving for another party.

"No you're doing this for yourself," Sofia had replied in a matter of fact way as she rocked Sylvia's baby boy tightly in her arms. Josh was now 16 and it seemed as if nothing had changed. No maternal instinct, the thought, like a silly child stuck in a revolving door poking fun at her. No maternal instinct.

Sylvia remembered when the prospect of doing a few videos came up. It was Max who had the idea. He'd been in contact with some producers and after seeing Sylvia at one of the parties, thought that they wanted to shoot her. The promise of racking up a small fortune, Sylvia thought, was worth the sacrifice. One of Sofia's wise sayings seemed to bear more merit now that she'd actually been through the entire ordeal. "A promise is a comfort to a fool," Sofia's mocking voice jeered then as it does now. And still Sylvia fell for the promise. You could make two to three thousand from just one shoot. And depending on what she was willing to do, she might get more. Sylvia felt apart of her die the moment she revealed herself to the camera. What little innocence she had left was put on display and marketed to fatten someone else's pocket. She did get a check for two thousand five hundred dollars and she cried alone. I should be happy, she'd thought. This is what I wanted. More money meant a good life for Josh; good schools, a nice but moderate apartment in the good part of Miami, maybe Aventura. She could maybe even go back to school herself, though the idea felt daunting. Why had she felt so empty? There was just nothing. There should have been more excitement and thrill. But the void, the lack of emotion where there once was something, swallowed her. She'd determined never to go that far again.

Sylvia's every step took on more and more confidence as she attempted to ground herself in what she'd been told to do. She strode out the club and made her way to the apartment on Brikell Ave. Her freshly washed and vacuumed Benz glistened all the way up the sloped drive way of a building called Oceana. The valet took her keys and she rode the elevator all the way up 18 floors to room 25. Sylvia walked into a living room the size of her entire apartment. Of course, her apartment was tight, even for a single woman living alone. Over the years, Josh had been to her apartment a handful of times, and had opted out of staying for the night. "Wow, how much did Max pay for this place," Sylvia's voice was full of awe. She pulled the drapes which revealed a beautiful view of the sun setting over the city of Miami. The orange light flooded through the floor to ceiling windows and glass door which lead to a moderately sized balcony. There were two chairs and a small glass table outside on the balcony. There was also an ash tray on the table with a half smoked cigar hanging off the lip. The city was on fire, she thought. Not in a destructive way, but a fire which gave it a new life and excitement. Sylvia fell in love with the apartment. It was somewhere she wanted to be. Somewhere she could come home to after a long day. She smiled at the sun, trying in earnest to feel better about the situation.

Sylvia finally made it to the bathroom of the master bedroom and felt a youthful excitement spring up inside her. She imagined that this is how a virgin would feel walking into the Royal Playhouse for the first time. She ran her fingers across the granite counter tops. The stone had a therapeutic kind of cold. There was a large Roman tub and a beautiful shower with semi translucent glass tiling. Sylvia's eyes transfixed on the three silver shower heads, the squares and its intricate design impersonated the pendant of a hypnotist. And there were actual smooth stones on the shower floor. She could not wait any longer. She got undressed, fiddled with the digital dials, until the damn thing turned on. After a few moments, steam began to rise and Sylvia slipped into the misty blanket. It was simply divine.

Sylvia felt as though she could spend her entire day just in this bathroom. But then her bliss was interrupted by a knock at the door. The sudden memory of why she was even in this apartment barged to the forefront of her mind, along with all the anger she had felt towards Max. She wrapped herself in a white bathrobe and slipped on a set of plush bath slippers. Through the peep hole, there was Gerald in all his grey speckled hair glory. Her hair was wet, but she'd didn't care. "He's early," she said softly, her voice quivering from the water cooling on her head and around her neck. She breathed in and opened the door. "Gerald!" Sylvia said in an exuberance which seemed to fail at the end. "Please come in!" The portly man's belly floated into the room a few moments before the rest of his body. He was a lot bigger than Sylvia remembered.

"Hello Sylvia," Gerald said with a smile plastered across his fat head. "We're going to have so much fun together." Sylvia was surprised to see him walk in with a small carry on suit case in one hand.

"Ahhh, what is that for?" Sylvia sounded puzzled.

"Oh this," Gerry turned his sight to the suit case. "This is our fun bag." Gerry walked into the apartment and the door closed behind him.

Sylvia woke to the sight of two spinning blades. The design seemed high tech and was probably celebrated as a great engineering feat. It spun effortlessly in a ceiling way too high for any normal apartment. Then it was as if she turned a corner and ran into this monstrous stabbing pain which definitely came from one area. It radiated down her legs and clawed up her stomach. At first she was confused. What her mind and body were experiencing was familiar, a feeling of days gone by when she promised herself never to do porn again. She should have known why she felt like this, but for some reason couldn't quite put a finger on it. All she knew was something was wrong. Something was definitely wrong. "Where am I? Oh yeah, Max's apartment," her memory played hide seek. "Ouch, wow, that really hurts," her insides complained more and more. Sylvia looked to one side a splatter of blood across the beautiful linen mingled with 20 dollar bills. And just like that, Sylvia realized that she was playing hide and seek with a little monster. Like a tidal wave, it came rushing in. She felt heavy. She tried lifting an arm but it was as if her limbs were weighed down. Her thoughts, the words and emotions roaming through her head, felt as though they were all under water. Her thoughts were muddled, nothing made sense. Everything was just so heavy. Tears came, wetting the sheets mixing with the blood. A sob erupted from the depth of her soul. Her anguish was stuck in her throat but finally relief came through belts and shrieks. The sound was like something out of hell; a soul doomed to eternal torment. Sylvia just wanted to curl up and die.

She thought for certain that she was making headway. But this, this was not her going forward. She had gone back to a nightmare she never intended to revisit. Her encounter with Gerry revived demons she thought were long behind her. Yet, those demons hid in some dark closet of her mind, unlocked by Gerry's abuse. But this was the life she chose. This was the price she had to pay.

Secrets

t e n

I T WAS THE end of another school day and Chad, Brian, and Josh were on their way to basketball practice.

"Hey Chad, over here," a boy with bushy brown hair signaled to Chad from the other end of the hall. Chad, Brian, and Josh were all standing at a four way cross intersection of hallways. The hall, the three walked from, led to the performing arts building. The hall to the right of them led to the auditorium and the path in front was to the psychical education building. To the left, where the boy called from, was the Math and Science hallway, which was apart of the building they now walked through.

"Hey guys I'll catch up with you later," Chad said to Brian and Josh, changing course and heading towards the frizzy haired boy.

"Chad, you're going to be late for practice. You know how coach gets when we're late," Brian said.

"I know, I know," Chad replied, "but we're working on a project for Anatomy and Physiology and I need to talk to him quickly. I'll catch up, don't worry about it," Chad said reassuring his friends. He walked in the direction of the frizzy haired boy and started to open his school bag. He turned his head and glanced behind him to be sure he was clear of curious eyes. They saw him reach for the bag on his back then resumed their walk towards the gym. No doubt they were probably saying how stupid he was for working on his project now, when he clearly had basketball practice on his agenda. Chad didn't care.

The boy that called to him was nicely dressed. His cloths were not brand name, but what he wore was well put together. If there was one word Chad could use to describe him it would be neat. He was just neat; not in a clever kind of way just very orderly. But really, he's a nerd attempting to look trendy. Chad was drawn to him for that exact same reason. Very little in Chad's life was orderly. Chad possessed the wild, I don't care, spirit of his mother. He was impulsive and sensitive. Atleast, that's what his father would say, "you're so emotional just like his mother." His father was the orderly one. He was a cold and calculating man. He'd worked hard and was once Mayor to the city of Jupiter, Florida. He served a few terms but resigned his position and started a textile manufacturing company.

"Hey Luis," Chad said, reaching the boy.

"Follow me," Luis said with a devious smile beaming over his countenance. There was a classroom a few steps off the path of the hallway and Luis led Chad into it. It was unlocked. *How did he manage to do that*, Chad questioned in his own thoughts. After teachers were gone for the day the doors would be usually locked. The only access was from the cleaning crew, who possessed master keys. Chad was sure Luis pulled some MacGyver style James Bond Mission Impossible type of stunt to get his hand on a master key.

"Hey how did you," Chad meant to ask, but Luis pulled him into the classroom, turned off the lights, turned around and started kissing him. Chad returned his passionate kiss with one equal in its ferocity. A minute later Luis pulled away giving Chad the opportunity to finally get a word out, "hey, I don't have much time."

"I don't need much time," Luis replied, before dropping to his knees, unbuckling Chad's pants. They hadn't been together like this in a few days and Chad really wanted to see him. The two boys had struck up a friendship in computer lab. Luis was the teachers aid and had helped him with some computer issues. From there, the two found they liked the same video games. They played against each other and in co-op over the Internet. Luis eventually made it over to Chad's house. Chad had a stunning 65" inch curved LED TV in his room with amazing surround sound. They blasted baddies on Destiny the game, trash talked, and had a great time in each other's company.

One evening Chad's father barged in on the two. "Why don't you ever bring girls over? Why is it you always invite boys to my house? Is my son a fag? Is my son a fag?" Chad's father barked questions, snarling like a rabid animal. He turned and walked out the room. The evenings enjoyment was over at that point. Chad tried his best to hold back the tears. That is when Luis reached over and kissed him for the first time. Luis was his first kiss. He'd been attracted to boys from the time he knew to be attracted to anything, but he didn't know what to do. Should he pursue a homosexual relationship? Was this just a phase? What does it even mean to be gay? Was being attracted to boys the same as being attracted to blondes or brunettes? Should he tell his other friends? Was there something wrong with him? There were so many unanswered questions in his mind.

Chad never introduced Luis to his other friends, partly because he knew they would think of him differently. Another part of him wanted to keep his sexuality in the closet, protected from any outside influences; so he could figure out what this attraction meant. He had no intention of telling any of his secrets and they were many. His relationship with Luis happened by chance and even that he wasn't quite sure. He felt goo around Luis but their relationship left him just as empty and thirsty as he was before.

"Okay, okay, really, I have to go," Chad said, finding it hard to halt Luis' passion.

"Oh c'mon. You're always too busy for me, running off to your little practice, getting hot and sweaty. Well…" Luis said then paused, "yeah, you go do that."

"Ha, ha, ha, you're too funny," Chad replied sarcastically. "I still have to go!"

"When are you going to introduce me to your friends," Luis said cautiously. He already knew how Chad felt about his secret life and if he wanted to still see Chad, he would have to respect his right to secrecy. Chad did not reply, but picked up his school bag, which he had left by the door and slipped out the room.

"I'm going to be in so much trouble," Chad said to himself, preparing for the beating he was about to get from Coach Barnes. The last time he was late, he had to do an additional 50 push ups, 20 pull ups, and running the perimeter of the gym 20 times while everyone else played. He thought back to what had just happened and figured, whatever punishment he was to endure would be worth it. A smile adorned his face as he jogged through the open courtyard into the physical education building. It's not so bad, he thought. He was only ten minutes late and all the players were seated on the bleachers. The coach stood in front with another boy Chad had never seen before.

"Mr Black, so nice of you to join us. You're just in time. This young man here will be trying out for your starting position as small forward," Coach Barnes explained emphatically. Chad had stopped walking at the coaches words but did not realize that he was standing still. The coach continued, "and because you're late to yet another practice, this tardiness will be taken into account. Please, Mr Black, have a seat. You also Mr Noble." The boy standing next to the coach sat down. The new boy was introduced as Jeremy Noble. He'd recently moved to Miami Beach from some school Chad and the others had never heard of. Coach was going to watch him play in today's practice and make his decision. Chad had always taken pride being apart of the starting line up. Brian was point guard and captain. Josh was center. If this boy was allowed into the small forward position, the big three would be broken up. Chad took a seat on the second level of the bleacher and Jeremy took a seat behind him to the right.

"I'm going to wipe the floor with you kid," Chad heard Jeremy whispering. He was a tall black kid, slender, but he looked strong and probably quick. Chad looked back to find Jeremy's eyes locked on him. "You might as well quit now," he continued, "I'm better than you. I've seen you play." Chad turned his head, anger and hatred blazed in his chest.

Chad's anger was to his disadvantage. His game was sloppy; completely out of the usual. Out of frustration, he threw the ball at the backboard of the hoop, it bounced back and hit Alex, the power forward. That act alone sealed the deal. He was out of the starting line up. For the reckless use of the basketball in practice he was suspended from play for the next 3 games. Coach was very strict and made it painfully clear that this kind of flagrant behavior will not be tolerated. Chad left the court after the embarrassment, though there was another 20 minutes of practice remaining. He called an Uber and went home.

The white Toyota Corolla pulled up to the iron gate of Chad's house. The gate was open and mom's SUV was in the driveway. Chad hopped out the car, the events of his day still fresh in his mind. I can't believe what just happened, he thought. "I hate that guy. I really hate that guy," Chad said to himself once out of the Uber. He walked towards the front door and realized the lift gate to the SUV was open. He peered into the back and spotted five packed bags. "What the hell is going on," Chad said to himself again. He simply couldn't process any new or different information at this time. Everything was becoming a blur. His body was tired from his failed attempts at practice and his mind was fried from a long day and the disappointment of loosing his position; not to mention the suspension. He opened the door to find his mother scurring around the living room, grabbing personal items and shoving them into a large tote bag. "Mom?" Chad said quizzically. His mother did not look up, she kept going as though she didn't hear him. "Mom! Mom," he called a few more times. He approached her from behind as she was getting something out of a drawer. He placed a hand on her shoulder and called once more,

"Mom!" She jumped as though he had suddenly awoken her from a deep and disturbing sleep.

"Chad," she said in a sigh, startled at his touch. "Hey!" she sounded tired and worn. Her eyes were red and face wet. She's been crying, Chad thought.

"What happened? What's going on?" Chad asked. It broke his heart to see his mother like this. He'd never seen her in this state and he was puzzled by it. He'd never been close to his mother, but he wished he was. It was safe to say, Chad was raised by nannies and babysitters. She would come around from time to time, but not enough for them to develop a deep familial relationship. She was always too busy living her life.

"I'm really sorry Chad. I really am. I realized all too late what the important things in life really are. I blame myself for this. I blame myself," she said with her eyes full of tears and a froggy tremble in her voice. She took a deep breath and recomposed herself. She wiped the tears from her face and stood up and walked towards the front door.

"Wait, what, where are you going?" Chad called to her; confused as to what was going on. Her words meant nothing to him, just hysterical ramblings. Remembering the bags in the back of the SUV he asked in disbelief, "are you leaving us?"

"Goodbye for now Chad. I love you my dear. I'll call you later, okay? Ah, I love you," she said finally as though stumbling to find the right words to say in an uncomfortable situation.

"But wait, mom wait," Chad said as his mother turned to exit the house. "Mom please don't go."

"I'm sorry Chad, please I hope you don't blame yourself because this has nothing to do with you. I simply cannot…" Mom said, but her words failed and dissolved into sobs. Chad did not know what to do about the woman who'd just walked out of his life. He was dazed; locked in a trance. An hour passed and he was stuck in the same position as when his mother left. She left them. She left me, Chad thought. Chad's brother was always out doing his own thing and dad was always working. He felt alone. Sure he had his friends, but they were outsiders, this would be another secret he would have to hold. Chad got up from the couch, more tired than he'd realized. He made his way up the stairs, every step was met with a hard breath. When he had finally gotten to the top, the door to his dad's office was wide open. He was surprised that inside was in complete shambles. This had to be mom's doing, he thought. Until now, he'd never considered why she was so upset and why she'd just left. He was too tired and emotionally drained to even contemplate the mild specifics of his mother's decision. But there it was. The cause of what broke his family was in his dad's office. His limbs found new life. He became powered by a mixture of emotions. He felt as if he simply had to know. He was entitled to know what his father did to push his mother way. What had his father done to break apart the family. His father's desk was facing the door. Chad made his way to the other side. The computer was already on. He moved the mouse and was greeted by a browser window with multiple views of an apartment. It was obviously surveillance, but some of the cameras were at waist level as though they were sitting on tables. There was a fish aquarium and the fishes were moving, so this was obviously a video feed. There was a small red rectangle in the lower right corner which read live.

"Why would mom be so upset about surveillance. Unless it's one of those real life porn sites, but even then. It doesn't make any sense," Chad said to himself. There was another window open. It was a folder with 36 files; according to the info bar at the bottom of the window. They were all numerically named. It seemed as if the numbers represented dates. The first file was named 10112015. That was only two days ago, Chad thought. He clicked on it. The video opened to a picture of the same apartment. A woman walked into the apartment. The video focused on one square frame instead of seeing the streams from all nine cameras at the same time. She walked around the apartment, as though admiring her surroundings. She walked into the bathroom and the camera view changed to the bathroom, following her journey through the spaces. She stripped down and stepped into the shower. There was a camera in there too. This camera gave a good close up of her face. She looks familiar, Chad thought. "Oh my god," Chad said, the realization hit him like a wrecking ball. "That's Josh's mom," he said in disbelief. Chad watched her take a shower. She seemed a lot younger than his mom. She popped her head out of the glass doors and slipped into a bath robe. She made her way back to the living room, looked through the peep hole, and opened the door. "No freaking way," Chad said as a sick revelation walked into the room. "That's dad! That's dad!" he said in an even greater disbelief. Chad did not stop the video. He continued watching until the bloody end.

Party

e l e v e n

"**L**ADIES, LADIES, PLEASE quiet down," said the man with beautiful blonde hair and blue eyes, as he walked into the living room.

"Oh, he's nice," Karen leaned over and whispered to Sylvia.

"I know," Sylvia forced a smile. To think of it, he looked familiar. Oh, he was at the club, she thought. Blondie lifted his hands in the air, a signal for the nine beautiful ladies seated on the white leather sofa and chairs to squash their bickering. The ladies always brought crazy energy, a bit despondent and a lot of fun. Sylvia could tell that he was loving every second. He looked cocky, which was exactly the kind of men Sylvia went for. The way he walked and dressed, the air of confidence that surrounded him gained her attention. Their eyes met when they were at the club, but this time, it sent an alarm through her head. A prideful man is a jealous man, Sofia once said. Sylvia knew this to be true from experience alone. She liked that kind of strength in a man but the relationship often ended with her being berated. After the breakup with Miguel, which almost ended in a fist to cuff knock down, Sylvia resolved to stay out of relationships. He might be different, she thought. But cocky is cocky, she reminded herself. And she could sense that cock from a mile away.

"Who is he," Sylvia said to herself. There was another man seated at the bar. Not quite as nicely dressed as the other but he was cute in a nerdy way. I almost ran into him, she thought, remembering the full scene at the club. He was wearing a pair of horn rimmed glasses which he kept fidgeting with. They must be uncomfortable, she thought. He finally got it to sit right on his face and his eyes met Sylvia's. It was almost as if he was surprised to see her looking at him, because his mouth lurched open and stayed that way for approximately seven seconds. Sylvia was not the type to back away from a good old traditional staring contest. But he was smart, he started messing with those damned glasses again. Sylvia smiled and turned her attention back to the blue eyed devil who demanded it.

"So ladies, thank you very much, be on your best, and this should be a really good night for you," the blonde hottie seemed to have finished saying what he intended. Sylvia leaned over to Karen who was sitting next to her.

"Ahhhh, what?" Sylvia said.

"Yeah, I know right, I kept getting distracted by the roll of quarters in his pants," Karen replied.

"I should have known better than to ask you. I spaced out for a sec, what did he say?" Sylvia asked in a whisper that only Karen could hear; or so she thought.

"How could you space out with that beautiful piece of meat standing in front of you. No pun intended," Karen replied raising an eyebrow. She looked at Sylvia then spotted the inconspicuous guy sitting over at the bar, "Could it be baby face over there? He doesn't seem your type. I on the other hand, I could be the bad teacher."

"What?" Sylvia said, with her face in a scowl.

"You know, Cameron Diaz, 'Bad Teacher,' the movie. You know, because he looks young. Syl why do I have to explain every single time," Karen replied.

"Because your jokes are corny and punch lines are weak," Sylvia said.

"Or maybe they're just too smart and you're too dumb to know it," she snapped back loud enough to draw attention from some of the girls. The others were simply too amazed at the ridiculous view of the Miami Harbor. There were different colored lights which lit up the bridge. "That beautiful beast you just ignored is Simon Hanson. He is a huge Real Estate success out of the ATL. He just bought this property and he's inviting some friends over for a housewarming. But from the looks of it, these will probably be other agents he wants in his pocket, to rent or probably sell back this spot."

"Hell of a housewarming party to have nine of us here on a Saturday night," Sylvia said hinting to something deeper than what her lips could mention. Suspicion was written all over her face.

"Girl, I ain't one to complain, let's just get that money," Karen said with that feisty Latina attitude she was famous for. This time Sylvia did not respond in her usual affirmative.

"Money?" Sylvia asked and the images of Gerry throwing the cash at her sent chills down her spine. For the last two days the memory terrorized her dreams like Freddy Krueger. Sylvia knew there was no one to blame but herself. She's the one who invited this nightmare into her dreams. I did it, she thought. I did this to myself.

"Girl you ok," Karen said, who looked truly concerned. The absence of her normal response felt awkward.

"Yeah, I know, I'll be fine," Sylvia said, but still sounded not like herself.

"Well girl, I'm going to need you to put on a, we going to get this money face. I'm going to need you to look a bit more happy that you're here, with me, making this happen...ok?" Karen demanded.

"Alright, alright," Sylvia forced a smile before breaking into a chuckle. "Thanks Kay."

"Anytime girl," Karen replied.

"Ok ladies," Simon returned to the living room. Looked at his cell phone and ended a call before his hand fell to his side. "There are a group of guys on their way up, please head to the rooms now."

"Oh yeah, you didn't finish telling me what this was all about," Sylvia again whispered to Karen.

"Don't worry about it chica. I'll explain later," Karen said. She held Sylvia's hand pulling her to stand. "Oh girl, you are hot. The gym has done wonders for them butt and legs."

"Kay, really, I was born with this butt," Sylvia replied.

"Ahhh No," Karen replied with eyebrows raised shaking her head side to side. "That butt of yours was looking a little saggy, like someone slapped the smile off a grumpy old man. But you did pull it together...You did pull it together," Karen shook her head, affirming the results gained at the gym. Sylvia playfully punched her in the arm. Both girls walked towards the master bedroom. Sylvia from the corner of her eye caught baby face nerdy guy eyeing her. Karen saw him too, "See, I told you. Them legs, that butt, in seven inch heels might cause the man to get a heart attack. Girl what were you thinking."

"I guess I wasn't. Sorry!" Sylvia said playfully apologetic. She raise her right hand placing the tip of her pointer finger between her teeth and looked at Mr. Nerdy Guy with a corner stair.

"Syl, you are the worst, by far," Karen remarked seeing what she was doing.

"I know," Sylvia replied in a high pitched girlie voice. She turned and headed into the room.

The bedroom was beautiful. Everything was so pristine. The two other girls who were with them oohed and awed at what they saw.

"OMG this bed is huge, this is definitely a California king. I want one of these," a girl they called Luscious said.

"I know, but look at this bathroom. There is a jacuzzi in the bathroom that can hold at least five people. I like," the other girl, Sugar said.

"And the closet," Luscious tippie toed over to the closet in her seven inch heels. Her eyes lit up as the lights turned on. The closet was like another room by itself. It was empty except for a few trench coats on hangers. "Guys, these are the coats he was talking about," Luscious was still very excited and could hardly hide it. The four girls came close and all filed into the closet. They pulled the coats off the hangers and slipped into them. They were all non distinct trench coats which covered most of the girls down to their knees. All except Karen whose extra inches over all the girls made her coat ride up to her thigh.

"He's going to call for the evenings entertainment and that's when we walk out," Karen started to explain so Sylvia could finally get it.

"Like contestants at a beauty pageant," Sugar added.

"Once all the girls are lined up in front, we drop the coats and just start dancing with whoever. And that's it Syl. We get the money and hit the streets."

Luscious had a startled surprise on her face, "get the money and hit the streets. I like the sound of that. Alright ladies, let's get this money and hit the streets."

Sugar let out a, "woo." They look so young, Sylvia thought. They couldn't be more than 21.

"Hey keep it down, it's suppose to be a surprise," Karen whispered loud enough for everyone to hear. The front door opened and Simon was calling to all the people to come in. "Good they are just getting in."

Sylvia peeked through the bedroom door to see who she was working with. "Guys welcome, welcome, come on in," Simon stood at the door, shook hands and gave hugs. "Rick it's been a long time, what like three months."

"Three months, not long enough," Rick replied from the back of the small crowd of seven men. It was very hard to miss Rick, it seemed as if he was a foot above everyone else. Really he was about six feet five inches. He looked Indian but as he walked through the door and into a brighter lit environment he was definitely of Pakistani decent. He was dressed in an all white loose fitting outfit with light brown shoes. Everything fit so well, it would seem as if his cloths were tailor made. Guess it would have to be for his size. This man was both tall and wide. His gut was not the biggest but it was big enough to make him look rich.

"Guys, that's one of my closet friend over there by the bar, say what's up to Marcus. He'll be making drinks for us tonight. Whatever you guys want, we have more than enough to get you wasted. Just don't expect us to drive you home," Simon said before closing the door behind the last person to come in. "We should have quite a few people left to come in you can grab some drinks and hors d'oeuvre. The pool table is open to you, and I'll get some music."He was right, except there were quite a bit more people left to come in. Just one after the other, more and more just kept coming in. After about 20 minutes there were an additional 26 bodies who strolled through the door. Most of them were men with a few women scattered sparsely through the crowd. It wasn't long though before everyone had a drink in their hand and they started to congregate doing what most business people do at parties like this, talk more business. Sylvia could see Marcus from across the room. He seemed as though he was contemplating life on other planets. Maybe he's Simon's younger, more dorky brother.

"Ladies and gentlemen, thank you again for coming to my humble housewarming. I hope that you're enjoying all the food and drinks. But I have a special surprise, now for the main attraction to get this party really going. Please welcome some of the hottest ladies from the Royal Playhouse," Simon held his arms up and out as though he held the world in his hands. He had the entire city of Miami as his backdrop. And here came nine of the sexiest temptresses, like models on a catwalk sporting slightly over sized beige trench coats. They stood to the right and left of Simon with his arms still raised. As his arms slowly descended the trench coats opened and fell to the ground. The overhead lights dropped, blue and purple mood lights lit up the walls, and the music started. The ladies joined the crowd, holding the hands of sheepish men too afraid to let loose and urging them to move to the beat of the music. Their flamboyance took the party to a new level. It went from a standing around, business party to something way more fun and lively. These ladies were famous for leaving an impression. These poor unsuspecting millionaire Real Estate agents and investors had no idea what had just been unleashed upon them.

"Can I have a glass of your Dom Perignon," Sylvia said as she approached the bar, took a seat with her back turned to Marcus. She sat as though posing for the front cover of a liquor magazine. Her drink sat idly on the bar counter next to her and her hands where appropriately placed over her crossed legs. Rick came over to the bar and sat one chair over from Sylvia. "How's about another drink, gin and tonic please," Rick said, his attention fully towards the bartender. "If I dance another minute, I'll pass out," he said to no one in particular. So no one responded. His words slurred, he was already drunk.

He took one sip of his drink and a voice came up behind him, "are you going to ask me to dance or are you going to sit there all night. Don't let me drag you to that dance floor young sir." Rick looked as though he was dangerously close to 50 years old. He turned to be greeted by a pretty young face. She had beautiful milk chocolate skin and teeth that looked like pearls. His eye traveled down her slender body, adorned by a skimpy blue dress; which fit her like a glove. A very tight glove at that.

"And who do I have the pleasure of speaking to. I don't dance with strangers," Rick said.

"You can call me Luscious. Now see we're no longer strangers," Luscious said.

"Well you certainly do look deluscious," Rick said, a feeble attempt to flirt.

"Would you like to taste? Come dance with me," Luscious said. Rick turned his head towards Marcus, gave him a big smile and got up from the bar stool with the cocktail still in his hand. "Let's dance!" Luscious drew Rick by his belt buckle and in playful reluctance he strode onto the dance floor. Marcus could not help but chuckle watching them getting close as they danced. Luscious was having her way with him and he was loving every second.

"What do you find so funny Mr Bartender," Sylvia asked without looking at Marcus.

"Oh nothing, I'd probably be frozen solid if she ever did that to me," he said as Luscious was bending over and grinding into Rick.

"Hmmm, so is that why you haven't asked me to dance. You don't have to be afraid, I won't bite," Sylvia said in her most sultry voice. She finally turned towards Marcus and stared into his eyes, allowing him the opportunity to drink her in.

"So why exactly are you stuck behind this bar while your friend over there is having all the fun," Sylvia asked angling her head, eyeing Simon as he and another guy danced with Karen?

"Well, I was hoping you would would be the one to approach me," Marcus said remembering what happened just a few moments ago.

"I thought it was the man's responsibility to pursue the woman he wanted. Am I not worthy of your pursuit Mr. Nerdy Bartender?" Sylvia said reaching for Marcus' glasses. She picked them off his face, placed it down on the counter and drew close to him. She was so close she could smell his cologne over the odor of alcohol that had spilled all around. "I like a man who comes after what he wants." Sylvia picked up the glass of champagne and started walking away. She slowed for a moment, looking over her shoulder, "are you coming?" She then turned and kept walking. As soon as she made it to the dance floor another of the male guests of the party almost instantly pounced and she started to dance. Her hands went in the air and she threw her head from side to side allowing her hair to wave from left to right and back again.

Spineless

t w e l v e

HALF THE GUESTS had already left and it was quickly approaching the 3 o clock hour. The dancing slowed and the music became more intimate. Simon seemed to have been pleased with the way the party progressed. He was making his rounds with the guests. The night flew more quickly than Sylvia had anticipated. It was not her standard every weekend party. Actually, it had been a well needed break from the norm. After what happened with Gerry, she wasn't confident getting naked for anyone. Sylvia had a great night when her greatest difficulty was the pain emanating from her red bottomed Christian Louboutin heels. She had to get off her feet, even if it was only for a short time. She had managed to stay relatively sober and was drinking water most of the night. She would be the designated driver but hopefully not the designated walker and carrier too. Karen was sure to be drunk off her feet and Sylvia would be her Supergirl; catching and carrying damsels in distress as they fall from tall buildings. Karen would need a Supergirl because she was no light weight. She wasn't fat. Not an ounce of bulge to pinch. But she was tall. Not freakishly so, but a healthy five feet eleven inches. Not to mention, she had a pair of thunder thighs which would make Zeus gurgle. Sylvia was disheartened at the thought of carrying her. She tried her best to shake the image of both of them falling over, heels broken, dresses ripped, and some unsuspecting stranger snapping a picture of them both. Sylvia was sure something like that would make it onto one of those You FAIL videos on Youtube. "Where is that chick anyways? That redhead shouldn't be too hard to find," Sylvia said to herself ignoring the men she had become relatively familiar with over the past few hours. Karen was nowhere to be found in the main living area. Sylvia stormed the master bedroom where the girls had gotten dressed in their trench coats. As soon as she got in the room, she was greeted by an odor of sweat, alcohol, and the sour stench of vomit. Sylvia crinkled her nose but could also hear groans. "Oh no, oh no," she said to herself out loud. The sound seemed to have been coming from the bathroom. She rushed over and threw the door open and was almost relieved to see a naked milk chocolate body bent over the sink and some guy having his way with her. The faces of those bodies turned in the direction of the door and she slowly retreated, "sorry, sorry…" That still left the question, "where the hell is Karen. You better not be passed out somewhere." Sylvia looked in the closet, then sped out the bedroom into the living room area; still nowhere to be found. Marcus spotted her and sensed that something was wrong. She took to the other room and found a few of the girls seated on the bed speaking to some of the guys. "Excuse me, have you guys seen the tall redhead anywhere," Sylvia interrupted the conversation with a bit of urgency. The girls began to eye the bathroom.

Sugar spoke up, "she's in there."

"Thank you," Sylvia said. She approached the bathroom fully expecting Karen to be bent over the toilet bowl. As she approached the door, she realized there was no sound, just a faint male groan. This time she slowly opened the door to find Karen's pale white body perched on the counter top with white powder on her face. Her dressed was pulled up and hung around her neck like a donkey's yolk. The man she came to know as Rick was also fully disrobed and was grinding against her. No, he was plowing into her like a police battering ram on the door of a drug lord's house. The thoughts and memory of a few nights prior rose in Sylvia's mind. She saw herself in Karen's position, bent over the sink with Gerry attempting to fit an over-sized dildo into her vagina. "No," Sylvia shouted which drew the attention of the others in the room. Startled, Rick retreated, he pulled a towel that laid on the tub and covered his waist.

"What the hell?" he shouted. He was more than a little pissed. "Can't you see I'm busy," he continued.

"Syl is that you," Karen turned her head in a daze. Sylvia recognized that look. She had seen it many times and it made her angry that her friend was in this predicament. Gerry had wanted to coke her up too, but that was the only thing she refused him. In her Sylvia like persuasiveness she convinced him that she'd rather experience all of him rather than a daze and a spotty memory. Now she wished she had taken him up on his offer. Forgetting that night was all she wanted to do. Sylvia had hoped that some kind of affection towards him might have done something to make him less rough. She would have done almost anything to make him have just an ounce of compassion towards her. But he was so cruel and so mean. He cursed at her as though she was a horrible monster. He was full of so much hate. An uncontrollable torrent of hate and disgust towards her. And nothing she had said changed it.

"You worthless piece of trash," Gerry had said. His southern drawl added emphasis to trash. Then in the end he thought his money absolved all the wrongs. Was that all it took to ease his seared and blackened conscience? Throw a few thousand dollars at the feet of the woman you'd sexually and emotional abused and consider all sins absolved?

Marcus came through the door, "is everything alright?"

Simon came in shortly after, "what the hell is going on. I heard a shout." Sylvia hurried over to Karen. She quickly adjusted Karen's dress, covering her tight slender figure.

"Wait, wait, wait, I'm not done with her yet," Rick angrily disputed.

Sylvia ignored him and instead focused her attention on her friend, "Karen, we have to go ok…C'mon."

"I paid good money for that pussy and I want more than just 15 minutes," Rick again attempted to stop Sylvia's progress. But Sylvia knew men like him. *He's just trying to save face*, she thought. Rick placed a hand on her shoulder and shouted, "are you listening to me." Sylvia turned and with one quick motion reached down and grabbed his balls and squeezed hard. Rick's words got stuck in his throat. His body stiffened, immobilized by the pain. His surprise soon turned to hate, but Sylvia held fast.

"Loud and clear, but I suggest you back off, unless you want to be as dickless as you are spineless," Sylvia said gritting her teeth. She used her other arm to push him off. By that time the remaining guests were all crowded into the room. Even Luscious and her significant other had found their way to the drama as it unfolded. Seeing the disapproving stare seemed to have dissuaded Rick from taking any further action. He grabbed his pants and shoes and stormed out of the bathroom, pushing his way through a number of eyes. He headed towards the exit and Simon took off behind him. Sylvia, meanwhile continued putting her friend together. She took one of Karen's arms, in attempt to lift her to her feet. Karen had no strength of her own and her dead weight tipped her causing Sylvia to loose her balance. Marcus came up on the other side of Karen, grabbing her other arm, stabilizing the two. Sylvia knew from the first moment he saw Rick and Karen that this was more than just vaginal sex. The way she moved now confirmed it. Sylvia knew Karen would hurt just as she was hurting a few nights ago when Gerry did the same to her. Sylvia could have only wished that there was someone there to rescue her from that maniac.

"I got her," Marcus said. He reached down and lifted her entire body into his arms. "Lead the way."

Sylvia always considered herself to be self sufficient, but she would have to accept his help this once if she wanted to make a quick escape. "Ok, thank you," she reluctantly accepted. The waters parted and the three promptly abandoned the apartment. Once to the lobby, the front desk was able to assist with a wheelchair. They finally made it to the valet and Marcus gently rested Karen on the back seat of the car. "Thanks again…ahhh"

"Marcus, nice to meet you?" Marcus reached his hand out to shake Sylvia's.

"Marcus, ok…thank you Marcus," she shook his hand and got into the car.

"Aren't you going to tell me your name," Marcus stood in the way of her door closing. Sylvia was at this point not in the mood to be nice. She was tired and stressed and pissed and sad. Her life was becoming something she did not anticipate.

"You can call me Scarlet," Sylvia replied with a half baked smile.

"Is that your real name," he questioned in disbelief.

"Wouldn't you like to know. Goodnight Marcus," Sylvia pulled the car door which made Marcus back off.

"Goodnight Scarlet!"

Just Try

t h i r t e e n

"YOU MADE IT," Rena said standing at the door moments after Josh rang the bell.

"Wouldn't miss it for the world," Josh said with a nervous reply. "I got you a present."

"Ahh…you shouldn't have. I'm just glad you were able to make it," Rena said. She held his hand and pulled him through the door way. "A lot of kids from school are already here. My dad is barbecuing out back. We've got an Xbox going in the living room and the music is only in here. So just hang for a while ok, don't run out on me? If you're hungry there is food set out in the dining room and in the kitchen which is right through there." Rena pointed to an area where Josh could see a dining table filled with all sorts of foods.

"Ok, cool," Josh said, still attempting to thaw out the nerves.

"Alright, I'll see you in a little bit, ok? I have a few things to do," Rena said smiling wide.

"Don't worry, I'll be good, I won't completely wreck your party," Josh replied. His stomach started to turn inside him. A mixture of unwinding nerves and hunger. He forgot to eat this evening. He was so on edge that the thought of nutrients to his body completely slipped him. Now that he was here, at the party, the emptiness began to envelope him. He wanted to make a B Line for the dining room to see what he could scavenge. From the looks of it he did not have to scavenge anything, the food was ripe for the eating.

"Look who we have here," a familiar voice and arm came up from behind him. The arm went around his shoulder grabbing him tight. "I've made up my mind, I want to be a porn star when I grow up. Getting paid to have sex. How amazing is that?" Brian said. Did he completely forget what they saw that evening or is he trying to rub it in. *I wonder about you sometimes*, Josh thought.

"Brian, do I look like I care. Do us all a favor and keep your clothes on, please," Josh said while taking Brian's hand off his shoulder.

"Well, look who I'm here with. You might know her as the hottest blonde in the whole school." Brian placed his arm back on Josh's shoulder and whispered, "my first porn scene is going to be with her. Just you watch." He started to speak a little louder now. "Yes ladies and gentlemen you guessed it, Brittany," Brian said as he nudged Josh. "And look at what she's wearing."

"Did I mention you're a jerk," Josh said.

"Did I mention you're jealous that my girl is hotter than yours," Brian replied.

"Rena is not my girl, we're just friends. Anyways, is Chad here," Josh desperately wanted to change the subject.

"He's in the living room. He's killing everyone on Street Fighter. Rena's dad has an Xbox," Brian said.

"Go figure, he probably has a full setup at home," Josh said.

"A little rich boy," Brian said.

"I'm starving, I need to get some grub," Josh tried to break away to the kitchen. Then a voice came from across the room. It was Rena.

"Hey Josh," she said.

"Oh, she calls you Josh now," Brian said attempting to further exasperate Josh.

"Everybody calls me Josh. Even the people I wish didn't know my name," Josh attempted a comeback.

"Bro really, don't talk about Chad like that. He's a good guy, ok" Brian said mockingly.

"Hey Josh," Rena repeated her call. Josh gathered himself and started towards her, leaving Brian behind.

"I'll just be over there, eating, in the kitchen," Brian said a bit loud drawing unnecessary attention. Josh looked over his shoulder with a scowl on his face.

"Hey," Josh approached Rena smiling, attempting to keep the look of hunger from showing.

"I want you to meet my dad and Dad this is Josh" Rena stood beside a tall very good looking man. He really didn't look old enough to be anyone's dad, but he must be because Josh was standing in his house celebrating the sweet sixteen of his daughter. He couldn't be much older than Sylvia which means he probably had Rena when he was pretty young too.

He extended his hand,"nice to meet you Josh, no need calling me dad."

Rena elbowed him, "be nice."

"I am nice," Dad replied.

"I mean to me. Be nice to me, after all I'm your favorite daughter and it is my birthday," Rena said cocking her head to the side.

"No one said anything about treating you nicely," Dad said smiling. A large smile adorned Josh's face.

"Are you going to take his side," Rena narrowed her eyes at Josh. He instantly wiped the smile from his face; or at least he tried.

"Hi Josh, my name is Andrei but you can call me Rena's dad," Andrei said.

"Ok Rena's dad, certainly a pleasure meeting you sir," Josh replied.

"Bye dad," Rena said with a tone he would understand as 'leave now.'

"Well at least I have the decency to know when I'm not wanted. I'll be around," Andrei raised one hand and walked back to the backyard were he was attempting to finish his work on the grill.

"Did you get something to eat yet," Rena said, probably sensing that life force had left Josh as a result of the black hole in his stomach which enveloped his entire being. At this point, he could not forget his hunger.

"No not yet," he said, not wanting to sound too desperate.

"Well…would you like to get something?" Rena slowly spoke the words.

"If that's alright," Josh replied sheepishly.

"Joshua Bradley, you really need to relax. I know I'm super hot and all, but don't worry, I like you. You don't have to worry about impressing me right now. I just want you to have fun…okay," Rena said as a matter of fact. Josh was completely thrown off by this which made him seem even more nervous.

"Yeah," Josh replied. Rena grabbed his hand and pulled him over to the kitchen where they picked out their choice of foods. *I wonder if she gets everything she wants,* Josh thought to himself. She seemed so happy. Josh had been to birthday parties before, but he never had one. It never really made a difference before. The desire to be celebrated, to be acknowledged just for making it through life one more year started to burn just as the hunger did. After they had gathered their fill, Rena walked in front of him with her plate of small bite size sandwiches, chips, and guacamole on the side. She took to the stairs in order to avoid the busy areas of the house. She went about six stairs up before taking a seat. Josh followed in like manner and sat on the fifth stair. His thoughts and mind must have tunnel visioned on the food. He saw nothing except for what was on his plate. The hunger and the temptation of food consumed his humanity, reverting him to a beast-like mentality. He mauled the sandwiches, not bothering to taste it. As the contents of one hand was inhaled, the other hand would prepare the fodder for the beast to gorge. Rena chuckled a bit seeing the raging beast rise from such a quiet boy. "Breathe, Josh breathe," she said mockingly. Josh paused for a second, his senses returning for but a moment. The beast held at bay by the realization that there was a very pretty girl watching him.

"Sorry, it's really good though," he said, with his mouth still full . "You should try some." He returned his attention back to his plate and continued.

"Joshua Bradley you are so unpredictable" Rena said. She picked up a sandwich of her own, bit into it, but she could not help but look and smile at this strange creature sitting so close to her. When he finally slowed his pace cleaning up what small morsels remained, Rena was only half way through her third sandwich and she had not even touched her chips. She looked over at him, still smiling, but trying to hide it.

"Would you like some more," Rena asked in a low voice, almost whispering.

"No thank you, I'm feeling a lot better now," Josh said, putting down his plate. He looked over to Rena whose plate was still half full. He instantly realized how ridiculous he probably looked. After all, he had taken more food than her, and he had finished eating before her.

"Don't worry, I always finish last at the dinner table. My dad always finishes his food after two bites," she said attempting to sooth his worries. "It was nice of you to think of me though. Not many guys would stop to consider another girl's feelings."

"Why wouldn't they?" Josh questioned naively. "You don't have a round bald head and big round green eyes, so from the looks of it I would say you qualify as human," Josh said. His reference to extraterrestrial alien life forms was proof that his nerves had finally settled. Plus, there was no sense being nervous after she had seen him gobble down the party grub like a very hungry fat kid.

"Well Joshua Bradley, I hope that stays true in your eyes," Rena replied.

"I like when you call me by my full name," Josh looked away as he spoke.

"Are you blushing Joshua Bradley," Rena said attempting to reestablish eye contact. "Have you ever asked your mom about your dad?" In the blink of an eye, the subject of their conversation changed.

"No," Josh kept his eyes low as he replied.

"Sorry, I didn't mean to offend you. I was just curious," Rena quickly tried to turn the tide of where she thought the conversation would lead.

"It's ok but my mom and I don't get along very well."

"Don't get along?" Rena sounded puzzled. "Why, is she really mean?"

"No, but she hasn't really been there for me. For most of my life, she's been out working, or getting wasted, or whatever. She's never really wanted me. There was always something more important to do other than being with her own son. She's been coming around more trying to make up for lost time but it's too late now. There's nothing she can do to fix what she's done," Josh's voice cracked as he spoke.

Rena reached her hand over, touched his cheek, "well you're still warm, that means you're alive. I would say you still have time Josh. I lost my mom seven years ago, when Kylie was only one year old. I was nine at the time and I still remember dad dropping the phone. He picked me up and we raced to the hospital." Josh's face turned to Rena as she spoke. She looked away when she saw his eyes, "I was screaming in the car, 'Dad why won't you tell me what's going on?' I knew something bad had happened but all he could do was cry. I've never seen him cry before and it broke me. When we got to the hospital, she had burn wounds on over

50 percent of her body. There was a pile up on the interstate and mom was caught in it. Her arm was broken and she was pinned inside so she couldn't get out. The car caught on fire. She had passed out from the shock of the pain. The doctors couldn't do a thing. The firefighters told us that she was bent over Kylie to protect her from the flames. It was a miracle Kylie survived. Don't loose your mother Josh," Rena wiped the tears from her eyes but they came regardless. "Sorry, for unloading so much on you all at once. What do you say to a story like that, right!"

"It's fine and I understand what you're saying," Josh said, finding it hard to stay objective.

"At least tell her how you feel," Rena pleaded.

"I found out some things about her that I want nothing to do with," Josh replied. "I don't want to be part of her world. I don't want to be her son. I don't want her as a mother."

"What if she really did change. What if she really did turn over a new leaf and you're simply judging her from the mistakes of her past. If a football scout came to watch your games, would you like him to judge you solely based on where you were when you first started playing or based on the growth from then to now," Rena spoke so sweet and calm that her words bore no offense in Josh.

"I hear you," Josh knew he was cornered; not that he minded being cornered by her.

"I feel like a sprinkler, with a whole lot of waters works," Rena said. Josh reached up and wiped another tear from her cheek.

"I like you way too much Rena Novak," Josh replied.

Dreams

f o u r t e e n

"**G**IRL, YOU WERE heavy," Sylvia sitting in a couch across from Karen who was laying on the bed. It was already 10 AM Sunday morning and heading back to bed seemed like a perfectly logical thing to do. "How are you feeling," Sylvia rubbed her eyes showing her own fatigue.

Karen was laying on her side, staring at her with red blurry eyes from beneath fresh white linen. "I'm really sorry, I don't know what happened. I probably had some bad blow," Karen said with her palm against her head attempting to stave off the impending headache. She started to sit up in the bed and shrugged as she felt the tug of her cloths against the sheets.

"Bad coke? Bad blow? You could've died. You should know better by now not to snort that stuff," Sylvia echoed disappointment towards her friend's decision making.

"I know, I know! But Syl it was a lot of money for just a little 'extra attention,'." Karen threw up half hearted air quotes around extra attention. "I didn't think it would go that far. He just seemed like one of those guys who just wanted to fulfill their fantasy," Karen said attempting to explain her actions.

"You know guys like this," Sylvia said attempting to calm the obvious anger building inside her chest. She always felt as though she had to protect Karen. The moment Karen walked through the doors of the Royal Playhouse, Sylvia took to her. Karen was this tall beautiful young girl, who was obviously naive.

"I know, I know, it was just a lot of money Syl" Karen again replied.

"Kay, is it really worth your life," Sylvia replied.

"My life? What is my life? Taking off my cloths for the next jerk off to gawk at. I can't even think about the future, cause there is no future in this industry for washed up worn out women. Sylvia, I have to get what I can when I can. I'm getting older."

"Older, you're only 24 Kay," Sylvia replied, setting the record straight that 24 is not equivalent to getting old.

"Yeah but I'm not like other people Sylvia. I'm not as strong as you. This life is all I know. I'd be lucky to hit it big with a rapper or bawler with some money," Karen's head drooped. "I guess I was sorta hoping that this guy would be my ticket." Tears filled her eyes and her lips quivered.

Sylvia left her chair and sat beside her in bed. "I remembered when you first walked into the club. I loved how tall you were. More than once, I thought 'the legs on that girl could slave any giant.' But beyond that, I always thought you had more potential than this club would ever know how to exploit. Trust me, Kay you do. You have something in you that makes people smile. People are naturally drawn to you and you don't need to take off your cloths to prove that. I figured this was probably something you would do for a short time to get you through college and then I thought you would have moved on by now. It hurt so much when I heard you dropped out. That's probably why I took to looking over you; plus the other girls would have chewed you up. Jealous bitches!" Both girls chuckled. "You were young and invincible, but I wasn't in any better position to tell you different. And I'm still not, but I love you and the strange thing is I want more for you than I do for myself." Sylvia reached for Karen's hand. They both sat there, in bed and held hands.

"By the way," Karen spoke up after a few moments of silence. "Whose place is this? This is nice!"

"Oh, you like?" Sylvia teased with interest.

"Is this your apartment?"

"Well I have the keys," Sylvia said slyly, avoiding the question.

"Wow, well damn girl," Karen's eyes searched the room then found Sylvia's eyes again. "If this is your apartment, then where is all your stuff?" There was a pause as Sylvia attempted to concoct lie, "liar! And you're terrible at it so don't even try."

"Fine, I'll tell you, but please don't tell the other girls," Sylvia told her how she came about the apartment. She told Karen what Max expected of her. But she did not tell her about Gerry. That memory was far to fresh in her mind. It was far too painful to recount. They had already been through a somewhat tumultuous night and she didn't want to go and add her own troubles to the mix.

"Well are you going to do it?" Karen asked, but before Sylvia could answer she spoke up with conviction, "Syl you're not a prostitute."

"Karen, neither are you," Sylvia replied. Both girls fell silent again. "Max said he would black ball me from working anywhere else if I don't!"

"What?" Karen's face showed both alarmed and anger. She had not gotten upset about her own plight, but tell her one small piece of Sylvia's and she was ready to erupt. Sylvia was sure now that she would not tell her about Gerry. "He can't do that!" Karen continued. "He can't do that!" She said again, the second time with less conviction. Sylvia openly gazed at her as though looking into the face of a pitiable child. Karen's disbelief slowly drifted away as though carried on a slow moving river.

A noise came from deep within, not a moment too soon. Hunger came and gnawed at both their stomachs like a cornered rat in a wooden box. Sylvia decided that she would go downstairs to the lobby to see what she could scrounge up. She determined to make her scavenge quick, because in all honesty she was a little worried for her friend. Even though last night was traumatic, they had been through much worse episodes of horror: the jealous girlfriends of men they danced for. Why would anyone take their boyfriend to a strip club and then get jealous. Hell, why would any self respecting girl take their boyfriend to a strip club period, she thought. It's as if they're begging their boyfriends to cheat. And then there are the fights with fellow dancers. Money, of course, is usually at the center of it all. Sylvia cringed at the thought of a repeat performance of last night. It had seemed like such an easy night, but there is always a jerk who screws things up. Over the years, overdosing had threatened the life of many a women in her field of work. The next time it could mean they do not make it out alive. "Okay, maybe I'm over thinking this," Sylvia said attempting to get out of her head. On the other hand, fearing for one's life should never be an every day or even every week occurrence, especially when you can help it. It's like living in hell. To live in a perpetual uphill climb. To be perpetually beaten and still run back to it. Even a lab rat will know not to touch the electric wires after being shocked a few times. Why do we continually throw ourselves into situations where we might get hurt over and over again, she thought shaking her head in disappointment at her own mind stupor. I've always wanted a better life, but never actually did anything to change and be better, Sylvia found herself staring out a window. She wasn't even too sure what she was looking at.

But what else was there? What else was there beyond this life. Well, there was plenty out there, just not for her. This life was all she knew. The stripping, the parties, the sex, the fast life. Her education did not go much beyond high school. Sylvia tore her eyes away from the window just in time to see a man walking in through the front doors of the apartment building with a very nice camera slinked around his neck and a good sized tripod in his hand. In high school she had wanted to become a photographer. Of course, Sofia didn't have the money to buy her a professional camera or even just a regular old point and shoot, but she loved taking photos. Sylvia only had experience with the single use disposable cameras, but it was all she needed to immortalize her subjects forever. Even now, her iPhone was chock full of pictures. Not, selfies, but photographs of structures she thought looked interesting, the beach, well mostly the beach, and people. She loved taking pictures of people; mother's shopping in Target or teenagers walking down the side walk or old men sitting at the park feeding the birds. A moments glimpse of their lives were immortalized in the iCloud. Sylvia imagined herself traveling to exotic worlds, capturing the essence of its inhabitance and sharing it with the world. "High school dreams," she said to herself. It was a dreamed which seemed all too impossible. A dream too far out of reach. She wasn't quite sure why it was impossible, but she had resolved within herself a long time ago that high school dreams where but fairy tales. Much like the boy wanting to become superman or the little girl wanting to be a princess. Dreams did not come true. And that she knew for certain.

Sylvia wondered if Josh had dreams of his own. He was most likely smarter than her at this point. "No wonder he hates me," she said as she walked into the lobby.

What kind of job would she even qualify for, bagging groceries at Walmart? Woman in her low 30's with not a single work experience she could put on a resume. Sylvia's mind started to race making it difficult to focus. The fear evolved from mere shivers to panic. There was a tightness in her chest making it difficult to breathe. Sylvia marched out the lobby, through the front doors and into the fresh sandy ocean breeze and scents of sun tan lotion. "Come on get a hold of yourself Sylvia," she said attempting to coach her nerves back to the solid steel columns of support she needed them to be. "I can't dwell on this now, can't afford to loose it with Karen on the brink," she spoke softly, eyes shut tight.

"Syl is that you," Karen was out of bed attempting to wash up in the bathroom.

"Yeah, I've got some bagels and coffee, is that alright," Sylvia asked.

"I just got off the phone with Max. Syl, he's pissed," Karen sounded upset again.

"About what," Sylvia felt fear and uneasiness threatening to drag her back into the mud again. This is turning into a weekend from hell, she thought.

"The jerk from last night was upset and the guy who threw the party called Dinero. He wants his money back. Said he didn't get what he paid for," Karen tried to get the words out before the tears.

"He tried to take advantage of you, did you tell him that. Did you tell Dinero what happened?"

"I tried but he didn't want to hear it," Karen said, the words escaped her lips in pieces. Much like a phone call with a bad connection.

"Karen that could be considered rape," Sylvia was boiling.

"But I consented to it Syl, that's not rape. Let's just forget it. I'll give him the money. It was only two thousand. And plus, who will believe my story anyways," Karen said with the tears running down her cheeks. The makeup was already off, whatever remained was on the sheets and in the sink; so there was nothing to ruin. She had such a beautifully sad face, Sylvia thought. It broke her heart.

"Either way, for what he did to you, he needs to pay," Sylvia fighting for her friend who could not fight for herself.

Sylvia's phone rang. Max Dinero appeared on the caller ID. "Oh c'mon, not now!" Sylvia said in a tired sigh.

"Is that Max?" Karen questioned.

"Yeah," Sylvia said, allowing the phone to ring a second time.

"You have to answer. He knows you're with me," Karen said nervously.

"It's my phone Karen and I can answer if I damn well please to," Sylvia replied. Her actions betrayed her words. She picked up the phone and, not before hesitating, she answered the line on the fourth ring. Max did not wait for her greeting before rolling of a string of curses and name calling. "Good morning to you too," Sylvia said, holding the phone off her ear.

"Do you know what you've done? You don't have a clue. Your morning wouldn't be so good if you really know," Max said before another string of curses and name calling.

"Max, that guy was a jerk. He drugged Karen and raped her," Sylvia said, pleading with him.

"Do you take me for a fool? You must really take me for a fool," Max replied. "Why would he give money to a girl he was planning to rape?"

"He was covering it up. He probably thought that we were just strippers and it would be easy to get away with it if he just shelled out a few hundred dollars" Sylvia lied again, it was actually a few thousand. Nevertheless, her voice was loud from the passion of her words.

"No ma-mi! You are just a stripper and I don't believe you. I don't believe a word out your mouth," Max said, who was also shouting so loud Sylvia had to constantly move the phone away from her ear. "I lost a lot of money because of you two and now you, Sylvia, will make it up to me." After he had finished speaking the line went dead. Max hung up the phone. Sylvia certainly didn't want Karen to hear all that, but Max's deafening voice was hard to miss. His words were as clear as a voice over speaker phone.

"What did he mean by 'you will make it up,' Syl" Karen questioned in a worried high pitched tone.

"I don't know," Sylvia lied. She knew good and well what Max was talking about. It had to do with the very apartment they were currently in. She shuttered when she remembered Gerry. Were all Max's clients men of special fetishes. Sylvia didn't want to go through another Gerry again or any of Max's other clients.

"Sylvia," Karen defiantly raised her voice. "I made a mistake, I want to cut my losses."

Sylvia gritted her teeth, walked up to her friend and hugged her, "Alright Kay. Their condo is not far away, we'll head back there as soon as I get a shower." Sylvia's heart pounded hard. She agreed for the sake of her friend but was in no way satisfied with just laying down and allowing another jerk, another lesser excuse of a man to just come and run over her and the people she loved. "Let's just spend some time on the beach before I take you home, Lord knows you need a tan." Sylvia pulled away and smiled. "Okay?"

"Okay," Karen sounded more resolute. She was certainly no sun worshiper, but spending a day on the beach must have sounded far better than facing Simon again.

CB

Sylvia got off the elevator with determined steps. She left Karen in the car. She was certainly in no condition to head back to the scene of her nightmare so soon. Standing before the door, her anger was subdued but it gave her confidence.

Knock, knock, knock

Her fingers hit the wood with force. There was a door bell, but a door bell would seem too easy, too nice, too not rough. She wanted to show strength. She looked at the light coming through the peep hole in the door. The light darkened and lit up again. Someone saw her. That jerk, she thought. She remembered Simon and how she was sickeningly attracted to him. She attempted to concoct thoughts suitable for the situation. She needed to look serious. She would put on her no nonsense tone and she would mean it. The door opened to black hair, horn rimmed glasses, brown eyes, wife beater, chiseled arms with a toothbrush in one of them, dark blue tight jeans and flip flops. "Oh it's you, the bartender." All the anger and foreboding drained from her face and voice. She wanted to roar like a lion, but could only manage flaunting like a peacock.

"Hello Scarlet, good seeing you again. Please come in," he said as though he was expecting her. She forgot that she told him to call her Scarlet, which in actuality was Karen's stage name; hence the red hair. He stepped out of the way, still holding the door, fully expecting her to come in. She paused for a few seconds then stepped inside. "Simon is out right now, but you can have a seat. You're here to pick up your money I presume. The other girls picked up their checks last night."

"Well…I was here to return that jerk's money, Rick!" Scarlet said, reminding herself of why she was upset in the beginning. The feelings had subsided, as if they had never even existed and it seemed futile at this point to attempt drumming them up. After all, he was only the bartender. "So did you stay here last night?" Scarlet took a seat at the bar and Marcus went around to the other side and leaned against the stainless steel gas stove.

"Yeah, where else would I stay?" Marcus said, as a matter of fact. "So you're returning the money, why?"

"I wouldn't have, but my friend doesn't want any problems with our employer," Scarlet replied. Though referring to Max Dinero as an employer seemed awfully nice. "So wait, are you really a bartender?"

"No of course not, I'm an investment banker for a firm in Atlanta. I was just here on the weekend. Well it was supposed to be a fun weekend but it turned into this. I'm heading out today," his voice trailed off at the end.

"Oh, hmmm…that's interesting," Scarlet nodded, acting as though she knew what investment banking was.

"But, why would there be problems?" Marcus was obviously trying to keep the conversation going.

"Yeah, but who's going to believe her. Who's going to believe that she didn't sign up to be treated like the scum under the jerk's shoes. Who's going to believe that a successful real estate investor, probably with a wife and kid in college, took advantage of some whore out for his money. The story of a successful business man versus Scarlet a stripper at the Royal Playhouse," Scarlet felt disgusted saying it. A sudden realization came over her. She referred to Karen as Scarlet. Did he catch that, she looked him in the eyes and knew, yes he did.

"Well, did she make an agreement to have sex with him," Marcus raising an eyebrow. *Wow, he could have totally blasted me for lying but he didn't*, she thought.

"I don't know, maybe…it just wasn't what she bargained for. Marcus I just don't know anymore, I mean why we do this," Sylvia's words seemed to stumble from her lips. Her uncertainty was quite apparent. The sadness from this morning washed over her face. I can't loose it in front of this guy, I cannot, she thought.

"Well, you don't have to keep doing this if you don't want to," he said softly. He said it in a way which showed he cared, but it did not really add much hope. She felt stuck, not just in a rut, but in a hole, where the light to the exit was dim and there seemed to be no way out.

"Thank you for saying, but who'll hire a stripper," she replied, hoping that, despite the odds, Marcus would have a magical cure for her malady.

Marcus stepped around to the other side of the bar and sat in the stool next to her. He turned and faced her, which caused her heart to pick up pace. "When I see you, I don't see stripper. I see a really beautiful young street smart woman brave enough to drag her friend out of a really tough situation. I see you as someone who loves enough to even come up here on her own, irrespective of whatever risks it might have posed to you. You know the threat, dangerous bartenders like myself can pose," Scarlet chuckled at his remarks. "You're only a stripper if you want to be. No one can make you something you haven't agreed to or something you sincerely don't want to be." He stared into her eyes and broke through her barriers. Sylvia felt him willing her to believe.

The lock on the door opened, the electronic key giving access from the outside. The knob turned and Simon walked into the room, "bro you won't believe the morning I've had," his words trailed off towards the end. "What the hell is she doing here. After what she did at my party last night, I should call the police for assaulting one of my most important business partners," his anger broiled much faster than hers did. It was as if he had it on reserve all the while, waiting for the moment he needed to unleash its force. Simon walked into the room. He had two cups of coffee and placed them both down on the bar counter. "Don't you dare think I'm going to pay her after what happened last night." Though she was in the room, he directed his speech towards Marcus. But there it was, the thing she was attracted to and the truth which laid underneath. "This little bitch and her red head friend almost screwed everything up for me," Simon continued speaking indirectly to her.

"Wait…what? Bro, are you serious? Where were you last night. Were you at the same party," Marcus' voice rose. "That guy was a jerk." She was quite surprised to hear the ferocity in him. This baby-face might be more than meets the eye.

"Are you seriously going to stand up for this bitch, Marcus," Simon replied, though he did not seem all that surprised at his friend.

"That old fart had that young girl drugged. Simon, that's rape," Marcus attempted diplomacy in the midst of what looked like an all out war.

"Red head agreed to it and this whore stuck her nose into something she shouldn't have. And why are you fighting for this, this, stripper?" Simon said, now sounding disgusted at his friend.

Marcus tensed and stood to his feet, stared his friend in the eyes. "Simon, there was powder all over her face!"

"So what, these girls take coke all the time," Simon rebutted.

"But how do you think it looks. She was so doped up, she barely knew where she was," Marcus said through his teeth. "Rick took advantage of her Simon. I had to carry her out, Simon. These women are not some dispensable pawns on a chess game. Women are not to be used to gain some advantage in this little game you're playing," Marcus's voice gained strength and fire without being loud.

"I want her out, out of my apartment," Simon loudly insisted.

She got up from where she sat and walked towards the door. Her nerves were surprisingly quiet. "Hey wait," Marcus called out to her as she reached the door. He broke his gaze with Simon and started after her. When he got to her, she was already out the door and it closed behind him separating them from Simon's deathly gaze.

She turned around to face him and was a little surprised at how close she was to him. She pulled the money from her purse, "here is the money Scarlet took from him." Marcus reached out and took it. His brow was furrowed and body hot. She touched his face softening the frown, "No one has ever done that for me before. No one has ever fought for me before. Thank you for believing me." She stood tipped towards him and kissed him softly. She was right, his lips were sweet.

She did not dwell long, but pulled away and started walking towards the elevator. He reached for her putting something in her hand. "Call me," she pulled away and walked quickly towards the elevator. "Wait, I don't know your name."

She turned and with a smile said, "Sylvia." She could see him silently mouth her name.

Protection

f i f t e e n

MORNING CAME QUICK and Chad still felt the pangs of the night before. One of the seniors at the Rena's party spiked the punch and Chad could not resist the urge. He and many of the others drank and laughed well into the night. It was a good thing Josh's grandfather Bernie was there to pick them up. Bernie seemed to him like a dumb old man, but he was useful. Luis did not come. He thought the party was far too trendy for him. "Only the popular kids will be there," Chad remembered him saying; among whom Luis did not count himself. Chad would've been happy for another blow job, he had to run out on the last one. They had only gone as far as oral sex, but Chad suspected they'll be going all the way soon. Chad remembered Josh sitting with Rena. He liked Josh and now he's got a girlfriend. The likelihood of being with Josh was minuscule. He always thought Josh was cute, but seeing him in the locker room made Chad burn for him. The thoughts stirred in him now. So he hopped out of bed, jumped onto his computer and pulled up his favorite porn site. He reached down into his pants and proceeded to pleasing himself. The climax came quick. It's been a while, he thought. He felt a certain pressure released, like the deflating of a balloon.

He wanted to stay in bed a little while longer. It was after all Sunday and he had nothing important to look forward to. He remembered Josh complaining about his grandmother forcing him to go to Sunday Mass. Church was a dumb thing to Chad, his parents weren't religious and he inherited the same attitude; yet at times he wondered what difference church and God would have made in his life and in the life of his family. Would it have really helped to preserve or even better his family life? Would it have made a difference or simply extended the inevitable breakdown of his family unit. He shook off the idea and reminded himself of the terrible nature of those who'd called themselves followers of a faith. After all, they were all hypocrites, or so he'd heard his father say. He's never really spoken to one. All families are like mine, he resolved in thought; I'll never get married, it will just end up in the dumps. He ran his fingers over his short black hair and forced himself to get out of his room. He felt he had to get out into the open.

"The fresh air would do you some good," he would hear his mom say. Ten minutes into his day and he was already pissed. Jerking off relieved one tension, but then another subsisted. Great start to my Sunday.

Chad walked down the stairs feeling heavy as though burdened by the weight of all he carried. Though it is a heavy burden, he carries it nonetheless. It is his and no one else bear.

Hunger clawed at his insides. On his way to the kitchen, he caught a glimpse of the living room and remembered the moments before his mother walked out of his life. He could see her rustling through the drawers. She had said that she would call, but Chad didn't expect to hear from her again and he would hold on to that truth until she proved otherwise. The thought made him angry. Mothers should be there for their children and fathers should be there to protect their families. A framed family photo on the wall caught his attention. A new devious intention flooded his mind. Chad opened the door to a storage closet, took out his basketball and flung it at the picture on the wall. The impact of the ball caused the glass from the picture to implode. Shards flew everywhere, littering the areal rug and wood flooring. The frame broke and clattered to the ground, disturbing the peace of the Sunday morning. He heard foot steps from upstairs. He expected to see his brother and was not surprised when his father appeared at the top of the stairway.

"What the hell is going down there," Chad's father asked, his voice was croaky as as if awoken suddenly from a night terror. Chad looked at him but did not reply. He turned calmly and walked towards the kitchen. "Chad!" his father shouted, his face turning red. "What do you think you're doing?" He was at the bottom of the stairs now. He'd seen the ball and the damage it did, "you're throwing basketballs in the house now? The court isn't enough, you take up playing in here?"

Chad turned to his father and said, "you're pathetic!" and resumed his walk to the kitchen. He felt a heavy tug on his shoulder which made him spin around. He only saw the blur of his father's hand and then a terrible stinging pain across his left cheek. Chad stumbled to the side. The slap caught him by complete surprise. Anger and rage welled up inside himself and it came flooding out with tears.

"Mom is gone!" he shouted. "Mom is gone and you're doing nothing to get her back. For whatever you did, you're not even sorry." Chad wanted to keep his knowledge secret. "You're just going to let mom go without a word. You know what, I think you wanted her to go," Chad shouted even louder. By this time another footstep came rushing down the stairs. It was Chad's brother Michael. It seemed as if he'd been awake for a while. Mike got between the two, placing a hand on Chad's chest.

"Hey, calm down now," Mike demanded, looking at his brother. "Don't do this!" Their father huffed and puffed like an angry beast. It was apparent, Chad had hit a nerve; the response he received told him there was truth in what he said. His father did not respond. Father was a big man. He'd been in business and politics, spending the majority of his time around a desk, but he kept himself fit. Plus, his competitive nature meant that he would not back down from a fight. Though Chad worked out, a requirement for playing basketball, he was not near the size of his father and would certainly loose in a fight. He would have to temper his words and actions and listen to the wisdom of his brother. Father turned around and walked quickly towards the door, there was ferocity in every step. He grabbed his keys from a rack which hung by the door and stormed out the house barefooted. Chad could hear to roar of his Jaguar as it came to life, the front gates opened, and the car screeched out of the drive way. The boys looked at each other, feeling awkward in the silence. Mike turned to the living and grabbed a broom from the storage closet.

An hour had passed, Chad and Mike had finished eating, and father was not back. Mike took off to meet up with some friends and it was quickly approaching mid-day. Chad took to his father's office, plopped himself behind the computer, but the browser window and surveillance was gone. The computer was totally unlocked and he was able to access it quickly. For a man with so much to hide, he sure does a crappy job protecting himself, Chad thought. He starting looking around different folders but was unable to find the files he had seen previously. Did he delete them, Chad questioned himself? He started looking around in the computer's cookies folder and history folder but couldn't find anything related to porn or surveillance. He was about to give up the search, but though to call Luis. Luis asked him to go back over what he saw in the cookies and history folder. The folders weren't complete clear and there were entries from that day but he didn't see anything which bore any relation to what he should see. "Well, there are plenty of ways to hide what you've been doing. Of course, erasing your history would be the quickest and best way to deter prying eyes," Luis explained.

"You don't know my dad," Chad replied, "he's the least technological person on this planet. And I do mean it. Monks in the mountains are probably more computer savvy than my old man." After saying that, an icon on the desktop suddenly stood out. "Oh hello, what is this?"

"What do you see?" Luis asked.

"There's an app on the desktop called Direct Connect, but the icon actually says VPN on it," Chad relayed.

"Oh, wow. Well that's interesting. Open the browser you saw before," Luis instructed. Chad opened an Internet Explorer window but nothing came up.

"It's not pulling up anything," Chad explained.

"This computer's browsing is probably setup to working through a VPN; which means Virtual Private Network. It's a great way to connect to another computer network somewhere over the web. Once you connect, you can get access to the other network's resources and possible open sites you weren't able to open before. VPNs are used in the dark web to publish illegal stuff without being tracked. The plot thickens," Luis sounded intrigued. He wanted to dig deeper.

"Okay, I'm going to click on it," Chad said.

"Go for it," Luis affirmed the decision.

"There's a username and password," Chad said, sounding disappointed. Luis sighed, sharing a similar sentiment.

"Well that's a bust," Luis said.

"Alright, I'll let you know if I'm able to connect okay. Thank for all your help you sexy sexy boy you," Chad flirted.

"You better tell me what you find," Luis replied. "Be careful though. Most of these things will only allow you to try the password a few times before locking you out completely."

"I'll make a note of that. I'll see you tomorrow, okay?" Chad said attempting to get his friend off the phone.

"Okay, c ya lover boy," Luis replied. Chad was doing his best to keep his voice civil. He did not want to show his bitter feelings towards his father to his little boy toy. His explanation to his friend was that he was attempting to find where dad hid his sicko porn. Of course, he left out the part that he was watching video and was engaged in sexual relations with another of his friend's mother.

"My old man is such an idiot," Chad said. The truth was, the password was saved and Chad had full access into the remote network. He opened the Internet explorer again and it opened up to an IP Address which displayed the the surveillance. A notification popped up in the lower right, virtual drive connection established. Chad clicked on it and the video files he'd seen before reappeared. He turned back to the surveillance window after watching the video through again. He saw Josh's mother sitting on the bed in the bedroom with another red head woman. They were holding hands.

℣

It was Monday, the beginning of a new week. Chad was not looking forward to the week ahead. He was up late the previous night, his mind reeling, staving off sleep. When he made it to school, he was grumpy and he knew it. His other classmates saw his face and stayed clear of him. All the better, he thought, he didn't feel like talking to anyone. The first few classes went by fairly quickly. If you asked him what happened during those periods, he'd be surely hard-pressed recalling any specific detail. His memory was like looking through a hazy glass, unable to identify what was on the other side but knowing there's something there. There was something peculiar which caught his attention. He saw Rena talking to the new boy. He'd turned into a hallway and ran into the two. It seemed as if they knew each other. But she was not smiling. She seemed very upset

At lunch time, he sat at a table by himself. He looked and saw Luis sitting with his other techie friends. Brian and Josh sat together with Brittany and Rena sitting across from them. Chad tried to shield his face so they wouldn't see him. Except he wanted to be seen. He wanted to be seen by Josh. His attention was fastened on him, unable to let him out of his sight. A figure stepped in front of him blurring his vision. It was Luis, "why don't you just go over there? Are guys no longer friends?"

Chad smiled and said, "I just don't feel up to it today."

"Does it have something to do with what you found yesterday?" Luis inquired. He was intrigued with Chad's father's secret VPN, which wasn't very secret.

"I couldn't figure out the password and I closed the application before it completely locked me out," Chad lied. "Don't want my father finding out that I've been snooping around his computer," he further explained. He received an approving nod and knew that his answer was satisfactory. An idea popped into Chad's head. He would have to be careful as to how he explained it or else his secrets might be revealed. "Hey, can you help me with something," Chad looked into Luis' eyes as he spoke. "Sit down for a second."

"Yeah, what is it," Luis sat down, curiosity tingling.

"I saw something earlier today that has got me a little worried for my friend over there," Chad said and motioned his head towards Josh's table. Chad explained what he saw earlier, between Rena and the new boy Jeremy. "See the thing is, he'd fallen for lying girls before. He dated Bianca who lied and almost broke the three of us apart. Do you know the new kid, Jeremy?"

"Yeah," Luis replied with skepticism written all over his face.

"I saw Josh's girl over there, arguing with Jeremy. Where does she know him from? Why were they arguing? And how comes none of us have heard anything about it, especially considering all we've been through. There are just too many questions surrounding this girl." Luis gave an approving nod. "I know this might be a selfish request because they are my friends, but it's important. I want to look into this new girl, but I don't know the first place to look. And that's where I need your help."

"Ah…okay, so is that the reason you're post up over here," Luis said sounding unsure of the reasons Chad had given. Chad nodded with sympathetic eyes. "I didn't buy that, but I'll help you find whatever there is to find on this girl. Shouldn't be too hard." Chad knew that Luis would've done anything for him just because he asked. "You know, you could just come sit with me," Luis said, sounding embarrassed that he had to even ask.

"Thank you cuteness, but I'm on my way out. I'll talk to you later okay," Chad said before standing and walking out the cafeteria.

New York

s i x t e e n

H E WAS ONLY a few days into the training for his new position and already Marcus was tired of the whole thing. He thought that he would be shadowing with the manager of the New York branch office, but for the last few days he was in a conference room doing computer work. He knew for certain Bobby had something to do with this. He would pop in every so often, acting all smug, to make sure Marcus was on task. He wouldn't really say anything, he would just look and then leave. Marcus always thought it a little creepy. When he finally had the chance to shadow the New York branch manager turned out to be very impressed with Marcus' knowledge, which only made Bobby more upset. Bobby didn't really expect Marcus to be so knowledgeable in the operations of the firm. Bobby figured that if Marcus was to take this position, he would have to fight for it. The position would not come easy. However, Marcus was branch manager and he will not be dissuaded. Marcus' knew that his years at Berkley prepared him well enough to handle the pressure of managing the relatively small branch in Atlanta.

On his way back from lunch on the third day of his training, Marcus, about to turn a corner heard Bobby's voice, "how is he doing?"

Syed Masood, a portly man, with cool skin and jet black hair was standing with him outside the conference room. Syed was the branch manager of the New York office and the one Marcus was shadowing. "He's doing very well so far. He's quite learned. The kid knows his stuff. I think he'll make a good manager for the Atlanta office. On par with or even better than Mike Rolando."

"Let's just hope he doesn't screw up like Mike did," Bobby said with disgust. Mike was caught funneling money into offshore accounts. Bobby had to work overtime to keep it out of the press. They stood the chance of loosing all their clients if word ever got out that someone within the organization was charged with embezzlement. "If he screws up anything or if any alarms go off in your head about him, let me know," Bobby finished before turning and walking away.

"Will do," Syed responded.

Marcus could hear the two sets of foot steps. One sounded as though it was walking away. The other opened the door to the conference room. Marcus waited a few seconds before stepping around the corner. He was pleased with what he heard. Bobby's anger towards him was to be expected. But to hear that Syed thought him capable of running the office gave him the drive he needed to finish out his day with confidence.

Cʒ

The up side to this whole trip was the view of the city from the 25th floor of the Mandarin Oriental. The company paid for this suite which had a foreground view of central park and the Manhattan skyline in the background. Marcus absolutely loved the concrete jungle. It gave him a rush his parent's earthy all natural vineyard didn't. He was pacing his room, looking over the company guidelines when an unknown number showed up on the screen of his iPhone. Marcus, like many others, was quite weary of telephone marketers. He had been called numerous times over the last four days and it had become quite the annoyance. How do they always know the perfect time to call and totally piss you off, he thought. "I really don't have time for this," he said to himself. I should just let it ring, he thought. But in case it was something important, he didn't want to miss the call. He answered the line, totally expecting some kind of automated phone call recording or someone with a foreign accent asking for a Mr Walden or some other variant to his real name. How could anyone mess up Warren. It was so simple and common. To his surprise he heard a hesitant but familiar voice, "Hello Marcus."

"Sylvia," Marcus replied with surprise in his voice. His focus had solely been on his work and hearing her voice was a welcomed distraction. It had been already four days since he left Miami and he was beginning to wonder. "I was beginning to think you had forgotten about me."

"Oh, how could I forget those glasses," she replied smiling through the phone, something Marcus was used to hearing. He could tell whether his business negotiations over the phone were going well by listening to telltale inflections in the person's voice. It was something very hard to hide; not that anyone would intentionally think to hide the fact that they were smiling. "So how did you find out where I lived?" Sylvia asked with interest. "Are you a stalker Marcus?"

"I have my ways," he replied sneakily. He was always fond of finding out more about someone than they would naturally care to share.

"Your ways huh?" Sylvia replied with an air of suspicion. "Do your ways happen to involve a person by the name of Max Dinero with whom your friend Simon is associated?"

"Ahhh, it might," sounding as though he was caught with his pants around his ankles. "I just figured I would send you a little reminder to call me since I hadn't heard from you in three days."

"Oh no, call the search party, something must be wrong, a girl hadn't called baby-face in three days," Sylvia jeered.

"Hardy har har, very funny," he replied sounding like an old pirate of the Caribbean.

"I've only now met you Mr Warren," Sylvia said.

"I don't remember telling you my last name," he said suspiciously.

"I have my ways," Sylvia said, implying, two could play this game.

"Oh, you have jokes…well, you can be rest assured that you'll be well taken care of. My room overlooks central park and there are plenty of restaurants and bars close by. We could even catch a show on Broadway. You can bring your friend if you'd like. Come on, what do you say?" he said with confidence knowing that if her friend heard about this she would probably be the one to make the decision.

"Well, I wasn't really planning on taking a trip to New York," Sylvia said with a thoughtful pause at the end.

"Oh come on, it will be fun," Marcus said playfully pleading. "Escape the hustle and bustle of the city of Miami in exchanged for the hustle and bustle of New York."

"And you said I could bring a friend? What are you trying to assure me that you're not a crazed mad financial rapist. Any friend? Even my red headed side kick? You know, the one who created such a stir for your good buddy Simon?" Having Karen around would risk sparks flying if Simon were to come. On the other hand, it was a chance worth taking to see Sylvia again.

"Girl-wonder is more than welcome, I'll make it happen. So I am to send you another first class ticket? Great!" Marcus said as a statement not a question.

"Wow, you just won't take no for an answer huh?" Sylvia quickly made the distinction.

"That's because you are worthy of my pursuit," Marcus said, referencing the conversation of the night they first met.

"Marcus, don't you ever think you can buy me with first class tickets to New York. It's going to take more than that," and in an instant her tone switched to something serious. "Okay?"

"Yes Ma'am," he replied.

"Now that we've got that all sorted out, I'll see you tomorrow," her voice changed again to the sparkling girl she was a minute before.

"Ahhh, okay," the feeling that he might be getting into something well over his head crept up in his stomach. The line went dead and Marcus pushed off his feelings of doubt and subdued them, locking them away in their cage. Marcus was the kind of man who always made sure everything was worked out to the smallest detail. This time, he found himself fighting off the urge to be logical. He didn't want to be reasonable or wise in his decision making concerning Sylvia.

He wasn't too sure what he was doing, but there was something about her that attracted him. There were so many other women in his circle, who would certainly look great as a trophy, but with whom he could not see himself spending more than one night.

She was the first to try to throw him off by giving him a false name and by standing up for something worth fighting for; her friend. Marcus had seen so many other women stab their friends in the back for a chance to sleep with a rich guy. "Bunch of gold diggers," he said to himself as his mind ran over all his failed relationships. And the one woman he was interested in had to be a stripper, he thought. His parents would have a laugh. He would not be telling them anytime soon, he thought. He paced back and forth with his eyes to the ground. "She is different," he primed himself; hoping and praying that she really was. If the woman of his dreams was indeed a stripper, then that is the woman he must pursue.

Marcus had not dated anyone for almost a solid year. Every date, relationship, and one night stand had ended always leaving Marcus astonished at the values of today's modern woman. Marcus thought for sure that there was something in the Atlanta water system which made women absolutely crazy. There were some who would go out with him on Tuesday and sleep with another man on Thursday. The uneasy confrontation in the bar, when he would catch her locked in the arms of another man, would always end with him looking like the idiot. And these days, dating for a month equaled lavish trips to exotic islands, stays at luxury resorts, and being disappointed when he would refuse the suggested expensive gifts from Tiffany's. After being shocked for a few years at the extravagant expectations of the modern day diva, Marcus resolved that relationships are best kept at one night stands. But even the occasional fling lost its taste. He simply found himself caring for the woman laying next to him and the desire for something deeper could no longer be ignored.

Do You

s e v e n t e e n

TODAY WAS FRIDAY and it was his last day of training. He would spend the rest of the weekend in New York before heading back to Atlanta on Sunday and start his new position on Monday. Marcus booked Sylvia and Karen on the evening flight from Ft Lauderdale to La Guardia Airport, so that he could pick them up after his training. His thoughts were on her all day and he simply couldn't wait to see her again. Waiting at the exit before baggage claim, he could see Karen's redhead bobbing through the crowd. A few moments later, he could see Sylvia. Her long black hair, curled at the end, her eyes dark and sultry, her beautifully thick lip. She walked with the grace of a princess and could easily command the atmosphere of any royal ball. His heart raced. "What the hell was I thinking?" he said to himself. "Yeah…I wasn't thinking," he answered his own question. She looked better than he'd remember.

They finally made it through the gate and Karen took off running. "What the," he said, but before he could finish, she threw her arms around his neck, kissed him on the cheek.

"Hello baby-face," Karen spoke softly into his ear. She pulled away smiling, some of her bright red lipstick left on his cheek. "I don't think we've officially met. I'm Scarlett," she held out her hand to shake his.

"Ohhh, I see! Red hair, Scarlett. Marcus, nice to meet you" he took her hand.

"I assure you, the pleasure is mine," Karen sounded refined which made Sylvia chuckle. Marcus looked at Sylvia, "thanks for coming."

"Now that the formalities are out of the way, I guess we can get going?" he asked, as though there was some other option.

"Lead the way," Sylvia replied.

They jumped in the car and headed back to the hotel where everyone was able to get a shower and change. That night, Marcus took them to a rooftop restaurant. They ate outside. The 65 degree Fahrenheit temperature was a bit chilly for the Miami girls, but the restaurant was kind enough to put out a single heating lamp to accommodate them. A few drinks later and they were like pigs in a blanket. The dj must have gotten to the latin portion of his playlist, because a few hit songs played in a row and the girls couldn't help but get up and dance. They were doing the salsa and merengue. Marcus was quite content with just watching them from the side lines. They are having so much fun, he thought, no reason for me to spoil that. He should have known that there was no way they would let him just sit there. Both girls came over after the song was finished, but another one of their favorites started, a bachata hit. They pulled him reluctantly unto the dance floor. He knew there was no way to escape the embarrassment, so he downed another shot of Tequila and allowed himself to be dragged. If Simon saw him doing what he was doing, gyrating, jigging, and bobbing, he knew for certain he would be made fun of for the rest of his life. His logic concluded that being sandwiched between two beautiful women should positively leverage the appearance of his so called dancing. Having only one woman would have been a stretch and it would have made him more resistant, but this two-to-one ratio made sense. It was certainly a great return on an investment.

The suite he was in was big enough to house 3 people. Karen slept in the guest bedroom, which she was more than happy with. They came in from dinner and as soon as her head hit the pillow, she was fast asleep. Marcus insisted that Sylvia use his room and he would sleep on the couch. Sylvia did not fight him on the matter, she simply smiled at the proposal and walked to her room.

The next day, the girls slept in, as was their normal routine. Marcus was up early. He ordered breakfast and surprised them with a feast fit for a king and his royal concubines. After breakfast they took to the streets. They saw a Broadway show, ate New York style pizza, did a little shopping, and even took a nice stroll through central park. Marcus told them about everything he was doing. The position he was training for and the responsibilities he would have. All of which the girls seemed very impressed with. The conversation lulled, as he spoke about the things he wanted to do. He soon realized how uncomfortable they became. Karen mentioned that she wanted to open her own hair salon. She was the one who styled both Sylvia and her own hair. She planned on going back to school, then she would get the certification to start the business. Sylvia stayed silent through all this and Marcus did not bother to ask.

Later that evening Marcus took them to one of the hottest clubs in New York. He and the girls vigorously danced. All the troubles of the week flowed away and all the stresses of tomorrow were forgotten.

-=-=-=

"Do you think your parents would like me," Sylvia was laying on the couch in the living room of the hotel room, a purple silhouette of lights from the city washed over her body. Marcus sat at her feet slowly massaging them. The question caused him to pause for a brief moment as he tried to think of a smart answer to her very candid question.

"Of course they would," he replied. Well at least he'd hoped so. He knew meeting the parents at this stage would be moving way too fast, but he assured himself that she probably didn't mean that. But what did she mean, curiosity loomed in his mind. He kept his eyes from looking at her directly so she wouldn't see any trace of uncertainty.

"Yeah right," she said and sat up. She held his face and turned it towards hers, "you're lying. I'm not the kind of girl your mother wants to see on your arm. I'm not what they picture for you." She saw right through him. He realized then that he'd better not lie to her. Her street smarts were sharper than a butchers knife. She read him like a book and they'd only known each other for a week.

"I'm sure you're a great person on the inside," he said sarcastically. Sylvia chuckled. He continued, though in a more serious tone, "I'm sure that once they get to know you that they would love you."

"Marcus, you seem like a really good guy with good upbringing. You seem to have also not realized that I am a stripper. I am a stripper Marcus. I am a stripper. I take off my clothes for the enjoyment of men and women. I am nothing more than a fantasy. A figment of your imagination. I am a living representation of the porn most men have on their computers. I am what their wives cannot be. I feed the lust in their hearts. I give them the thrill without the commitment. I am not even a real human being in their eyes. I am just a beautiful thing that entertains their fantasy. I am not the girl your parents want in your life. At least not for any extended period of time. I'm probably good for the night on the town, but probably not good wife material. Isn't that what your parents want? Wife material?"

Marcus was at a loss for words. He knew he had to be careful and choose his words wisely. Her heart was wide open and there was no fluff. She was not beating around the bush. She had entrusted him with her fragile truth and he had to be careful not to break it. "Sylvia, when I see you I don't see a stripper. I see a strong courageous woman. You grabbed that old geezer by the balls and I knew for certain I was in love." They both laughed but hushed remembering Karen had passed out in her room. Marcus told her about his sister, an example of a woman who did not take the easy route of simply taking over the family business. She decided to build a career all on her own and is now quite successful. "The life you live now is full of so many risks. I can only imagine the amount of stress you girls go through. It takes courage to keep going when the path ahead is dark and dangerous," he continued, remembering her hesitations from previous conversations. "Those qualities are precious. When you came to the apartment, I realized there was something about you that would make me fight my best friend for your honor. You stood up for someone who had the odds stacked against her, made me want to stand up for you too. I really want to get to know what that something is; however long it takes; however hard it is." Wow, those were bold words, he thought. Marcus could hardly believe they came out of his mouth, but he could not take back a word and neither did he want to. Each word bore witness to something inside him.

She continued to stare him in the eyes, "what do you want Marcus Warren?"

He could feel her longing for something. She wanted to hear something and this was his chance to prove his worth to her. "Well, I want what all men want. Or maybe I should say, what we all want, as humans. I want to fall in love," Marcus said. That was so corny, he thought. He spoke softly, carefully articulating each word to precision. "I want to find that person who will make me whole. I want to find someone who will make me happy and I can make them happy." A smile crept across Sylvia's lips signaling her approval.

"What if I told you I cannot return your love, would you give up on me?" she paused for a moment before continuing. Her lips would open and close, small sounds escaped, as if struggling to find the right words. "I don't even know what love is anymore," Sylvia said. She looked away from Marcus and out towards the city. "People tell you all the time they love you, but why? Love makes no sense. A good relationship might even come out of it, but give it some time and I guarantee that relationship will end up in the dumps. The other times, love is used to just manipulate. You fall head over heels for someone and you become blind to their faults. Sooner or later those faults come around and bite you on the butt. Marcus, I am convinced that love is not as wishful as you see it. It is not some magic force that draws people together. It is just juices, hormones, DNA, or something. But there is no magic." Sylvia looked him in the eyes and smiled. She took one of the cushions and placed it underneath her head making it her pillow. "I'll sleep on the couch tonight."

"No, you're not," Marcus replied in a whisper. He got up, releasing her feet from his hold. Then to her surprise he reached under her body, hot from the impending sleep, picked her up and took her to the bedroom. She curled up in his arms, like a kid in front the fireplace in the middle of winter. The warmth of their bodies mingled.

-=-=-

Sylvia's flight was before Marcus' so he walked her to the her gate. The moment had come to say goodbye and he felt his heart longing to spend more time with her. She was by far the most interesting woman he'd ever met. She was more than the strong warrior princess he'd seen in Simon's apartment. There was something distinct about her. It went beyond the curves of her waist and the five inch heels. "So can I see you again," he said while looking into her eyes.

Karen looking at the both of them said, "of course, you can see her anytime baby-face."

"Ahhh…" Sylvia looked at Karen and cleared her throat.

"Ok, ok, fine, I'll give you guys a little privacy, in the middle of the freaking airport" Karen said loud and sarcastic.

"Marcus, thank you for an amazing time," she started out.

"Why does this sound like a no," Marcus replied pulling away.

"Well, let's just see if you live up to your words," she replied. Sylvia reached forward and kissed him on the lips.

Karen stood there watching the two of them with her hands at her waist, "seriously Syl, if you don't rape this guy, I will." Sylvia let out a huge laugh but quickly placed a hand over her mouth to stifle the sound.

Marcus looked as white as a ghost. "Bye Marcus honey boo," Karen said in a cute and girlie way, kissed him on the cheek and both girls headed towards their gate. Sylvia looked back at him and gave a small wave before disappearing out of sight.

Father

e i g h t e e n

THOUGHTS OF RENA made Josh's stomach overflow with fluttering butterflies. He had not thought of Elizabeth once when with Rena. The conversation with Rena replayed in his mind like a song stuck on repeat. She had advised him to try talking to his mother. It was probably one of those things where it was best to act in the moment. He really didn't want to but whether he felt comfortable or not he had to get this off his chest.

Rena knew what it was to lose a mother and he supposed she was right. "I'm still alive, it's not too late," Josh said to himself, attempting to pump life back into his will to do the right thing. He saw his mother in a burning car, screaming for her life. He saw her attempting to protect him. Would she really protect him, he questioned himself? And though he did not admit it to himself, he felt a stir inside him when Rena spoke of her mother protecting Kylie. Josh was certain his mother would save her own skin. He felt the heat of the hell they were in and smelled the strong odor of motor oil, gasoline, and burning leather. He supposed he would feel nothing if she died. He imagined life would go on and that his only regret would be that she hadn't died earlier. The thought made him angry. Life should not just go on in the event your mother dies, he thought. Years after Rena's mother died, she still mourned the loss. But why should I mourn Sylvia, he thought. He felt hot. The back and forth in his mind made him feel as though he was running laps on the football field.

The fact of the matter is, there was no way to truly know how he would feel because he'd not ever been in that position. Maybe one day he would be. Would Rena be right then? There was a possibility that he would greatly regret not doing something when he could have. It is like being thirsty and not knowing it. And it was only when you have finally had a cup of water you realized the magnitude of your thirst. And when you have had a full glass, you thought that one glass would do. Except, that the one glass of water only served to expose the true depth of your thirst lurking within. Rena was the first girl he had ever felt strongly for and though it was only a taste it left him wanting more.

He had grandma Sophia but she was not his real mother and neither was she the nurturing loving type. Grandma was simply the woman who took care of him. The woman who fed him. He supposed though, the moment she had a chance to get rid of him she would do it in a heart beat. Sylvia, in her eyes, was a mistake. He was probably Sylvia's mistake also. But how did this mistake happen. And the reality of the matter is it takes two to tango. So what guy was this mistake with. He had never really heard about his father from Sylvia nor from grandma.

He saw the relationship Rena had with her father and he envied it. He wanted that. He wanted something. He did not think he wanted it but he did. He wanted someone to speak to about how he felt about Rena. He wanted someone who knew about his temptations who were not as dumb as Brian and Chad. He wanted limits. Someone who would tell him not to do something and someone who would challenge him to be something. So far this person was coach. Coach's voice resounded in his mind, "keep your head in the game Bradley." The sentiment, coach's most used phrase, made Josh chuckle. Maybe with my dad, I wouldn't have to learn things the hard way, Josh thought.

"Rena I really hope you're right," he said out loud. "It sounds dumb to say it's too late after hearing what she'd been through," he said out loud, attempting to reason outside his head. His head was bursting with what seemed like an innumerable number of thoughts. "Would knowing who my dad is change anything," he continued pausing in between as though expecting an answer from some unseen force. "If he really wanted me he would be around wouldn't he? If he's dead then that would make the difference I guess and it would explain why no one speaks of him. I still have to find out what kind of guy he is. At least I'll know what kind of DNA runs though my veins. Hell, I don't even know if that makes a difference…ahhh," he got louder.

"Hey Josh, is everything ok in there," Sophia shouted from the living room. She was watching her favorite TV drama.

"It's all good Sophie…I mean grandma," he replied loud enough for her to hear. There was no further word from her, which was not a surprise considering Grey's Anatomy was on.

The phone rang once and he could feel his willingness to speak to Sylvia wane. It rang a second time and his stomach flushed down the toilet. "What am I doing," Josh said to himself before pressing the red button on the land phone to hang up the call.

Not ten seconds later the phone he had just hung up rang. He could hear grandma pause the TV with the full intention of picking up the phone from her end. It's probably Sylvia calling back, he thought. His hand hesitated before finally grabbed the the receiver, causing the phone to stop its incessant badgering.

He cautiously placed the phone against his ear, "Hello…hello," Sylvia's voice in the ear piece sounded groggy.

"Mom, sorry for waking you up, I had a question, but since you're out I'll call another time," Josh said in a hurry. He looked over at the clock in disbelief. It read 8:30PM. His day was about to end and it sounded as if he had woken her up early for hers.

"No Josh it's fine, I'm here," Sylvia said with a level of strain. Her heard a rustling noise, the sound of her repositioning.

"Mom, I want to know about my dad." There I said it, he thought, now kicking himself because he sounded stupid. On the other hand, he was certainly relieved that he'd finally asked the question. Now the ball was in her court. The father question was a good starting point, he thought. It might be the bridge he needs to get to the porn question; a inquiry he had no idea how to tackle.

Sylvia sighed and said, "I knew I would eventually have to tell you this, Josh."

"What is he dead," Josh blurted in an alarmed and chilling voice.

"No, no, that's not it," Sylvia said followed by another sigh. "You see, I got pregnant with you really young. Actually, I was your age when I got pregnant and everything turned upside down. Life with Sofie was crazy at the time. I wasn't a very good girl in school. Actually, half the time I wasn't even in school. The other half, I was drunk or high. I had a boyfriend that I really loved and I thought he loved me too. He got me into a whole lot of trouble. He was a freshman in college when we met and he took me to one of his college parties. I had a few drinks and my head got really woozy. It wasn't like anything I'd felt before. The next thing I remembered was waking up in the hospital with tubes down my throat. A few weeks later I realized I was pregnant with you. I blame myself for what happened. I got mixed up with the wrong people. So, to be honest," Sylvia's words lost their steam, "ahhh."

"You don't know who my father is do you?" Josh said the words Sylvia could not.

"No, I don't," Sylvia confirmed. Josh's heart sank in a malaise.

"I am so sorry Josh. I know that doesn't really help things, but…" her words failed again, swept away in a gurgling mumble.

"I can't believe this. You're just a whore. That's all you are, a whore. You just go around sleeping with a bunch of guys…" he couldn't find the words to finish. He was drowning in an ever growing pool of anger, frustration, and disappointment. He had been so hopeful. He had hoped for something in his life to make sense. This desperation brought out the worst in him. Sylvia's words, though heart felt as they were, did not help. She doesn't know who my father is. *She doesn't know who my father is*, he thought over and over again; unable to shake the spiral in his brain. That spiral soon translated to the room. His world started to spin, thoughts raced in and out of his head before he could properly translate them. "I…I…hate this," his words sounded as though some unseen force was holding them back and he struggled to release only the few.

"I should have told you earlier Josh. I should have not waited. I just didn't know what…how to say it," Sylvia hearing the struggle felt powerless to do anything over the phone. Hence, she resorted to blaming herself.

"I know Josh, I'm a whore, and I'm not proud of it; believe me. I don't know who your father is, but… " Sylvia was at a loss, nothing seemed sufficient. What could she possibly say to make things right? "But…," she tried again. "But I'll try my best to be there for you."

"Josh, whats going on in there," Sofie spoke through the door.

"Everything is fine grandma," he replied. Sofie's intrusion broke his train of thought and like a small candle lit flame in the back of a dark room, he heard and saw Rena's words.

"Sylvia, I have to go to bed," still angry, he yearned to be untethered from the broiling emotions. He really preferred being calm. Getting angry was not his style. Josh didn't really think he got angry very well. There are some people who got angry and you could just feel the power of their anger pulsate, filling the room. His anger was wimpy. His anger looked like a temper tantrum and not the real thing.

Sylvia not knowing what to saw simply replied, "okay."

He placed the receiver back in the cradle. I hurt her, he thought loud in his head. "I really hurt her," he spoke it out loud. His hands were trembling. "She deserved it!" He clenched his fist.

The next day he could not wait to see Rena. Grandma Sofie's car was fixed so she took him to school. Plus, Sofie didn't want to depend on Sylvia to do it, lest Josh come home with another letter. He got to school and met Rena by the lockers. Though he spent the entire time at the party with her, he was still in disbelief that she was indeed his girlfriend. He stood by his locker, waiting for her to show up and when she did he simply waved at her. Rena rolled her eyes and walked over.

"You can come over and say hi Joshua Bradley, I promise I won't bite," she said sassing him. "Or are you embarrassed to be seen with me."

"I'm afraid you'll be the one who'll be embarrassed. Either way, I'm very shy," he spoke in a girlie British voice making Rena laugh.

"Did you ask her," Rena looked to his eyes as she questioned him. Her glare pierced right through him. His thoughts, intentions, his will and motives were naked before her. He couldn't lie. Well, he couldn't lie without losing her trust.

"Yeah," he said with a tired sigh. The memories drained him of all strength. He wanted to see Rena because he thought she would have distracted him or something. He guest he wanted to see her so he could tell her he really tried. He tried to make things right, but his mother is impossible. His mother is a lost cause and she is not worth his time. He wanted to see her reaction to how angry he became. He wanted to see Rena's shock at his mother's completely ludicrous story. He wanted to hear her say how right he was for telling her off; that she deserved everything and more.

"Well, how did it go," Rena said, shifting her weight from one foot to the other. Her eyes were so bright, like a school girl hearing the latest in gossip news. She's going to so get a kick out of this, he thought.

"Well…" he drew the word.

"Joshua Bradley," Rena started but the bell rang for the start of their first period class. "Tell me later okay."

"Okay," he said agreeably. But to be honest, if Rena had said, go dunk your head in the toilet, he probably would have agreed to that too.

This would give him more time to amend the story, so it doesn't sound like he was a spoiled little brat.

First period was always a pleasure. Mrs. Anders was as radiant as ever. Today was a skirt which made her look like a weather girl on the Channel 6 news. Her clothes were in no way revealing but they were so tight there was nothing hidden. A thong imprinted itself on her backside as she forecast sunny skies with only a 25% chance of rain. Of course she failed to mention the reason for the heat was her obvious sexy body and the raging hormones of teenage boys in the room.

Brian poked at Josh snapping him out of his trance. "Hey, are you seeing this," Brian whispered. He might as well have used his regular voice because the speaker phone he called a mouth caught the attention of at least five other kids around the classroom. The attention made him pull back in his seat, playing the good little boy.

"Yeah, I see it," Josh whispered back.

"A thing of beauty," Brian replied, this time lowering his voice so no one else could hear.

"Is there something you'd like to say Mr. Townsend," Ms Anders' words caused everyone to turn and look at Brian. Josh chuckled and said under his breath, "that's karma you jerk."

"No ma'am, Ms Anders ma'am," Brian replied chipper as though he was fully alert to what she was teaching.

"Mr Bradley, why don't you catch Mr Townsend up on what I was saying since you think it so funny," Ms Anders finished what she was writing, turned and gazed at Josh.

He took a deep breath and said, "The veil over his face was simply a metaphor for the hidden and deeper things in life. People resented him because they couldn't understand why someone would live their life with a veil over their face. Even his wife who was supposed to be supportive of him eventually left him when she could no longer imagine what he looked like. It wasn't until he was dead that people finally realized he was a great man who did great things. It wasn't until he was dead that people stopped focusing on his appearance and realized his accomplishments, which was a presentation of his heart." The other students in the class were stunned.

Even Ms Anders found it hard to speak after she had fully expected both boys to fumble around the question. But Josh recovered quite well; far better than expected. Brian nodded approvingly, as though to say, "that sounded great buddy. Good job!" But he said nothing out of fear that Cleopatra, the beautiful queen of 10th grade English, would slay him. Though if he was to be slain, he would sure choose her as his executioner.

"Thank you Josh," she said, sounding surprised. Still there was no response from the class, who probably reflected the same fear as Brian. Josh did not really know what to make of the whole thing.

Either way, he had better things to think about. Things like, what he was going to tell Rena. He had been perfectly honest with Rena in the past, but he wasn't sure if he should mention everything about what Sylvia did. He wasn't sure how she would handle it.

Ms Anders had gone back to teaching and was wrapping up by handing out assignments. The bell rang and everyone was leaving. Ms Anders caught Josh's eye and she motioned for him to come to her desk. "That was a pretty good answer you gave in class today."

"Well, you know I didn't want to disappoint you Ms Anders," Josh said.

"You've never disappointed me before, but I suppose one day you will," she spoke as though she could see into the misty uncertainty of the future.

"What do you mean by that," Josh said, looking puzzled.

She smiled and said, "goodbye Josh." With that he turned and started out the classroom. He turned his head once more, attempting to see something in her eyes which might betray the truth. He locked eyes with his teacher who was smiling, rosy cheeks and happy eyes. Josh broke eye contact and continued walking out the room. There is no way I'm telling Rena about this.

"You said what?" Rena said horrified.

"Didn't you hear what she did," Josh was a bit surprised at her response.

"I can't believe you're trying to justify this Josh," Rena said with the still horrified look on her face. "She is your mother Josh, whether you like it or not. She is your mother"

"At this point I might as well not have a mother," Josh said rather calmly but surprised that he had to defend his position. His mother was an embarrassment. "Rena, I haven't told you have the story! Rena, she did porn. Chad and Brian saw it too. She had a rubber ball in her mouth Rena, a rubber ball." There he said it, still calm so no one else could hear, but it was out and now she would understand his anger.

"But Josh, those are things she did in a time when she had lost her way. Didn't she regret it? Maybe she's still struggling to find the right path but either way you're her son and she's your mother. If you don't support each other then who will?"

"I don't want that whore for a mother," Josh was breathing hard, his hands expressive, but his voice was kept low as other kids marched to their parent's cars.

"Josh, you're being totally selfish right now," Rena argued.

"What the hell do you know," Josh's face contorted. His eyes narrowed as though attempting to bring his target into focus. "Who are you to lecture me on what I should and should not do."

"I am a girl who doesn't want to be treated the same way you treat your mother," Rena replied through her teeth in an attempt not to shout. "Goodbye Josh." She walked away towards her father's car as he was pulling up.

She called me Josh, he thought. He liked it so much better when she called him by his full name. She obviously said it out of frustration. The one girl he thought he could get close to now thought he was selfish and a jerk for saying those things to his mother. Maybe I am selfish. Maybe I am just a jerk and she is just a whore. Maybe we're all just screwed up.

Later that evening Josh found it unbearable to see anyone. He supposed he should call Rena and try to make things better, but what would he say. It seemed like the logical thing to do, but he lost all courage. He just felt like escaping. While doing his homework, he often found himself staring at the wall, his mind lost in thought on the events of the last 24 hours. He tried not to think about Rena and his mother but it would be a long time before he would forget. The thoughts were all in a screaming match and he found himself immobilized unable to do anything productive. There were no logical conclusions, just a messy scene.

In an attempt to distract himself, he found his thoughts on Ms Anders. "Now she's a woman," he said to himself. She has a degree, someone I can actually learn something from, and she's beautiful he thought. He stripped her down to a super sexy bikini, something he had seen at the beach and in men's magazines. He kissed her, touched her, and felt her warmth. He became as hard as a rock. He wanted her. His mind was now singularly focused on one thing Ms Anders; no, Katerine Anders. "She must be on facebook," he said as he exited his fantasy and pulled up to his computer. He searched desperately: Katherine, Kathy, even Kate Anders which turned up women of all persuasion but not the one he was looking for. The only thing he came across was her portrait on the school's website, which he found through the Google search engine.

"Just give it up," he told himself. It was getting late and he still had homework to finish. But curiosity stalked in the dimly lit corners of his room. Lust was at his door wanting to consume him. He thought, maybe I can find a Playboy model who looks just like her: her beautifully curved body, those seductively brown eyes, and moderately sized lips. He went on a manhunt through a host of Playboy models but found more than he expected. He was lost in the variety. He saw things which lead him to more things. Like Alice in Wonderland he fell through the rabbit hole into a world he was certainly not ready to experience. He glimpsed the clock in the lower right corner of his computer screen: 12:00 AM. Oh no, he panicked and quickly closed the browser windows. His room was fully dark, laying on the bed he could still see the images.

Josh was suddenly transported to a world where he wasn't watching from the outside, but he was an actual participant. He saw himself naked with other girls from the websites he had not long ago perused. He could not hold himself back and they gave themselves to him. The feeling was amazing. Beyond what he had ever imagined it would be like. He was lost in it all. Suddenly, the skin of the girl he was with turned slimy and her body started to age. The beauty he had so lusted for became something other. Something different, beyond what he's ever seen or imagined and he was inside this thing. He was inside this monster. He became frightened and tried to free himself from her but her hold on him was tight. When he finally did, her slime was all over him. The horror woke him promptly, a little stunned as to how realistic the dream had been. He sat up in bed sweating. There was a large body sized imprint of sweat where he once laid. He got up to go to the bathroom and felt that his pants were wet. He pulled the elastic waist of his pants and underwear and was surprised to find semen. It dawned on him. The very thing he chastised his mother for, he now found pleasure in.

Alone

n i n e t e e n

"SYLVIA, WHEN I see you I don't see a stripper," Marcus said on their last night together. Such a simple statement Sylvia thought. It could have very well been a careless statement. People make careless statements all the time. But that simple statement stood opposite to what Sylvia believed about herself. What she believed about herself, Marcus did not believe about her. That thought troubled her. Hadn't she seen something in Karen that Karen had failed to see in herself. Hadn't she seen something good, something worth pursuing. Did Marcus really spot something in her during the short time they'd known each other. He was probably just making a careless statement, to make himself look good; the hero who saved the damsel in distress. Was he just trying to earn himself another boy scout badge? There must have been a 'save stripper in distress' patch; a step up from helping an old person across the street. Were the parties, the roof

169

top dinners, and dancing all an act, put on by a man who couldn't really cut it otherwise?

"But he saw something. He saw something in me I didn't...couldn't see in my self. I am such a loser," she said to herself, rubbing the temples of her head. "Why am I falling so hard for this bull? Am I that desperate?" What if he turns out to be a more sadistic version of Gerry. After all, she'd judged Gerry to be the unassuming, grieving, positively wealthy exec. But after that night, she would only be trading the frying pan for the fire. She remembered Gerry's hands around her neck, choking her, making her gasp for air. She remembered the touch of his penis and the warmth of his cum on her face. Gerry did not respect women. She doubted he even saw her as a woman. Maybe Marcus' kindness stemmed from an unhealthy desire to get women to fall hopelessly in love with him. Then he would break their hearts for absolutely no reason at all, save only to see the horror on their faces. Marcus probably specializes in psychological torture, while Gerry lusted after the body. "Ahhhh," she shouted out of frustration. "How could I think that way after all he'd said." She felt as though there was a glass ceiling over her head. A glass ceiling she couldn't break through. Beyond it would be the answer she needed and it was pissing her off because she didn't have a hammer.

Voices crept around in the dark crevices of her mind. The voices which she knew for certain were the reason for her insomnia or maybe it was the blood and money splattered over the bed linen. The sheets have been washed but the blood is still there. The money was in the bank, yet the thought of it was repulsive. And why the hell was she in this apartment. She found herself staying here more than she wanted to. It was beautiful here and the views were breath taking. It had only taken a single encounter to completely ruin it for her. Maybe she intended to beat Gerry. Beat the psychological damaged he'd inflicted on her. She would show him that she was not so easily conquered. Being a courageous conquerer was certainly not evident at the moment. The voices crept up from beneath the bed. They came from out of the closet and from the dark areas of the room. They told her bad things; terrible things. Things which she thought she had to simply come to terms with. "It's all your fault. You're the reason you're stuck in this mess. You're no good for anyone. Your son doesn't even like you."

Sylvia sat on the couch in her comfy clothes, sweat pants and a Miami Dolphins jersey, watching the sun rise, her vision blurred from the tears running down her face. She couldn't sleep. All night her mind kept reeling. Her thoughts seemed uncontrollable. What if she presumed herself to be more than what she really was. What if she'd been overconfident? What if she'd been too arrogant, then deciding to leave what she knew would be detrimental. She might not have any skills which translated to anything worthwhile outside of the Royal Playhouse. On the other hand, she was getting older, and there was no way she could continue doing what she'd been doing. Her son had suffered long enough. Josh had only recently found out some of the deep truth behind his mother. "He hates me. He hates me. He hates me," tears came to her eyes. She took another swig of the fifth bottle of Heineken. "He hates me. My son hates me and I deserve it," she muttered in a low voice. Her sobs were quiet as though she was afraid to show that she was crying.

She cautiously reached for her phone, the time read 6:32 am. She unlocked it and dialed Marcus' number. She had witnessed first hand that he was an early riser and there was a great chance he was awake. The line rang a few times and he picked up. "Hello," Marcus answered the line with a yawn. "Oops, sorry, Hello," he repeated.

"Did you really mean it," Sylvia spoke in a way which could be mistaken for someone just waking up or someone who is flat out drunk. Marcus made no mention of it, so Sylvia assumed he couldn't tell.

"Good Morning to you too Sylvia," he said being playfully sarcastic. He sounded happy to hear from her, this time within 24 hours of seeing each other.

"You said you saw more in me than just a stripper. I need to know if you really meant it," Sylvia's words slurred together and she figured it was pretty obvious now that she was drunk. Calling a guy she barely knew at 6:30 in the morning and asking weird open ended questions.

"Of course I meant it," he replied quickly in a defensive tone.

"If I'm not a stripper then what am I?"

"Sylvia, stripping is something you do. You, your identity, is not stripper. You are not bound to it. Being a stripper is not some inescapable fate you're doomed to live out for the rest of your life." Sylvia knew what he was saying, but hearing him say it set off a bunch of tiny explosions in her brain. Though what he said shook her to the core, she felt incapable of making the connection. His words and her reality might never meet. She simply accepted what he said to be true, but would that truth ever apply to her. She doubted. "That morning in Simon's apartment, I felt like I would have ripped Simon's head off for disrespected you."

Marcus kept speaking, but his words got lost in the crowd. She knew he was speaking but, what he was saying was foreign. Her mind simply couldn't wrap around it and it was of null effect. "Yeah," she said absent minded.

He must have realized that she was distracted because he kept calling, "Sylvia! Sylvia! Sylvia! Are you still there?"

"Yeah, I'm still here," she replied. Sylvia got up from where she sat and walked outside to the balcony. The air began to warm from the slowly brightening orange sun washing over the city's walls and concrete. She looked down and could see the pool which had a large metal gate and brush separating It from the driveway. Fellow occupants of her apartment building were leaving to work or to do whatever activity they chose to busy their days. Sylvia looked over the edge and yearned to fly. Oh how she wished she could just ride on a gust of wind and just fly. The freedom of the air beckoned.

"Sylvia! Sylvia!" Marcus' voice broke through again.

"Yeah, I'm here," she wearily answered.

"Are you alright, you went completely silent for about two minutes," Marcus said sounding alarmed.

"My son asked me about his father," Sylvia ignored his concerns. "He didn't like my answer. He hates me. I don't know what to do." Tears welled up in her eyes.

"Oh Sylvia," Marcus replied with sympathy in his voice.

"I don't know what to do. Where do I go from here. Marcus, I want to just run away. I just want to be free from everything; everyone's expectations, everyone's opinions of me. I don't even know why I'm telling you this."

"I know what you mean," Marcus said softly recognizing her words as something he said to himself long ago when he first made the decision to leave his parents to go off. Sylvia's situation was quite different in its intensity, but not in its nature. The desire to be free, the desire in his sister, the desire in himself, the desire in Sylvia, seemed to be a cord that linked all of them.

"Really?"

"Really, I felt that way when I first had the dream to do something outside of our family business. My mom and dad had conjured up expectations of me. They wanted me to follow in their footsteps, fulfill their dreams, but I had no desire to be what they wanted me to be. I knew I had to fulfill my purpose on this earth."

"Purpose," Sylvia said, not questioning the word, but speaking as though it was something she had not thought about. Her alcohol induced and sleep deprived mind could not bring meaning to the word purpose. The word echoed continuously through her, before finally coming to a conclusion. "If I did have a purpose, I've wrecked it. My purpose is probably at the bottom of some ocean or in some dark pit."

"As long as you're alive Sylvia, you have an opportunity to live a better life. A life that does some good. Your son is a good starting point. You can't give up on him. Just because he rejects you once or twice doesn't mean you give up. Love doesn't give up," Marcus spoke with such resolve his words had finally pierced through the dark clouds of Sylvia's state. Her bottle of Heineken was left inside but lucidity was a ways away.

"He is worthy of my pursuit," Sylvia said remembering the words she spoke to Marcus the night they first met. "Thank you Marcus."

"It's my pleasure Sylvia," he said with relief in his voice.

"Will you still answer my calls? I assure you I am relatively normal once you get to know me," Sylvia said hoping to make recompense for calling this man early in the morning, depressed, and drunk.

"Of course I will," he said Sylvia heard him smiling through the phone. She wasn't sure about everything he said but she was beginning to feel more relieved. He had shown her more love than she'd had in a long time. Karen was always there for her, but he was like fresh air to her otherwise breathless atmosphere. She was beginning to need him, though she wouldn't dare say a word in regards to the truth of her feelings. She feared scaring him away.

The Ride

t w e n t y

SYLVIA CALLED SOFIA and asked if she, Sylvia, could take Josh to school. Sylvia received a resounding yes. She got to the house a few minutes early, but did not go in. She certainly didn't want her mother seeing her like this, so she sat in the car attempting to rehearse what she would say to her son. She tried to think of way to start the mending process of their relationship. It's too bad she couldn't think. The liquor she consumed left her mind cloudy. She was beginning to sober up, but sleep was also attempting to claim her. She turned on the radio, hoping to hear something that would jolt her mind awake.

"Miami's number one hit music station Y100," the promo played before Elvis Durant, of the Elvis Durant Show, started speaking.

"Guys," he spoke to his co-hosts, "Do you remember that missing person's case about a week back. The police have reason to believe that last night's murder, though in different states, is actually linked. Guys we have a serial killer manhunt on the way." Elvis spoke in a serious tone, imitating the voice of a detective in one of those old movies. "Last nights murder and the disappearance were both strippers," Elvis said, causing Sylvia's ear to perk up. "Not only that, but the police believes, that though these deaths were gruesome, the killer might have done it that way to make it seem like an accident. The problem is, the fire was so expertly done," Elvis said before being interrupted.

"Fire expertly done, what does that mean? You never hear of anyone expertly lighting a fire," a funny sounding male voice appeared on air; probably the one they called Froggy.

"Wait, wait, please Froggy, don't interrupt!" Elvis chastised him.

"Okay, sorry, I just thought it sounded a little weird that's all," Froggy apologized, with a drawl in his words.

"Apparently, the fire completely burn the victims in the den of the house but there were, I guess, measures put in place to prevent it from spreading to other areas of the house. And there were no fire systems in the house. You know, like sprinklers and what not! So anyways, Froggy," Elvis continued with his previous statement, "police have reason to believe that he's some kind of expert in arson or maybe even a contract killer. Guys what is this world coming to?"

"Dun, dun, dun, the plot thickens," a cheery female voice said, probably the voice of Bethany. "So there's probably someone trying to make these girls disappear."

"But guys, that's not all," Elvis teased.

"You're killing me with the suspense already," Froggy said. "I'm seriously about to crap my pants over here."

"Yeah, just come out and say everything this time Elvis," another female voice spoke sarcastically. Danielle, Sylvia thought.

"Well…The police also has reason to believe that this psycho is a police officer," Elvis spoke in a crescendo with its big finish on police officer. The co-hosts all burst out in disbelief.

"Are you kidding," one voice said.

"I can't believe that," another voice said.

"A police officer?"

"Guys we should all whisper a prayer for those families in the New England area who has lost someone to this psycho," Elvis said before moving on to another subject.

When Josh came out, he had a strange look on his face. His hair was disheveled as though he had gotten dressed in the cargo bed of a moving pickup truck. His clothes were sloppy though he was usually very particular about the way he looked. Even his shoes were still untied. He was wearing that school jacket though. Sylvia was coming to realize it was his mark. Others would recognize him on campus by the custom numbers and his last name in all upper case letters embroidered on the back. The jacket was distinctly him. The jacket was a symbol of who he was and his accomplishments. So far, he'd done well on the basketball team. All the custom embroidering was like an army man's stripes. The kids saw those numbers and they instantly remembered that he was a valuable player. The number 15, more than once, won the game.

He pulled the handle to the front seat of the car. The last time he got in her car he had sat in the back, but having him close made Sylvia feel good, irrespective of the fact that he hated her. Him sitting in the front seat was maybe some kind of sign that things would get better. He got in the car and as she looked at him, he frowned his nose.

"Have you been drinking," he asked.

"I had a rough night," Sylvia replied with a croak in her voice; she cleared her throat.

"Rough night?" Josh replied, skeptical of her choice of words.

"Not like that you dirty little boy," Sylvia said smiling. "I just couldn't sleep and ended up having far more beers than I anticipated."

"Do you need me to drive?"

"No, I'll be fine," Sylvia replied with more cheer in her voice. She backed out of the driveway far slower than her normal pace.

"Well can we roll the windows down, it really stinks in here," he replied with a snarl.

"Okay Mr. Grumpy, you don't seem to be having that good of a morning either," Sylvia retorted again in good fun.

Josh sighed and looked straight ahead he said, "I had a rough night."

"Rough night?" Sylvia questioned in the same manner he did to her. He chuckled. "You walked right into that one."

"Yeah," he sighed.

Sylvia placed the car in park."I think I'll take you up on that offer."

"What offer?"

"To drive," Sylvia said quietly, regretting it the moment the words fumbled from her lips. Her 15 year old son in the driver's seat scared her to pieces, but seemed like a step in the right direction. "Do you even know how to drive?"

"Of course I do," Josh replied with excitement roaring from his voice. "I took drivers ed at school, I take grandma to the store all the time. And…" his voice trailed off.

"And what?" Sylvia was curious to know what the 'and' was.

"And take her car out by myself," he said a bit coy but sounded more pleased with himself than he should have.

"Okay sir, let's go or we're gonna be late," Sylvia said as she wenched herself from the driver's seat. The beer made her muscles feel like jelly. He jumped into the drivers seat, adjusted his mirrors, pushed the chair back and they were off.

"Do you want to talk about it," Sylvia said softly. "I mean, your rough night." She was embarrassed to have even said anything. As they went down the street, she could see that he was as good as he said.

"No, not really," he replied. But she could see something was bothering him.

"Okay," she said, not wanting to prod him too much.

After a few minutes of silence, driving down the street with Josh around the wheels, he finally said, "there is this girl at school that I like, her name is Rena." Sylvia was relieved that he broke the silence. She wasn't quite sure how to approach him as he was not receptive. "I went to her birthday party last weekend and I think she likes me, but I think I might have screwed things up with her."

"Well, why do you say that," Sylvia said trying to be a good listener.

"I said something about someone else and she didn't like it. She thinks that if I treat this person one way then I will probably end up treating her the same way," Josh tried to explain without giving away too much details.

"Do you think she's right?" Sylvia asked already knowing the answer.

Josh let out a heavy breath and went quiet for a second. Sylvia could tell he was tumbling the mystery in his mind like a Rubik's cube attempting to make sense of the different sides of the problem. "Yeah, I guess she's right."

"The good thing is, most women are very forgiving if you show them you really care and are sorry," Sylvia said. "Wait, hold on."

"What!"

"Turn down this street," Sylvia said as she pointed to an old stretch of street she recognized. The city was preparing to repair and had blocked off.

Josh turned the car down the street and asked, "what are we going down her for?"

"Just wait for it," Sylvia looked ahead as though expecting to see some magical surprise. "okay, here, you can stop." She looked over at him, "when I was younger, my friends and I use to drag race down this street. It looks like the city is going to remove it to expand the highway. This might be our last chance to drive it like in the old days. Plus I'm sure you want to see what this car's got."

Josh's eyes brightened, "really?" He shouted with glee. Something Sylvia had never heard from him.

"Well we have a few minutes before school so, let her rip," she said, but almost immediately regretting her words. Josh placed the car into its sport mode and manual, allowing him to use the paddle shifters behind the steering wheel.

"Okay, let's do this," Josh stepped on the gas. The tires screeched loud enough to wake up the neighborhood. The engine revved in a way Sylvia had never heard it. Both their bodies sank into the plush red leather seats as the car quickly lurched forward accelerating at a neck breaking pace. Josh changed each gear with the paddle shifter with surprising precision. okay, Sylvia thought, he's done this before. Within a few seconds the speedometer quickly leapt above 60 mph and recklessly approached 80. Sylvia nervously held arms out, bracing herself against the dashboard.

"Okay, Josh, we're getting to the end of the street. I think you better slow it down." Sylvia jerkily said barely able to keep herself composed. Josh heeded the warning as he could see cars up ahead. He slowed his pace and turned onto the major street. He had actually cut a few minutes from his ride time to school, they were only a few turns away.

"Thanks for letting me drive, Mom." They pulled up to the school, Josh's excitement seemed hard to contain. Sylvia was still recovering from her close brush with death.

"Ah…sure, no problem!" she said. As the car came to a halt in front of the school, she jumped out of the passenger side almost wanting to kiss the ground. Josh climbed out of the cockpit and Sylvia came around and faced him, "I know now that I should have told you about your father, but I was so scared and I'm so sorry Josh." Fresh tears started to well up, but Sylvia fought them back out of fear Josh would grow embarrassed.

"Scared of what," he said softly, as though he was sympathetic towards her.

"What you might think of me. What you think of me now. I figured if I didn't say anything then the whole thing would somehow solve itself or just go away. Stupid I know, but I want to do better Josh. I promise you, I will do better."

"Okay, thank you Mom," he replied, squeezing her hand. He turned and walked up the steps and through the doors.

Sylvia got into the car and started crying, releasing her tears like a breath she could no longer hold, "he called me Mom. He called me Mom." Emotions overwhelmed her. This was by far the best morning she'd spent with her son. It was certainly a step in the right direction and she was overjoyed.

Rumors

t w e n t y   o n e

JOSH HURRIEDLY CLIMBED the steps to the entrance of the school. He was fresh and full of excitement. He had a good start to his morning and had something cool to tell his friends. He had a few minutes to spare and he was hoping to see Rena before going to class. The adrenaline still coursed through his veins and he better use that to his advantage when approaching her. Other students clamored all around attempting to get to class. He took off to his locker which was their usually meeting place. Once there he moved slowly not wanting to miss her as she passed. Josua's eyes took focus of his books and started to put them in his school bag. He was surprised to find a pair of red tearful eyes staring at him when he closed the door to the locker. It was Rena. She had been crying and quite a bit it would seem. The sight of her left him without words. He had not expected her to look quite like this.

"Rena?"

"I can't believe you would do something so ridiculous," Rena's voice got louder with every word that escaped her lips. Josh was shocked. How did she know, he thought. His heart rate rose and panic overtook him. A horrid look overtook his face. His guilt was apparent and there was no way to hide it. Rena saw it too, because her tears flowed without restraint.

"Rena, I," his words failed. Rena in her anger beat both her fists in his chest.

"Josh, I never want to see you again," Rena said and with gritted teeth she walked away. Josh stood there, dumb founded and watched her walk away. He just wanted to run. Shame and embarrassment could not describe what he felt in that moment. He didn't have the courage to face anyone and was surprised to find the kids standing in the hall were all staring at him. She was gone and now out of sight. The bell rang, which was a much needed wakeup call from his mental stupor. That's right, I have to get to class.

But how did they find out. Was someone watching him. Did he make a mistake and post something to Facebook. Was his computer hacked. His mind raced as he attempted retrace his steps. It was long after the halls were empty and all the other students had filed off to class. Josh stood, completely unaware that he was alone. His third period math teacher, Mr Horowitz, spotted him and called out, "Josh, you better get going to class young man before your teacher marks you as tardy."

"Oh, yeah, you're right, thank you Mr Horowitz," Josh stumbled for words as for the second time in a five minute span he needed some kind of outside help to rein him back to reality. He placed his bag over his shoulders took off in a slow jog to his first period class. He made it in time and would not be marked late, but still his entrance caught the attention of the entire class. Even Ms. Anders sitting at her desk looked up briefly. Her eyes darted to a digital clock on her desk. Once seated, the class seemed to spring back to life. The chatter beginning again, but was not quite the normal sort of chatter. The focus seemed to be on him, heads turning to stare back at him before resuming their talk with their neighbors and friends.

"Bro, you are one heartless SOB," Brian, who was sitting next to Josh, said under his breath with an air of disappointment. "I wouldn't have expected that from you. Hell, I wouldn't even go so far. Now Brittany's not even talking to me." Brian shook his head but kept his eyes staring straight ahead.

"Wait," Josh said with a look of confusion on his face. "What did I do again," he said in a whisper so only Brian could hear.

"Are you kidding," Brian replied, turning to him. "You recked my chance with Brittany. Now there's no chance I'll get her to sleep with me. I was so close too."

"How did I do that," Josh said still looking puzzled as to what Brian was talking about. Brian must have seen the look in Josh's face, because he gave Josh a long look. Brian searched his face like the hands of a blind man attempting to memorize its structure.

"You didn't do it, did you?" Brian said after some time. Ms Anders had begun handing out last class' quiz results which gave them a few more seconds to speak.

"What did I do. Everyone's been looking at me funny. Rena just told me she never wants to see me again. Now you're telling me that I'm the jerk in the friendship, a position that I certainly don't want to take over from you," Josh was even more confused. He was somewhat relieved though, because the thing he was worrying about might very well not be the reason for the absolutely insane morning he's had.

"Ok class, go ahead and turn your books to Chapter 4. We'll be starting this chapter today," Ms Anders said as she made her way to the front and center of the class room.

"Bro, I'll talk to you after class," Brian said before looking ahead. Not even Brian was his normal self. This whole thing was difficult for him even. Though a bit relieved Josh's mind still wondered what this cosmic upheaval was all about.

"If I were you I would take meticulous notes. Much of what will be in next week's exam will be coming from this chapter. If you get this chapter, it will have accounted for almost 50% of your exam grade. It is pivotal that you know this chapter, so you need to be detailed in your note taking." Ms Anders took her place by the black board in her standard weather girl form and taught vigorously, like a gladiator in the Colosseum. Yet, the class was a blur. Josh's mind could not leave Rena. What is it that had made her so upset? Why had she been so mad which made her not want to see Josh ever again. Rena is a smart girl, he thought. Whatever she was angry about must have been something major. She thought that what he said to Sylvia was terrible, but she'd known of that for a while now. She had plenty of opportunities to break up wit him. Hell, she could've easily called and done it over the phone. That couldn't be it, he thought. It sounded as if I did something directly to her. It doesn't sound as though she was upset about Sylvia, someone she had only heard about and had never met. He had lost his temper with her and now she doesn't trust him to be good to her. She's probably right, Josh thought. I'm probably like all the other guys, staying up late, watching porn. And what was up with that dream. Josh's mind ran over what he could remember from that weird dream he had. And there was cum in his pants. "Mr Bradley...Mr Bradley, wake up Mr Bradley," Ms Anders' voice came as a surprise to him. He looked up quickly, as he was absentmindedly staring at his desk, the entire class was staring at him.

"Sorry, I'm not asleep," Josh replied.

"Well, clearly whatever is on your desk is far more important than the chapter that will take up 50% of your mid term exams next week."

"Sorry it won't happen again," Josh said. He knew exactly what to say to stop the onslaught which was on it's way.

"Okay, as I was saying," Mr. Anders continued with the lesson. For the rest of class, Josh took detailed notes to keep his mind off Rena. He would not see her until lunch. And though he was scared, he now more than ever wanted to make the right. Of course, it will not be possible until he knew what he did not do.

The class went on with no further interruptions. The bell rang signaling the end of the class period. Josh picked up his bag and started heading out the door anxious to hear what Brian would tell him. "Ms. Bradley," called Ms. Anders.

"Looks like you'll be getting some extracurricular work tonight Josh," Brian whispered in a flavor similar to his old self.

Josh gave him the, you're a jerk look, and said "I'll see you outside," to be nice. The class was now empty of any students and Josh made his way to the front of the class where Ms Anders' desk was stationed. Ms. Anders got up from her seat and sat on one corner of her desk.

"You've been doing well in my class so far. " Ms. Anders spoke softly. There was no hint of harshness in her voice. The way she spoke was almost musical. This was probably what the writers of old meant when they wrote about the Sirens which led sailors to their watery grave. It was hard not imagining himself being with her. Just as the thought crossed his mind, she reached for his hand, clasping his left hand between both of hers. "Because of your sacrifice and the difficulty of playing for the school team while keeping up with your work, I am willing to give you a bit of leeway in my class. The only thing I would like in return is," Ms. Anders placed Josh's hand on the inside of her thigh. She stared straight into his eyes and smiled at his response. Her eyes traced his body to find the bulge in his pants. "Well, think about it. It will be our little secret." She removed his hand and hopped off the desk. The other students from her second period started to file into the classroom.

"Elizabeth," Josh whispered. He was no longer smiling.

"Oh?" she said, staring into his eyes, reading his face, "I was expecting this to happen. Well it was amazing while it lasted."

"It certainly was," Josh replied, smiling again. Josh backed away, pulled off his school bag and held it in front of his pants before walking out of the classroom.

-=-=-=-

Josh got out of class and headed towards his locker. He could still feel her warmth on his hand. But his mind was completely empty. He didn't know what to think. "Bro, everything alright? Did Ms. Anders lay it on you."

"Yeah," Josh said, but then suddenly regret letting this secret out moments after being entrusted with it. "And so did your mom."

"Ouch," Brian said wincing at the remark.

"Anyways, can you just tell me what the hell is going on. We have to get to class soon," Josh pleaded.

"Okay, okay so pushy. This is Rena's first year at Miami Beach Senior High," Brian started out, but saw instant confusion on Josh's face. "What, you didn't know."

"Is she a freshman?"

"No, she's a transfer student. Apparently it's been going around that Rena was suspended for inappropriate activities involving her previous school's basketball team," Brian said attempting to be diplomatic in his word.

"Inappropriate activities? What are you talking about," Josh's voice riled up.

"Hey lower your voice. Jeremy the new player confirmed it. He was at that school last year too and remembers when she got suspended. He said that she was a cheerleader and was staying at a hotel with the rest of the team. Apparently, the coach came to check up on the team and heard moans and groans coming from one of the rooms. The coach entered the room and found her and four other football guys trying to get their clothes on. The reason she came to this school was to escape the toxic environment the scandal created," Brian finished and placed a hand on Josh's shoulder. "I'm sorry bro."

"That doesn't sound like Rena at all. We've shared a lot of personal stuff and this never came up. I don't know Brian. It just doesn't seem like her," Josh said shaking his head in disbelief.

"Well, some people saw you and her fighting last week and thought that it must be you who started the rumor," Brian added.

"What…that wasn't a fight. Yes we had a disagreement but this is something completely on a new level. I would never go that far. Hell, I didn't even know this was her first year."

"Alright bro, I have to get going, I'll talk to you later," Brian waved and walked off to his next class.

"C ya!" *Rena was the one who told me to try and make things better with my mom,* Josh thought as he started towards his next class. *She'd always wanted the best for me even when I didn't want it for myself. She'd been through so much for her age. She lost her mother.* "And I called my mom a whore. No wonder she was frustrated with me. I'm such an idiot," he said to himself attempting to plow his way past the rumors to find the truth. "I have to see her." He felt light as a new resolve flooded his mind. He ran down a corridor towards Rena's next class; dodging through the crowd. The crowd eventually dispersed as students made their way into class. He got to the door of Rena's class, he peered through the glass opening in the door but couldn't see her. He pulled the door and went inside, looked around but she was nowhere to be found. The bell rang, signaling class to begin. Maybe I have the wrong class, he thought. There was a slender black kid sitting at the back of the class. Josh motioned to him and asked, "Hey, is Rena in this class?"

"Yeah, she's not here today though. Actually," his face lit up as he remembered something. "She was in first period class, but I think she went home sick."

"Thanks a lot, I really appreciate it," Josh's shoulders slumped and walked out of the classroom. Josh went to his next class and thought that he would wait until lunch to ask Jeremy. His mind did not leave her. All he could think about was how bad he was going to beat the person who started the rumor. Since Jeremy was the only one who knew Rena, then he must be the one or he must know who did it. Lunch came and Josh spotted Jeremy sitting at a table talking to a few other girls. Josh didn't care. He wanted answers and he wanted them now. Josh took lively steps over to the table where he was sitting. A few of the girls sitting around him saw Josh coming and stood up to move out of the way. Josh slammed both hands against the table making a loud noise. Just then Chad and Brian entered the lunch room. Brian saw what was about to happen and hurried over. "Why the hell would you start a rumor like that."

"What the hell bro, you better back off," Jeremy said in like threatening tone.

"I know you're the one who started that rumor. I know it was you. Now admit it so I can beat the crap out of you jerk," Josh spat, every word making him more angry. All eyes turned towards the two boys.

Brian placed a hand on Josh's chest, "hey I told you he affirmed it but I didn't say he started it."

"So what she did it. Rena screwed everyone on the basketball team," Jeremy said. As soon as he finished his sentence, Josh swung hitting him square on the jaw. The crowd of kids shouted and jeered, egging the two boys to fight. Brian grabbed Josh from behind keeping him from doing any additional harm. Jeremy was stunned and didn't seem able to fight back. It was a clean hit. Teachers and administrators tried making their way through the crowd to see what was going on and who was fighting.

"Let me go," Josh shouted, struggling against Brian's hold. "Let me go!"

"Bro, relax…relax. You need to go now, before you get in trouble," Brian said sternly. "Look, do you want go get suspended?"

"Alright, alright," Josh said and relaxed his arms. He grabbed his school bag which he had dropped and disappeared into the crowd. As he made his way out of the cafeteria, he saw the boy Chad had been doing his science project with. The boy motioned to Josh and Brian as they made their escape. The two boys joined Luis in a brisk walk away from the scene of the fight.

"He didn't start the rumor!" the boy said.

"Yeah," Brian replied, "how do you know that?"

"Because I did," the boy said.

"What?" Josh said in surprise, he stopped walking at the boys words. The other two stopped with him.

"You saw what just happened to that other kid in there right. So why are you telling us this now," Brian asked. Good question, Josh thought and turned his attention to the boy to see what he would say.

"I saw the way Chad looked at you," the boy said, his gazed fixed on Josh. "I knew I was only his play thing. Still, I tried hard to make him happy. But he loves you Josh more than he loved me. Hell, assuming he loved me at all." There was a look of startled confusion on Josh and Brian's faces. If they heard this boy correctly, he is insinuating that Chad is gay. Chad had not said anything of the sort. Neither Josh nor Brian said a word. They did not know what to say. "He said he was concerned about you dating Rena. He said he'd seen her fight with the new guy and I looked up information on her. I found records of court cases and put things together. It was easy really, all I had to do was text the information to one of the gossip girls around school. I sent it to Lauren, she'd been jealous of Rena after her party was a big success. She hated Rena for making friends with you and I just left it to them," the boy spoke in this nonchalance as though what he did was no big deal. Josh thought he saw a smile on the boy's face, as if he was pleased with his own genius. Without warning, Brian landed a swift punch to the gut. The boy doubled over. Just then Chad came running over, his eyes darted back and forth between the boy on the floor, Josh, and Brian. He came at such a pace, it would've seemed as if he wanted to say something important but in the moment words eluded him.

"Where were you?" Josh said, the anger still evident in his voice.

"I saw what was going on and went looking for him," Chad replied, setting his eyes on the boy who was still kneeling on the ground. Josh turned and walked away.

Truth

t w e n t y   t w o

HE REST OF the day went by in a blur. It seemed as if his whole world was turning upside down. He thought he could trust Chad, but there was this whole plot going on behind his back. A plot which turned into Rena being hurt. *Why the secrets? Why didn't he just come to me in the first place instead of going of and doing all this crap*, Josh thought. Josh would've been hard pressed to tell anyone what actually happened in his classes today. His mind was in a cosmic upheaval. Even though he tried to escape the scene, word got around that he was the one who caused the aggravation and landed the first punch. He was suspended from school for five days for fighting, but he didn't care. His only concern was for Rena. He had to see her somehow. He had tried calling her but her phone went to voice mail each time. A few days passed and he could not take it any longer. He called Sylvia. He decided that she would be more fit for this task than grandma. Sophia would not question him if he went out with Sylvia, so he needn't explain himself.

"Hey, what's going, it sounded urgent?"

"I really need your help. I'll explain on the way." They got into the car, Sylvia in the driver's seat and they sped off. He explained everything and Sylvia was quite shocked to finally see the big picture of her son's life. This was her first time hearing about the suspension. They drove to Rena's house. Rena's father had a BMW which was parked outside in the driveway. "You can leave if you want to," Josh said looking back at Sylvia. "I'm sure I can catch a ride home from Bernie."

"I'll stay," Sylvia assured him. She saw that this was important to him and it was the only thing she could do to support him.

"Okay, thanks," he turned and headed up the drive way to the front door of the house, knocked and waited. Moments later, Rena's father came to the door.

"Good evening Mr Novak," Josh said, remembering the first time they met he had told him to call him Rena's dad. "I was hoping to see Rena, I heard she wasn't feeling well so I had to come by and see her."

"You're right, she's not feeling well and she's not accepting any visitors at the moment. I'm sorry son," he said quite innocently before closing the door. Josh walked away with his head held low. He felt so stupid to have come this far only to be turned away.

"I can't believe this," he said under his breath and pulled the door to his mom's car open. "She doesn't want to talk to me."

"Well, from what you've told me, this girl seems like one in a million. Am I right?" Sylvia peered over at him from the drivers seat. He tried to predict Sylvia's thoughts before she could say them.

"Yeah," he said simply.

"A one in a million girl like this is not someone you give up on easily. She'll probably be the best friend you'll have. Don't give up on her. Take it from someone who has been given up on," she said, placing her hand on his arm; prompting him. Josh got out the car again, knocked on the door, and Rena's father returned.

"Sir, it is really important I speak to her and if it's okay with you, I'd like to stay out here until she feels good enough to talk." Rena's dad smiled broad at Josh's words.

"Okay son, I'll let her know that," Rena's dad pulled the door close. Josh could hear foot steps inside the house. There were whispers but he couldn't quite make out what they were saying. Time seemed to have stood still as he waited. Five minutes felt like 20, which the five eventually became 20, and 30, and 40 minutes. It was 56 minutes before the door opened again. Rena walked out, dressed in shorts and a tang top.

"I can't believe you're still here," Rena said softly, holding one arm.

"I had to see you," Josh said, realizing the words he had rehearsed floated away.

"Well, what do you have to say," she said in a desperate attempt to sound unyielding.

"I didn't do it. I wasn't the one to release that rumor about you. As a matter of fact, I didn't know who did it and I followed your advice and tried making things right with my mom. And she's waiting for me over there," he felt as though he was running out of things to say. Yet he had to try and keep her for as long as possible. "And thank you for being the most amazing friend I've ever known. You were so kind to me and I couldn't imagine that you actually did all those things the rumors said.

That's why I had to see," his words trailed off. His face became downcast with worry. "But even if you did, I wouldn't care," he blurted out. "I just don't want to lose you," his voice low again.

"What do you mean by 'you didn't know who did it?' Do you know now who started the rumor?" Rena asked, not missing a beat.

"It's a long story and to tell you the truth, it involves me, but I swear I didn't know what was going down," Josh's disclaimer only proved to add more suspicion to Rena's face. He started with the fight and gave her the play by play until the moment he came knocking at her door.

"Joshua Bradley," Rena said, and Josh beamed. "I appreciate you fighting for my honor and even getting suspended in the process, but please don't do that again."

"Yes ma'am," Josh said and saluted like a soldier in the armed forces. "Now, can you tell me what happened," he said cautiously.

"He wanted to do things with me I wasn't comfortable with. They were things he saw on some disgusting porn site. So," tears started to run down her face. "So, he forced himself on me. I tried to push him off, but he was too strong. So I screamed. He placed one hand over my mouth, but I guess the coach could still hear us from outside the room." Rena's lips quivered as she spoke. Her tears flowing as freely as before. "The coach stood up for his star player because I guess he didn't want to loose him. I blamed myself for so long Josh. I blame myself, I thought that there was surely something that I did to bring this on myself. It took a long time for me to even look myself in the mirror again. I had to even switch schools." Her voice was pleading for his understanding. "But it was their own…their own lust that drove him to raping me," Rena's voice could hardly get the words out. "I was too ashamed to tell my dad and by the time I told him, all evidence of the rape was gone. We tried to fight it in court but it was my word against his. Plus the coach testified that I always behaved sexually towards the players and hungered for attention." Rena's emotions overwhelmed her ability to speak. Her lips were sealed and his face wet from tears. Josh wanted to just hold her. Comfort her through the this tough time. He reached one hand out, not knowing if she would allow him. But she came running, almost falling into his arms.

Josh knew for certain the wisdom of this girl, her ability to see through his bull, was birthed from pain. He did not let the small broken areas of her life deter him from liking her far more than he probably should. This news did not make her less of a person in his mind. Actually she became more valuable. She had a strong and beautiful exterior, yet her heart was tender and fragile. It took a few days, but Rena eventually came back to school. Josh was off suspension and showed up early on her first day back. He was there at the door when her dad dropped her off. As soon as she got out the car, Josh took off his jacket and placed it around her. "Can you hold on to this for me today," he said. She snuggled up in his warmth. He felt good giving to her. He wanted to continue giving to her and protecting her and one day declare his undying love for her. He placed one arm around her neck and she beamed. He knew, that with his number on her back, his reputation would cover her despite the rumors.

Not The One

twenty three

THE PHONE RANG twice before Marcus got the ear piece in to answer the line. He had just returned from a company diner and was tired. Tired of talking and sounding polite, nevertheless ecstatic that he was chosen for the position as branch manager. Though, he was happy to hear that the other execs thought he was doing a good job it was three weeks before other employees started to warm up to him and the way he did things. Things were looking up but he was still exhausted from the night. Networking was never his strength, but he knew he would eventually have to develop the backbone for it. So he endured the pain for now. He finally got the ear piece in, pressed a button on the wire to answer the call and was shocked to hear the voice that came up in his head. "Marcus, hello," Marcus instantly recognized the voice.

"Hi dad," Marcus said nervously. He knew exactly what his dad was going to say. "How are you."

"Well, you've got your mom worried sick, we haven't heard from you in a while Marcus, what's going on," his father was an incredibly patient man. Marcus could not ever remember him loosing his temper.

"Oh nothing," Marcus replied.

Another voice in the background spoke, "what did he say," it was Marcus' mother. If Marcus' father was the most patient man he's ever met, his mom was probably the most impatient woman. The perfect balance, like yin and yang.

"He said he's alright dear," Marcus' dad replied in a tone of controlled annoyance.

"Well I can't hear," Marcus' mother said indignantly.

"I'm just trying to settle into this new job," Marcus continued, attempting to halt the ensuing back and forth banter between he and his parents.

"He said he's just trying to settle into the new job," Marcus' dad repeated back, relaying the message to his mother.

"How is the vineyard," Marcus asked.

"Oh, it's doing good," Marcus' dad replied.

"Wait, what did he say. He's talking but I can't hear him," Marcus's mother's voice protested in the background. "Gil, I'm going to pick up the phone in the living room." It was always an adventure speaking to his parents, one of the reasons he didn't call them as often as he should. "Hello?" Martha's voice became more prominent over the line.

"We're all here Martha," Gil said.

"We hear you're dating a stripper," Martha said. She was never one to beat around the bush. Gilford Warren was more the diplomat, but Martha Warren was always a bomb itching to go off. And she did not care who was in her blast radius. Marcus' brain went from mild annoyance to 'what the hell.' "I couldn't believe my ears when Simon told us."

"You spoke to Simon behind my back?" Marcus questioned with brewing frustration in his head.

"Son," Gil spoke up over the line. "You've always been a secretive boy. You could have ran off, gotten married, with children and your mom and I would probably never hear of it. We just figured it best to get the story from an outside source."

"Honey, strippers don't make very good wives," Martha said, insisting that Marcus sees the truth.

"I'm not getting married, we're not even officially dating," Marcus feeling as though he was being backed into a corner.

"What do you call flying a girl to New York," Martha rebutted.

"Are you guys spying on me? I'm not a teenager you know," Marcus pleaded for their understanding.

"What your mom is trying to say son, is we want you to be happy and we're afraid that this woman might get your heart in a tangle then leave or worse" Gil said.

"Yeah, leave with all your money," Martha added.

"Guys you don't have to worry about me," Marcus said, attempting to stay calm.

"Son, this is not like junior high when you went out with that nineteen year old senior. You hid that from us too," Gil said.

"Oh yeah, the one with all those tattoos. I mean she was pretty, but what parent would allow their high school kid to get all those tattoos," Martha butted in. "Imagine being married into that family."

"You have to start thinking about your future. You're not getting any younger. It's important to choose a good woman who is going to bear you good children and a woman you see yourself growing old with," Gil finished.

"What ever happened to 'love who you want to love,'" Marcus rebutted.

"But, son, you have to be wise. You can't just go pick up any girl off the side of the street and make her a wife," Gil said.

"Dad, I know that," Marcus replied.

"So trust your old man when I say this girl is not a good choice for you."

"What ever happened to that nice brunette you were dating? What was her name again?" Martha hummed attempted to jog her own memory.

"Lara," Gil resounded.

"Yeah, Lara, she was nice, what happened to her?" Martha probed, which was her way of showing approval for the women she would rather see her only son date. Lara was a very successful real estate lawyer someone Marcus had met through Simon. If they only knew, she was a crazy control freak. Marcus didn't mind a woman with a strong personality. But when she had a softer spot for her furry white Pomeranian over the guy she was dating, it just didn't seem like a relationship Marcus thought would work.

"Anyways, son," Gil said attempting to veer from the subject, and thankfully, because Marcus had all he could bear. "Your mother and I have also decided that we're going to split ownership of the vineyard between you and your sister. The vineyard has become self reliant and doesn't really require you to do much. Your mother and I are going to take our part and go into retirement, but you and Ema can still reap the benefits of our life's work. Our goal has always been to leave you and your sister a sizable inheritance."

"Oh, I see where this is going. You plan to leave us all this money, but hoping I don't completely send your legacy to hell. You're hoping I don't completely screw up like you thought I would when I decided to go into finance. Is that it? You're afraid I'm going to get married to someone who will steal everything you've worked for," Marcus' anger raged and voice raised. "If you're going to leave an inheritance, leave it. But please don't hang it over my head and think you can control my life with it."

"Do you blame us Marcus," Gil sounded more stern but not angry. "Do you blame us wanting the best for our children. Do you blame us wanting the best for you. We have seen people with humble beginnings get allot of money and turn into monsters. Your mother and I have worked hard for what we have and are not disillusioned by money. Money is a tool, Marcus."

"I know it is," Marcus rebutted.

"This level of wealth can ruin a person and if you don't have the right woman along side you, she will in turn ruin you too."

"I know you want the best," Marcus simmered, his heart still pounding. "But please no more relationship advice." The conversation continued, but fizzled quickly. Marcus had lost all his steam and had very little tolerance for whatever his parents wanted to say. Some five minutes later they said their farewells and goodnight.

༄

There came a knock at the door, Marcus let out a heavy breath as he got up to answer. He could hear someone talking. He touched the LCD panel to the side of his door. A live image popped up and he could see

Simon's teeth really big in the display. He was clutching his cell phone, cleaning his teeth and attempting to talk at the same time. Marcus turned the handle and quickly opened the door. "Oh hey," Simon said, voice muffled from his thumb and pointer finger attempting to grab a piece of left overs from between his canine and incisors. Marcus left the door open and walked back to his desk where he was working on something for the office.

"Please come in, make yourself at home," Marcus said in a sarcastic tone.

"You do know that thing outside my door you were using to clean your teeth, it's actually a camera?" Marcus said without looking up from his work.

"You're not still mad about Miami are you?" Simon said in disbelief. Simon knew Marcus long enough to know that he was one to hold a grudge but he would soon forget it.

"We were suppose to be there to relax and have some fun and instead, I ended up in one of your schemes. But most of all, I can't believe you would treat Sylvia like that."

"Sylvia?" Simon replied. "So you're still seeing her?"

"You know I'm still seeing her," Marcus said emphatically. "Where do you get off calling my parents."

"Hey, they called me. Your dad said you hadn't called in a while and wanted to find out what was up with you. I wasn't going to lie to your dad," Simon said, attempting to explain away his betrayal.

"Oh the venerable Saint Simon. Your piety surpasses all else," Marcus jeered.

"My friend," Simon pulled up a chair and sat beside Marcus. "Take it from a man who knows women very well." Marcus started looking around, as though looking for someone else in the room.

"Yeah, where is he, I have a few questions to ask," Marcus snapped back, then went back to his work as though Simon was only kidding.

"Ouch," Simon winced. "Anyways," he drawled. "Women like that get stuck. Especially women as beautiful as Sylvia. They make decent money stripping and sometimes never think to leave. Some of them think they can never make as much money doing anything else. There's the issue of getting a job. If the potential employer ever finds out that they were former strippers they will most likely not be hired. Others simply don't have the education, because they've been stripping from the time they were young. Sylvia was stripping out of High School or probably younger." Marcus lifted his head and looked into Simon's eyes. He looked for something. Something that said he was lying or joking.

"How do you know that," Marcus questioned.

"Come on Marcus, who do you think told me? I asked Max a few questions. I don't think he knows that you two have seen each other, but think Marcus. Think! Girls like her, with a 10th grade education look for sugar daddies as their only way out of stripping." Marcus was no longer writing or typing on his laptop. He sat there staring at the screen, lost in thought. He found it hard to believe what his childhood friend just said. "Come on bro, trying to start a relationship with a girl like that is only going to lead to heart break," Simon said seriously. "I'm just looking out for you bro."

"Looking out for me?" Marcus questioned, his face rigid. "I didn't ask for you to look out for me!"

"Hey," Simon sounding surprised at Marcus' tone, "if it wasn't for me you'd be still scraping at the bottom of that poor excuse of a investment firm. You should be happy that someone like me looking out for you."

"Yeah, thanks I feel so fortunate," Marcus said in sarcasm. "By the way, I want nothing to do with you and Max. Money laundering and tax evasion are for those who are trying to cover up illegal business they don't want the government finding. I'm not going to risk jail time because you feel some obligation to the devil." Marcus' thoughts roamed back to that morning Sylvia called him, waking him from sleep. He thought of the anguish she was in; anguish he attributed to the lifestyle she was living. Max was a determining factor of Sylvia's lifestyle and Marcus did not want to do anything to propagate this man's wealth.

"What," Simon's voice was loud and face contorted in anger. "It's because of that girl isn't it? It's because of this little fling you got going isn't it? But let me show you. Let me show you what kind of girl you're trying to get with. Simon pulled his phone out. He disconnected Marcus' phone from his computer and connected his own. He went inside a file folder on his phone and copied a video file unto Marcus' computer. He pulled up the video. Marcus saw Sylvia standing by the door in a silk bathrobe. A man walked into the room with a suitcase in his hand. He grabbed her by the neck, the camera angle changed, and he forced her unto the bed. Marcus' eyes widened.

"What the hell is this," Marcus said. He closed the video. He couldn't watch it any further.

"This is the kind of woman you're trying to get with. Don't be mistaken, she's a whore bro. She's a whore and you need to drop this,"

Simon's words bore weight. Marcus paused and thought of everything that had just occurred. He considered the words of his parents and the convincing argument of Simon.

Marcus tore his vision from the computer and ceased Simon in his gaze, "when was this video taken?"

"The day before the party," Simon replied. Marcus was somewhat relieved. Though it was close, she'd done this thing before they'd met.

"I want you to leave, now!" Marcus said sternly. Simon looked taken aback by Marcus' words.

"What?"

"You've decided to do some things I just can't get with. If I have to give up this position I will, but I am not going to become a slave to you and Max. I want nothing to do with whatever you guys are up to. So please leave!"

"I thought we were brothers," Simon said before ripping his phone from the computer and storming out of the apartment. The door slammed on his heels. Marcus looked back at the computer and the video froze just as Sylvia's robe had fallen. Marcus wanted to believe that she wouldn't go sex someone else while they were actively engaged in building a relationship. But he'd been through hard situations before. He knew what it felt like to be heart broken and he didn't particularly care for it.

℘

"Hello?"

"Hi Marcus," Sylvia's voice over the phone sounded cheery.

"Hey you," Marcus replied with pleasant surprise. His spirit instantly lifted when he heard her voice, but he became heavy again when he remember the video Simon had showed him. "How are you?"

"I'm good thanks to you," she replied.

"Thanks to me?"

"Yes thanks to you," she reaffirmed. "Things are looking a bit better with Josh, my son."

"Well thats great," Marcus replied which was news he was truly pleased to hear.

"One thing concerns me though," Sylvia's tone changed to something resembling apprehension. "What do you want?"

"What do you mean, what do I want," Marcus was surprised by the question.

"Yeah, what do you want," Sylvia kept her voice light and airy, "from me. I mean, you have money and you seem very successful. You can pretty much have your pick of the litter of women and most women would absolutely love to be swept away by Atlanta's most eligible bachelor. So why is it you seem to be interested in me?"

"Why not you?" Marcus questioned simply.

"Well...I don't know, but I want you to know that I'm happy you're interested in me. I also want you to know that I am very interested in you also."

"I also have a question for you Sylvia," Marcus said in a more serious tone.

"Oh? Not the response I was expecting," Sylvia said. "What's your question," she still sounded in good spirits.

"How long do you plan to keep on stripping," Marcus tried his best to be as direct as possible. Something, he thought, Sylvia would appreciate.

"Oh, so you want to know my one, five, and ten year goals," she did not sound as cheery as before and Marcus knew now that this was a difficult subject for her. "The only person I've ever thought about was my son. It's been a while since I've considered even being in a relationship, where I've had to think about someone else and how they would feel about me taking my clothes off. I wanted to make enough money to get Josh on his way to college. He was the only one that mattered."

"So isn't there something else you've thought of doing outside of stripping," he prodded.

"Why are we getting into this now," Sylvia sounded as though she no longer wanted to play this game.

"Please, humor me. I know it's hard for you to discuss this. It's just really important," Marcus couldn't help this line of questioning. He had to see for himself, outside of the influence of his parents and Simon. Most of all, he had to see for himself outside of his feelings for her.

"I knew this would have been too good to be true. Fine then…" Sylvia said with frustration. "I don't remember what it's like to do anything else. I was a teenager when I started. I think about leaving every single day, but what would I do," Sylvia's voice cracked.

"What about when you were a kid. Do you remember wanting or dreaming about being or doing something else." He said but heard nothing except a faint breath letting him know she was still there.

"I always loved photography, but that was so long ago," Sylvia answered failing to see the significance of this exercise. "Either way, whether it's photography or stripping, it's all the same. They are both professions. The only difference being money and I can bet that I'd make way more money stripping than taking a bunch of pictures."

"Sylvia, money cannot be the only motivation for you doing this," Marcus was more insistent with her than he'd been with anyone else. Did this mean he cared for her more than he had anyone else? He wasn't sure.

"So you want me to give up the only thing I know for a childish dream, which there is no guarantee that I'll be any good at?"

"It's worth a try," Marcus said.

"Yes, but what's wrong with stripping?"

"Sylvia, you're literally selling your soul to these men for way less than it's worth," Marcus pleaded. "I saw the way they treated you. The way they treated Karen and the other girls. Sylvia you're meant to be loved." His words were soft and caring, not harsh and imposing which left Sylvia defenseless. "Why are you afraid of walking away from something you were never meant to be.

"It's not as easy as you're making it out to be Marcus," she said.

"You're right. It takes courage. The question is, do you have the courage to overcome the thing you fear the most, knowing that your destiny is right on the other side?"

"I don't know," she replied softly.

"Are you still interested in me?" he said softly.

"I don't know anymore. If this keeps up, I might have to run for the hills," she said in a chuckle.

"You know, that might not be a bad idea," Marcus replied with a devious undertone. "Either way, I'll be coming for you."

My Body

t w e n t y   f o u r

SYLVIA STOOD UP, pacing the floor, unable to sit. Her nerves seemed to have worked themselves from her stomach into her legs. "Will you just sit down," Sophia said with a glare more powerful than words.

"He'll be here soon," Sylvia replied. Her mothers words only made her more nervous. To think of it, the sole reason for her pacing was Sophia. She had insisted on meeting this great guy of hers. Of course, great guy was in air quotes which solidified her skepticism.

"I want to have him over for diner," Sophia said. "I don't want my daughter falling for any old schmuck off the street." Never has Sophia been so interested in the guys Sylvia went out with. Maybe she felt like a failure after Sylvia got pregnant with Josh. After Josh, she just gave up trying. Maybe she thought Sylvia was beyond helping or at least, that's the impression Sylvia got from her mother. Sylvia couldn't imagine seeing Josh in the hospital half dead from an overdose. She must have been terrified.

"Oh mom," Sylvia said, then she leaned over to Josh and whispered so only he could hear, "I think we better order some food."

Sylvia had been by everyday that week to pick up Josh. They spoke more to each other more like loving siblings, because neither of them knew what a mother son relationship looked like. Nevertheless, she loved him like a mother should. What pleased her most was that he kept calling her mom. During their ride to school, she would update him on what was going on between her and Marcus. She told him how she felt about him, not holding back anything. He understood his mother more and saw her in a light he'd never seen before.

Sylvia should have expected Sophia would grill Josh for answers and Josh was keen on telling Sylvia of grandma's snooping. "What happened to Sylvia? Why is she so happy? Is she dating someone? Who is he? What kind of car does he drive? Where does he work? Where does he live?" Josh imitated his grandmother to Sylvia. He even crunched up his nose the way Sophia always did.

There came a knock at the door and Sylvia nervously jumped as though spooked by a ghost, "He's here," she said excited.

"Mom, relax," Josh said walking towards the door. What would Josh think of him, she thought? Her greatest wish was to see them get along. "Guys, Josh said, drawing everyone's attention to the door, I would like you to meet Rena," Josh said smiling from ear to ear. A very pretty brunette with freckles stepped through the door. Sophia's eyes almost popped from her head.

"Ahhh, who is this Josh," Sophia stepped quickly towards the door smiling and holding out her hand.

"She's a friend, grandma," Josh emphasized friend.

"Oh, nice to meet you Rena," Sophia said shaking her hand lightly. "Oh, and who is this handsome man. Is this your dad?" A tall figure appeared out of the evening light.

"Josh, Mom, Bernie, and Rena this is Marcus," Sylvia said giddily. Before anyone could properly greet him, Sylvia walked forward, threw her arms around him, and kissed him. "Thank you so much for coming," she said apologetically for what was about to happen. She was about to put this wonderful man through the valley of the shadow of death, an evening with her dysfunctional and possible psychotic family. Sylvia had already warned him about her mother and her insistence on seeing this man she was talking to. They spoke quite often and though he lived in Atlanta and her Miami, their affection for each other grew. It had been two months since Sylvia was in New York and they hadn't seen each other since, except through Skype calls. Sylvia was quite eager to be near him and it showed. Marcus wanted to take a weekend break from work. He slaved many weekends, though the office was closed. It was fine time to escape. For now they would eat and attempt to enjoy Sophia's fine dining.

"Ahh mom," Sylvia said in an attempt to get Sophia's eyes off Marcus. "Mom," she raised her voice in alert.

"What," she drawled. "Don't you see Marcus and I are trying to get better acquainted." Sophia was holding his Marcus' arm and showing him to a seat where they could both sit together.

"The food?"

"The food? Oh the food," Sophia released Marcus' arm and ran to the kitchen, but it was too late. The main entree, a pork dish Sophia said she had learned from her mother was burning in the oven.

"Did you make the order from Cafe Blanca," Sylvia whispered to Josh again.

"I'll do it now," Josh replied, smiled, and held Rena's hand and took her outside to the patio. When the food got there, they all ate and got full and satisfied. Sophia thought it best to pull out a few bottles of wine. Josh and Rena tried to sneak a glass, but Sophia was quick to lock down their efforts. Josh spoke more than Sylvia ever remembered. There seemed to have been far more drama in school than Sylvia remembered. No, Sylvia thought while staring at everyone around the table, he enjoys it like this. He enjoys having his entire family here, together, eating at one table and not in separate rooms or homes. Sophia kept badgering Marcus about the specifics of his work, his travels, his likes and dislikes. Sylvia was actually surprised to hear some things she had never heard from him before.

"I didn't know you lived in Japan," Sylvia exclaimed.

"Three years," Marcus replied, then spouted off something in Japanese. Of course, he could've said absolutely anything and Sophia would've believed him. Sylvia found herself smiling in amusement. She thought at first that Marcus was the sole reason for her joy. But around that table, she saw Josh and Sophia, her mother and son, the two most important people in her life. They were smiling and laughing and joking. They were happy. Marcus had quickly joined ranks of most important people. Her feelings for him, though she tried to stifle them, bloomed.

"I don't know how you guys are doing this long distance thing," Karen would say. "I would've fallen off that wagon along time ago."

"But he's worth it," Sylvia would say and even now, she mouthed the words to herself. Sylvia became incredibly overwhelmed by a warmth the wine could not provide. She never imagined her family could look like this.

The evening progressed quickly and by 9:30PM an alarm sounded on Marcus' phone, his face became positively alarmed. "We have to go."

"We?" Sylvia questioned. "We have to go where?"

"You have to go," Sophia asked in surprise.

"Thank you so much for a wonderful diner. Sylvia come on," Marcus said excited. He grabbed her hand and pulled her up from her seat as he stood.

"Marcus, what's going on," Sylvia said laughing nervously.

"Come on. You'll see," Marcus persisted. Sylvia shrugged her shoulders to her mom and the other dinner guests.

"Mom, Josh, I'll call you," she said before picking up her purse and keys and allowing herself to be dragged out the house. Marcus decided he would drive and for a moment it seemed as if he was heading to the airport. "You know, my mom doesn't like her guests running out on her diner like that."

"Well, the truth is she already knew we would leave. For now, we've got a go or else we're going to be late," Marcus said sheepishly.

"What!?"

Fifteen minutes later, they pulled into the Miami airport, parked and rushed out the car.

"Ahhh, we have no luggage," Sylvia protested.

"Don't worry about it." They got inside and entered the line for American Airlines International flights. Sylvia held his arm tightly.

"I don't have my passport," she again rose another concern. This time she stood in front of him blocking his onward procession. Marcus opened his jacket and pulled out two passports. One was his own and the other had Sylvia's face in it. "Wait, how did you get that?" She paused for a moment, stared into his face, "mom! That woman, how did she get so sneaky."

"Well Josh was also involved," Marcus said.

"Josh betrayed me? I thought we were getting along so well," she pouted. They finally reached the counter and the guest service agent confirmed.

"Here are your two first class tickets to Monterrey, Mexico," the teller said.

"Mexico?"

୫ଠ

The flight wasn't long and Sylvia's mind was buzzing. She had never been to Monterrey Mexico. For that matter, she'd never been to anywhere in Mexico. She had planned on going to Cancun, multiple times, but for some reason the trip was always put off by something more important; like a crazy party with amazingly wealthy clients. And now, Marcus had surprised her with this trip to some remote spot that she hadn't even heard of. Sylvia was part excited but more nervous. She knew Marcus to be the guy who didn't get caught up in hype, luxury resorts, and parties. He did like a good adventure though and that was something Sylvia wasn't quite sure she would share as a similar interest. I guess this trip will prove that or not, she thought. "So are you going to tell me what we'll be doing in Monterrey," Sylvia pried.

"No," he replied resolutely.

"I feel like I'm being kidnapped," she glowered and sat back in her chair, arms folded.

"Hey, don't look at me like that," Marcus said staring into her unflinching face. "Alright fine, fine fine. Let's just say Monterrey is one of my favorite places for doing one of my favorite things. I'm actually quite sure you're going to hate it and that's why I don't want to say what it is."

"Well that's comforting," she continued to pout, but some of the tension had gone from her face.

"We're going to be there a few days, but if you absolutely hate it then we'll leave. Okay?" Marcus spoke calmly and Sylvia could not help but be to be soothed by his smooth voice.

The non-stop trip was a mere three and a half hours. The time seemed to have slipped by spending it with Marcus. And in only three and a half hours, her world was entirely different. She had left the rich art deco culture of Miami and had traded it for something a lot different. From the window of the plane, Sylvia could see the shapes of mountains she would soon find to be beautiful. As the airplane overtook a few mountains, the lights came. The city of Monterrey seemed to have been quietly nestle in the midst of the hills. The plane landed and once through the airport, there was a driver waiting for them. Marcus seemed very familiar with the driver. Marcus was able to communicate a few words in Spanish but he was in no way a fluent speaker. They hurriedly got into a mid-size Toyota SUV and sped off. On their way, Sylvia saw many beautiful hotels, all of which she would have been more than happy to hole-up in for a few days, but her hopes were dashed as they simply passed by. Sylvia became quite nervous when they started to exit the city. Where is this man taking me, she thought. For a moment she wondered if the driver had lost his way. Did he really know where he was going. They were leaving the lights behind as they traveled into the hills. She thought to herself, she would certainly not survive if the car had broken down and they had to hike by foot in the dark, not knowing where to go. She remembered that show on TV, 'Man vs Wild.' I guess it would be 'Woman vs Wild.' She hoped it wouldn't turn into 'Naked and Afraid.' Stripping on stage was entirely different to getting naked in the wild. She was in an unfamiliar land and who knows what strange animals lurked in the darkness. There might be a bear or tiger out there for all she knew.

After what seemed like eternity, they finally pulled into what resembled a hotel. Sylvia looked down at her watch, they had only traveled about 30 minutes outside the city. The hotel was certainly not the most chic lodging Sylvia had ever seen, but it was quaint. The entrance way had many rounded arches and a walk way paved with red bricks. It was a fine example of Mexican architecture. It seemed to be the shining example of what homes in Miami attempted to exemplify, with it's terracotta roof and rustic outdoor lamps. By the time they had finally gotten to the room it was well after 2 am, but their bodies felt more like 4 am. The time change wasn't much, but after a full day a one hour time difference felt significant. When they got to the room all Sylvia could think about was getting a shower and going off to bed. Sylvia got into the shower and Marcus went out to fetch some food for the small refrigerator in the room. Sylvia undressed and wore the robe the hotel had provided. She stood out on the large balcony of their room. The stars were so bright, she thought. They didn't seem jaded by the lights from the city. All Sylvia could see of the landscape is a silky blue silhouette of jagged lines, peaks, and valleys.

A few minutes passed and Marcus made his way back to the room. Sylvia heard him, but she was so transfixed on the beauty of the landscape, that she didn't even think to turn around. The lines of the hills and highlight of the trees slowly became more visible as her eyes adjusted to the light of the half moon.

He came up behind her and slipped his arms around her waist. His lips found their mark; a spot behind her ear which made her knees weak. "Those lips," she groaned. She turned around meeting his gaze, she kissed him deeply. His lips traveled from her lips down to her neck. The robe started to give way. Her body yearned for him, so much so it hurt. He was so close, she could breath him in. But had she not felt this way before? Had she not yearned and longed for the intimacy and touch of a man who loves her? Had she not given herself to a man hoping that her passion would stir something within him to make him love her? Had she not basked in his groans, the way she made him feel, the pleasure of all that she is. And was she not rejected; thrown aside like the cheap toy of a spoiled child. Memories of years gone by surfaced. They are always so selfish, Sylvia thought. All the so called lovers of her past, have all been so selfish. So quick to take and slow to give. Just like Gerry. The moment he walked into that apartment, he was prepared to take everything from her. Sylvia was sure he'd be willing to even take her life to satisfy his lust and thirst. Almost unaware, her arms reached for his and loosened his grip. His lips were going further down her body, but those pesky arms started to push him away. "Wait, wait, wait," she struggled to get the words out. Marcus didn't seem to hear her at first, so she held his head for a moment, "wait Marcus."

"Is everything ok?" he lifted his face meeting her eyes.

"I know you want to take our relationship to another level but," she said before looking away ashamed.

"But? But what?" Marcus sounded shocked.

"I'm just not ready," she said almost embarrassed that she'd even said the words. Her thoughts were a jumbled and though he'd been good to her, voices of mistrust were still running rampant through her head. *He's just going to hurt you like all the others. All men are the same. All they want is sex. All they want is to use you and leave you all alone to deal with the consequences. I can't trust him. He doesn't love me, he just wants your body.* Fear overwhelmed every other voice of reason. Sex now might be of greater harm than good.

"Not ready? I thought you liked me?" his voice had changed. He was angry.

"I do like you, but…" Sylvia could not find the words to explain. Her mind was just not at the point for intimacy, not when there were so many demons gnawing on her common sense as though it was fodder.

He had never used this tone with her and Sylvia had hoped she'd never be on the receiving end. "So, when will you be ready?" Marcus said. Sylvia could tell he was attempting to calm himself.

She breathed heavy not wanting to fight on their first night away and together, "I don't know, I don't know okay!" Her voice trembled. The need for sleep only complicated her emotions. She couldn't make sense of her thoughts versus her emotions. She had always been the girl who just followed her feelings. But nothing good ever became of it. Sophia saw failure in her. Flippantly chasing after what felt good had only disappointed the ones she loved. But that certainly did not stop her from feeling and wanting to be loved. "I mean I want this but I…I don't. I don't know Marcus."

"Seriously, you take off your clothes for other men and I'm sure you've slept with some of them too," Marcus' voice became harsh and indignant, "and the man you're supposed to be in a relationship with gets nothing?" Sylvia's own anger started to flare. She could feel the top of her head getting hot. Blood rushed to her face.

"Why the hell do you get to be upset. This is my body and I'll give it to you if I want. And if me being a whore is what you're worried about, then be rested assured that I've never slept with anyone since meeting you," she replied anger still boiling but her voice was low. "You have no right to be upset." There was tension all across his face. He turned and left her standing there on the balcony.

Move On

t w e n t y   f i v e

A N ORANGE LIGHT shone through the glass door of the balcony heralding the dawn of a new day. Marcus was accustomed to waking up early, but something about a new environment always threw him off just a bit. On a normal work day he would have been up before the sun. The light beaming through the glass door signaled to him that he was late. He woke in alarm. He slept on the couch and allowed Sylvia to take the bedroom. The couch was soft and though he'd been to this hotel before, he had never slept on the couch before. He felt as though he would need to visit Gladys, his massage therapist, when he returned to Atlanta. For now, a few stretches will have to do. Last night's events replayed in his mind. The anger, though in a milder form, resurfaced. It seemed absolutely ridiculous to him that Sylvia would not have given herself to him. They've known each other for about four months now, how long would she need. He could see her point. It was her body and forcing her would be something entirely different. He peeked over to the room and she was so beautiful, he thought. He imagined himself waking up next to her, but the thought only upset him more. He could not have her, but why? Why had she resisted him so strongly. He'd met her family. She seemed perfectly happy up until that very point. I must have said something that triggered a nerve, he thought. That was the only thing he could think of. Something he said must have been the undoing of everything they had built. She would not allow it.

She stirred, turned and looked at him looking at her, "hey, you're up early!" she said. He tried to speak but the animosity from the night before lingered in his chest. He left the door way and sat down on the couch attempting to compose himself. He wasn't even sure why he was feeling the way he was feeling. He had been angry from last night and it must have carried over into the morning.

There came a knock at the door. "Oh, he's here already." Marcus got to the door, opened, and there stood a familiar face.

"Marcus, good morning." Marcus had never been happier to see his dad standing outside his door. Marcus' dad, had dark brown hair and gray speckled through his beard. One would expect a man like this to live in Sonoma Valley, California. He had a very nice tan, but not over done. He was a man of the fields. He worked in the sun. The wrinkles in his face were a direct result of him smiling a lot. Many would have called them happy wrinkles. The smile on his face was a stark contrast to the turmoil that churned in Marcus.

"Hey Dad," Marcus returned his smile and both men gave a hearty hug. Sylvia appeared from the bedroom, dressed in the hotel's robes. Gil looked over Marcus' shoulder and saw her.

"Oh, sorry for just showing up. I tried calling but couldn't get to you," Gil said apologetically. In the heat of the moment, Marcus had forgotten to plug in his phone last night and he had also forgotten to tell Sylvia that his dad would be coming along. "The woman at the front remembered me and told me what room you were in."

"We come here enough," Marcus replied.

"They had a room ready for me even though it's so early," Gil said delighted at the service that kept him coming back. "So are you going to introduce me or?" Gil hinted playfully. Though he was still upset with Sylvia, he didn't want his father to see it; especially because he knew his father did not approve of Sylvia. Marcus invited Gil in order to put his apprehensions about Sylvia to rest. Martha, Marcus' mother would not be caught dead in Mexico unless it was in one of those fancy resorts.

"Oh, sorry, Dad this is Sylvia, the girl I told you about. Sylvia this is my father, Gilford." Marcus moved out of the way allowing the two to officially meet. Gil stuck out his hand and held Sylvia's, not bothering to shake. He simply stared into her eyes and smiled.

"It is certainly a pleasure finally putting a face to the name and what a beautiful face it is," Gil said before releasing her hand.

"Oh please, the pleasure is all mine," Sylvia said, smiling pleasantly.

"Will you guys be joining me for breakfast before the climb?" Gil asked. At his words, an uneasiness crept over Marcus' face.

"Climb?" Sylvia asked.

"Yeah, the climb. Oh!" Gil said realizing that he might have spoiled a surprise.

"Yeah, Sylvia we came here to do a little rock climbing," Marcus said while slowly turning towards her, afraid to see the expression on her face. Another detail he meant to tell her but completely forgot.

"Oh," Sylvia said and struggled to mouth a smile.

"Oh great, well, let's meet downstairs in 30 minutes," Gil said then turned and exited the room.

"Okay dad, we'll see you in a little while," Marcus said before closing the door. The look on Sylvia's face was murderous.

"So when were you going to tell me about the rock climbing and your dad showing up out of no where. You know what, I don't care," Sylvia turned and went back into the room. "I don't even have any damn clothes." Marcus sat on the couch, attempting to gather himself. The trip had turned into a nightmare and in his mind he just wanted to give up. He could tell his dad that he made a mistake. He could just admit that he and mom were right. The idea of starting over with someone new was a scary thought. It was a thought he did not want to entertain. But he had no idea what to do to make things better.

ۍ

They both got dressed in the clothes they were wearing the previous day and headed downstairs without saying a word to each other. They met with Gil who was seated outside on the terrace. The restaurant floor was paved with uneven stone but had mossy green grass growing in between the rocks. The terrace over looked mossy green hills. Sylvia could trace the road they drove on the night before which lead straight into the city. The two sat down promptly at the table picked up their menus and started looking.

"See anything you like," Gil smiled and looked over towards Sylvia. She was perusing through the menu.

"Well this one looks good," Sylvia pointed to a picture of eggs, sunny side up, fried over ground beef and vegetables.

"Oh, great choice. I know this menu back and front," Gil said rolling his eyes at his own snobbery.

"Thanks, I think I'll get that one" Sylvia replied. They all made their orders and Gil reached under the table and picked up a backpack and handed it to Sylvia.

"Well here you are my dear. I suppose you'll be needing this if you'll be rock climbing," Sylvia hesitantly took the backpack.

"Oh, thank you so much Mr Warren, but I don't think I'll be doing any rock climbing," Sylvia replied. Marcus looked over to her in surprise. He was not expecting her to break the trip so soon. They had only spent one night.

"Really?" Gil replied with surprise. "Why?"

"Well, I'm not so fond of heights," Sylvia spoke unashamedly.

"Oh girl, that's no reason not to do it," Gil replied. "Hell, I hate heights too," Gil sounded excited, as if he had found a kindred spirit who shared the same struggle as he did. "Every step I take, I go higher up that mountain, I defeat myself and my struggle against the things that scare me the most. Every step I make up that giant rock, I place fear in a headlock and take victory by the horn and make it mine." Gil gesticulated every action. Sylvia seemed captivated by his words. Marcus had heard them before and he was well familiar, but it did soften his heart to see the effect his dad was having on Sylvia. They ate breakfast and Gil went over the basics of rock climbing. He was very animated with a passion that was infectious. Marcus found himself longing for the challenge of the climb. Marcus glanced over at Sylvia every so often found her hanging on every word of his father. She was even laughing at his stories. The same stories he had heard a million times and thought them to be corny. Like the time he had slipped and his foot caught up in the rope and he was dangling upside down. Or the time he really had to go and a flurry of bats came rushing out a cave which had him running with his pants around his ankles. She actually found it funny and Marcus, in a small way, resented his father for it.

"There is a resort store through there, if you'd like to pick up a few things. You can just charge it to the room," Marcus spoke to Sylvia for the first time during the breakfast. They were heading back to the room to get dressed to head out. Sylvia simply followed in the direction he pointed and without a word she marched off to see what the store had. This gave Marcus and Gil a bit of time to catch up.

"Trouble in paradise?" Gil asked.

"Trouble? What do you mean," Marcus attempted ignorance. He was hoping his dad didn't notice. But Gil would have to be deaf and blind not to notice something was up.

"Well, a normal couple who hadn't seen each other for 3 months would be all over each other. You didn't even pull out her chair, which is certainly not how I've taught you. And you haven't said a word to her or me all breakfast," Gil spoke with such sincerity, it was hard to dispute anything he was saying. So Marcus only shook his head and kept his mouth shut. "What, was the sex bad?"

"Dad?" Marcus drawled embarrassed that his father would even mention the word sex to him.

"I know you're not a kid anymore. I realize that now. Though it took a little while. But whatever the problem is son, it's not worth you treating her like that," Gil spoke in a way Marcus had never heard him. He was used to the fun dad who loved playing with kids, not the serious dad talking about grown up relationship issues.

"Dad, you don't understand," Marcus rebutted.

"How about you go get ready and we'll talk later," Gil said patting Marcus on the shoulders. Marcus nodded in approval and went towards the resort store to pick up a few things of his own. In the resort store they were able to find undergarments, attire suitable for sleeping, and clothes fit for the climb. Gil promised that they would start out small today so Sylvia could get the hang of it. Gil hadn't as much talked Sylvia into staying, he just wouldn't take no for an answer. Sylvia picked certain things up and threw them down. She was still upset, Marcus thought.

"You know, I think that would look good on you," Marcus finally said to her, referencing the shorts she held up.

"Oh, you can see me? For a while I thought I was invisible to you," she replied sarcastically. Tension arose once more in Marcus, irritating the pain in his back. He decided not to reply as she had every right to be upset.

The location of the rock they would tackle was a short one mile hike from the hotel, but they had a guide who would coach Sylvia on proper technique. She walked with the guide as father and son lagged behind. "You know Marcus, I think I was wrong. She seems like a great woman. Very down to earth. She doesn't seem obsessed with having more money than she knows what to do with."

"Yeah, she has a son who she really cares about," Marcus replied. "I have a feeling he's the only reason she still does what she does." He couldn't bear to say the word strip to his father. It just didn't seem right. "She said she's not ready," Marcus said watching the ground.

"Not ready for what? To stop stripping? Well that might be…"

"No dad," Marcus cut him off before he got carried away. "You know, not ready to, dot dot dot," Marcus attempted to give, what he thought, were clear clues. He soon realized that his father was no good at guessing hints.

"Just come out and say it son," Gil said shaking his head in ignorance. Marcus stopped him for a moment, whispered to him what he'd been trying to say all along. "Is that what this is about? Man I'm good. I really hit the nail on the head didn't I?"

"Dad!" Marcus called him back to reality.

"Marcus, why did you pursue this girl in the first place," Gil questioned.

"She seemed brave and strong. Even though the odds are stacked against her, she perseveres. I don't know, those are probably qualities I lack and it attracted me to her. But I'm her boyfriend. If there is anyone who should know her intimately, it's me."

"Marcus, you're allowing your own selfish desire to interfere with your perception of the girl you fell in love with," Gil said.

"Dad, she takes off her clothes for other men and what do I get? Is that selfish?"

"That is peculiar that she would do that. But just because she won't give you an orgasm, doesn't mean you should all of a sudden start defining her as a stripper," Gil said. The memory of their conversation in New York played back in his head.

He had told her that she was courageous and that there was something about her that would make him fight his best friend. He would fight his best friend, but would he fight himself. Would he fight back his own desires for her sake. "Love is more than a feeling son, love is a decision you make. Your mother and I decided to love you and your sister, which ended up being more give than get. We changed your nasty diapers and took you to baseball games and stayed up with you when you were sick. That love was a decision your mother and I made. Many parents don't, but we did. We gave our all to you and Ema, and still do, and our affection and feelings towards you and your sister are endless. There isn't any good thing we wouldn't gladly do for you. Son you have to allow your love to grow deep for Sylvia. You'll end up giving a lot, but I guarantee you'll receive a lot more. Make a decision to love her and stick to it, then when she is ready the sex will mean more than banging a hot chick with a fine pair of legs and big boobs."

"How did we even get to talking about love. I never said that I loved her," Marcus said, attempting to defend his loosing position.

"Then why are you doing all this. If loving her is not the thing you pursue. What are you looking for, a trophy? The whole point of dating is not just getting to know the person, it's exercising what it means to love someone. When you've finally mastered what it means to love that person, then you make the final commitment of marriage. I didn't have sex with your mother until we were married," Gil said quite candidly. "I learned to support your mother through all her faults and short comings and she did the same for me. We made the decision to love each other. It wasn't easy and it doesn't even sound all that romantic. But I gave myself for her and she gave herself for me. That's when we decided to get married and only then were we intimate. Sex before marriage was taboo in our time, probably why it's so popular now. Sex, drugs, rock & roll and all that. Your intimacy with her can have significance if you pursue loving her first."

Climb

t w e n t y   s i x

MARCUS' MIND WAS in tumult after speaking to his father. They caught up to Sylvia and the guide. Standing at the base of the rock, it seemed only to be about three stories but Sylvia was obviously nervous. She kept wringing her hands while staring up at what Marcus and Gil would describe as a small rock. It would be a great start for her though. Her apartment was only on the seventh floor in a building with 21. "How are you?" Gil said as he stood by her side to help reassure her.

"Well, nervous I guess. But I've been nervous before," she said now looking at the guide as he demonstrated proper foot placement and climbing technique.

"Good!" Gil replied with a cheer. "You wouldn't be human if you didn't have a little fear in you. Fear can be good. It can keep you from making dumb mistakes. Just as long as you don't turn tail and run. Alright here we go!" Gil started towards the rock. The 56 year old man was in great shape and looked nothing like his age. Sylvia started to chuckle as Gil started his climb.

Marcus looked over at her curious as to what she was laughing about, "what's so funny?"

"Gilford Warren, the most interesting man in the world," she said as she started towards the rock.

"Ha, I guess he is," Marcus feeling more light hearted than he'd been this morning, or for the whole trip for that matter. Gil was the first to make it to the top. Marcus had surpassed Sylvia by only a half body's length. But she had allowed him to pass and he coached her on places she could fix her feet. She listened to every word he said and followed his direction as she was afraid of falling. She relied on him and it gave him great satisfaction to see her succeed.

"Wow," Sylvia said looking out from on top the great rock. The rock had given them a view over the top of the trees which seemed like a floating meadow of green. There were larger rocks and bigger mountains to each side of this great meadow. I just want to run head long into it with arms sprawled open without a care in the world," Sylvia said closing her eyes breathing in the cool November air. "Wouldn't that be nice."

"Well, it would certainly mean your untimely death," Gil smiled, turned and pulled out a pair of binoculars from his backpack. He sat to one side looking out through the spectacles.

"Hey, can we talk," Marcus said to Sylvia. They took to the other side of the rock, placed their bag packs down, and made themselves comfortable.

"If you'd like to leave, I won't hold you back. But I'd like to be honest with you, I'd come to expect certain things from women, and I guess I expected you to fall into that similar mold. Now I feel like I have the biggest case of blue balls known to man. Sylvia, I am honestly jealous of the men you strip for. I am frustrated that they know you more than I do. They know you more intimately than I do." Marcus spoke as delicately as he could manage, attempting not to start another outburst.

Sylvia must have seen his effort because there were no smart jabs to the face nor quick rebuttals. "I'm not stripping for you Marcus. I don't want to feed an expectation based on a career choice I made. If I were a princess or queen, you wouldn't have those same expectations. But because I've stripped for other men you expect me to feed your lust like I did for them? I don't want you to look at me the same way they do."

"But I thought we were at a point in our relationship where…you know, we could be more intimate with each other," Marcus fought to find the right words. Sylvia fell silent for a few moments, looking out over the meadow of trees.

"It's unfortunate, but I've developed a mistrust for men. I decided that I don't want to be with someone unless I knew for sure he loved me and I loved him. I don't want to be used again Marcus," she paused for a moment gathering her thoughts.

"But I wouldn't use you Sylvia," Marcus said in his defense.

"Really? Then why were you so upset when you didn't get your way?" her eyes begged for his understanding. "I have been manipulated by men time and time again. And I admit, some of it has been my fault. I hung out with the wrong people and placed myself in terrible situations. Because of that, I've been used for my body. I've been used to satisfy fantasies in other people. Men and women alike," the words rolled of her tongue with disgust. "Marcus you've helped me see, over the time we've spoken, that I am more than someone's craving. But you seemed to have forgotten that," she said in disappointment. "I feel as though I found a slither of truth and I've got to hold tight to it. If I allow myself to be used by you Marcus Warren, I might just slip back into that dark place I fought so hard to escape. I want to be loved by you not just desired, but truly loved. For once I want to be treated with respect. I want to be a queen in your eyes," she said embarrassingly. "I don't want to be judged by my past. I wish I could erase the memories of ever being a exotic dancer from your mind. I wish that when you see me you don't see someone who took off her cloths for other men."

"Who took?" Marcus said hopefully.

"Yes, who took! I'm going to leave Max and his Royal Playhouse," she smiled and a tear slowly rolled down her face and was swept by a passing breeze. "There are voices telling me that I'm making a big mistake, but I know that I have to face these demons.

"The only reason I'm still here right now and not on a plane back to Miami," Sylvia motioned towards the old man with binoculars fastened to his eyes, "is him!"

"Him, my father? But you only now met him!" Marcus replied somewhat surprised that his father could have such an influence.

"When he looks at me," she paused again searching for the right words. "His eyes don't see me like other men do. He doesn't have that craving. I don't feel dirty. He was the only one on this trip who showed genuine interest in me."

"Ouch," Marcus could feel his heart sink. There were times he felt as though he was the liberator. He had met this troubled girl and he would be the one to show her more than what she'd known. His pride had driven his actions. Flying her to New York and now here to Mexico. And she had warned him that she would not be bought by fancy trips to exotic places. He knew that, but he assumed that he knew what was best for her. "I know. And I honestly don't know what to say to make it better," Marcus turned and looked her in the eyes. "Sylvia," she turned to face him. "I want to love you. I want to be the one who lifts you up when you're down, who carries you when you cannot walk, who praises you like the queen you are. I might not know how to do that yet, but I want to find out and I want to love you." There was a long stream of tears running down her face. She cradled his face in her hands and kissed him.

The next day they took on a mountain which seemed about six stories tall. The process was slow taking almost three hours. They stopped from time to time, giving Sylvia a break as this was only her second time going so high. When they made it to the top, they looked out and there was a fog that settled on top the the meadow of trees. It gave the trees and mountains an eerie look which Sylvia became totally awestruck by. "I have something for you," Marcus said in great delight.

"Ooh, I like surprises. What is it," Sylvia eyes lit up. She had noticed a bulge in his backpack but thought nothing of it. He pulled out a box wrapped in bright Christmas paper. "Oh my, and it's not even my birthday." She took the box which had a nice weight to it. She shook it first and heard something rattle inside. "What is it?"

"How about you just open it," Marcus said impatiently. Sylvia quite gingerly loosened the tape and started to remove the paper. She spotted one side of the box and ripped the remainder of the wrapping to shreds. Her mouth dropped open as she saw her first, brand spanking new, DSLR camera.

"Oh, thank you, thank you, thank you, I love it," she dove at him, threw her arms around his neck and screamed so that his ear rang. Gil stood a few steps back watching it all unfold. Sylvia spotted him and ran to him and held him tight. "Thank you Gil!"

Undercover

t w e n t y   s e v e n

THE TRIP TO Mexico started out a little rough, but they made it through in one piece. Sylvia felt as though her relationship with Marcus was stronger because they had worked through their disputes. They were more open with each other. They even decided that though fights might break out they would rekindle the relationship as quickly as possible and not let feelings of dissension thrive. She sat alone in her apartment recounting the conversations of the week gone by. Sylvia became suddenly aware that she was no longer afraid of being alone. The voices she had so long feared only seemed like roaches now, annoying, but certainly not dangerous. She felt stronger now. Stronger than she'd ever been. And there was one pervading thought which she simply could not shake, "He wants to know who his father is," Sylvia muttered to herself. She had to see what she could find out on the matter.

Sylvia got to the club hell-bent on finding something that might lead her to discovering who the guys were at the party some 15 years ago.

If Max kept any record of these things, her full intention was to find it. In the locker-room she adorned herself in the normal strings which made up her costume. Truth be told, her costume was not much of anything. The determination she had leading up to this point was high. But it soon melted away leaving a tight tension in her stomach. Actually, she wanted to throw up. She urgently rushed to the bathroom, slammed the stall door, and liberated this afternoons Asian cuisine from its resting place. "Good going Sylvia," she cheered herself on. She knew though, that in sunshine or in rain, this had to be done. She made her way back to the locker-room, put on her robe, and walked slowly towards Max's office. He was there, sitting on the desk taking a phone call. She would have to wait until he was out. She made her way up to the VIP section and found a few men who wanted lap dances. It was not her usual flare but she was good enough to get them aroused. She tried her best to keep an eye out for Max, as he would be leaving soon to do additional business in the city. Sylvia was able to do two lap dances, which got her 'a so-so amount of money,' but it was nothing compared to what she would usually make at the parties. She had just finished a second lap dance and spotted Max walking out the front door. He probably came to the main room to check on things before leaving.

Sylvia left the VIP area and headed to the back office. She tried to casually stroll but couldn't help feel the urgency which propelled her legs faster and faster. She tried the door to Max's office and it was still open. He probably won't be long she thought. She went in, closing the door behind her. Threw her robe over the back of the visitor's chair and still wearing heels she clambered over to the back of his desk to where he kept his files. She just needed to find a list of clients. She checked his desk drawer first and found nothing having to do with the parties. There was a safe, which most likely only contained the cash for the day. Well maybe it will be in one of the older cabinets, since it was so long ago, she thought. She allowed her eyes to scan over all the cabinets, searching for the oldest one. Her eyes landed on a black filing cabinet in the corner of the room. It was chipped and rusty. It must be there. Sylvia quickly rummaged through the files in the cabinet, looking for something that might give her a clue. Then finally she came across some information on various clients who have been to his parties. He had contact information for all of them, their preferred way to be contacted, and venues for upcoming parties. Sylvia's pulse raced. Her head elated by the sudden onset of adrenaline as she came closer to what might lead her to her son's father.

In the past, she had tried to guess how old the guys where at the party. They were fairly young then, probably in their low 30's. If that was the case, then the person she was looking for would be roughly mid to upper 40's. The files she picked up had portraits, names that had been blacked out with a black marker, contact information, and some kind of pin number. The pin numbers, Sylvia thought, must be encoded unto one of those white cards each of Max's clients show up to the parties with. The white card gets scanned at the door by a host which shows a picture to verify the attendee's identity. "Oh perfect," she said much louder than she intended. She stopped for a moment to make sure no one heard her outburst of excitement. There were dates which showed when the file was created. She realized quickly that each of the files was ordered by date. This made things simple. She left that file drawer and went straight to the bottom file. She skipped towards the back of the draw and found files from 15 years back. Some of the people she recognized, but none she believed she was involved with. "They've got to be here somewhere," she said making sure to whisper this time. She got to the last file folder and found it empty. This one did not have a date, it simply read X-Files. "Max is a fan of X-Files, who'd have thought?" she chuckled but then considered what the X-Files were. Nothing came to mind. It must be code for something, she thought. She closed the cabinet drawer and sat in his chair to think. Her mind explored all the possibilities, but there was something she was obviously missing. Then she heard him.

Max was in the hallway leading to his office, "make sure you come to my office and cash out before you leave."

"Yes sir," a voice responded. Must be one of the new girls, Sylvia thought. It was a voice she didn't recognize. If she tried to sneak out now, he'd catch her red handed. She placed her feet up on his desk, fluffed her hair, and put on one of her signature sexy looks.

Max walked into the room, saw her and said, "what the hell is this." His eyebrows furrowed and mouth snarled.

"Max, I know I screwed up, ok," she said attempting to appeal to his humanity. But he knew her. He knew of her power, which made him suspicious of her. It was nevertheless quite difficult to tell if she was being genuine or deceptive. "Honestly, thank you for allowing me to still work the club. I know it's going to take a while for me to redeem myself. But I'm asking you, let me back in the parties again. I'm good at that. You know I'm good. I make you more money than all the other girls," she said, at first pleading but then started whining like an old car needing a tune up.

"That's why you're in here dressed like this. You should be out on the floor making me some money," Max said, annoyed at her actions.

"But Max," Sylvia whined, "I don't like it here. Oh come on."

Max let out a big sigh, "fine, I am throwing myself a birthday party at my house with a few friends. They are not the usually big names, but they have money. You can come by and dance there, you money hungry little…"

"Thank you Max," Sylvia cut him off before he could finish.

"Alright, get out of my office and get back to work if you want to make any money tonight."

Ↄ

Sylvia showed up to Max's birthday party well after it had already begun. Showing up too early would make it easier for Max to see if she was missing. It didn't seem as if it even mattered, because he was well watered and high as a kite by the time Sylvia got there. Sylvia dragged Karen along for back up. Both girls showed up at the party hotter than noon time in California on a mid-summers day. Karen wore a super sexy green dress, which with her red hair made her look like the Batman character Poison Ivy. Sylvia was wrapped in a mini skirt and a completely sheer top that revealed her black bra underneath. She wore a furry black and white sleeveless jacket and retro fitted it with interior pockets to store whatever she found. The girls jumped out of Sylvia's Benz and heard someone call out from the door.

"Hey, keep it close, we won't be long," Sylvia said to the valet as she handed over the key. She included a $50 dollar tip with the key, "you'll get the rest when we get out."

"Hey Syl," a large muscle bound guy standing at the front greeted her with familiarity. Sylvia was surprised and delighted.

"Mikey, how are you. Where have you been?" Sylvia asked.

"I took the lady on a little vacation," Mikey smiled wide. He had great teeth, Sylvia thought. The memory from that day she first met Marcus flooded her mind. She had spoken to Mikey outside the club moments before almost running into the gorgeous specimen of a man she had come to love. She had known Mikey for about four years now and he was possibly one of the best bouncers she'd known. He'd gotten her out of some tough situations, where she could have been hurt. He was the big brother she never had. His presence certainly gave her a much needed boost of confidence, because now that she was at the hotel Max called a home, she was suddenly feeling faint of heart.

"Oh my god, it's so good to see you," Sylvia ran up to him, gave him a big hug and kissed him on the cheek. Sylvia meant every word. It was so good to see him, more than he himself knew. Though something was different. During the time he'd been gone, Sylvia had learned to get along without him. She remembered the times her nerves would completely overwhelm her for the simple fact that Mikey was not there.

"Guess what," Mikey said smiling, completely unable to hold back some great secret.

"What!"

"I popped the question and she said yes!" Mikey said, pulling out his phone showed Sylvia the picture of the ring. Seeing the joy on her face, Sylvia sighed hard, letting out a huge breath. Longing suddenly claimed her heart.

"I am so happy for you two," her eyes glossed over and there was sincere happiness on her face. Happy that someone she'd known for so long had found a reason to commit himself to one woman. Would anyone find that in her, she thought? Would Marcus find that in her? Would she even make a good wife? Or would she embarrass him like she did Josh?

"Sylvia," Karen said understandingly and drew her back to the reason they were there.

"Hey we have to get to work. Thank you so much for sharing that with me Mikey," Sylvia said to her old friend. "By the way Mikey, this might be my last party, but I want an invite to that wedding ok," Sylvia said softly, sounding sad and somewhat unsure of the words coming from her mouth.

"Definitely," Mikey replied smiling a little less as the news of Sylvia leaving sunk in. The girls got inside the house and couldn't help but be floored by the beauty of the home. Max certainly had good taste when it came to his home. It was a Mediterranean style house with a huge fire place which separated a sitting area from the TV room. The ceiling was high with dark wood beams. Hanging from one of the supporting beams was a beautiful vintage wrought iron chandler.

"Nice," Karen said. The French doors leading to the pool were open and the music from the pool side was loud. There had to be close to 150 people lingering in and around the house. The pool side was filled with beautiful girls and guys. There were small platforms around the pool and girls stood on each dancing. There were also cabanas with thick curtains pulled and it was easy to imagine what went down behind the separation.

"Okay, he will probably have an office, let's split up and find it. Keep your phone close and text me if you find it first and I'll do the same," Sylvia issued the command as they scampered up the stairs. Both girls headed in separate directions hoping to cover more ground quickly. Sylvia opened door after door and was disappointed to find them lacking the thing they hunted. After the third room, she realized that probably all the rooms were being used as private rooms for lap dances. Leave it to Max to make money at his own birthday party. Sylvia met with Karen in the middle of the hall way, "any luck?"

"Nothing, just a bunch of girls from the club giving lap dances," Karen replied. "But wait, there is probably a room on the first floor."

"Of course, a lot of homes have first floor offices. Clients wouldn't have to go to a private area in the house to do business," Sylvia said, then after realizing she had given way too much explanation. Karen was looking at her as though she was bored. "You know what…whatever! Let's go." Both girls laughed and started down the stairs. They got half way down and could see Max at the DJ's booth trying to hype the crowd.

"Well he looks like he's having fun," Karen said rolling her eyes.

"Let's just get what we came for and get out of here," Sylvia said. On the the east side of the house was the kitchen which left the west wing. There was a double door inconspicuously hidden in plain sight. That area had almost been completely deserted, except for a bathroom that received constant flowing traffic. Sylvia found her way through the moving people and tried the door but it was locked with an electronic key.

"Whatever is in there must be super important to have it locked away with an electronic key," Karen said.

"And I would guess that a key as important as the one to this door is probably on him now," Sylvia concluded guessing exactly what was in Karen's mind.

"Okay, leave it to me," Karen said before turning, zipping down the back of her dress, leaving her in a two piece bikini. Sylvia stood by a window and watched as Karen strode out to the pool side. Max was seated with two girls flanking either side of him. Karen bent over and whispered something in his ear. Sylvia could see a huge grin on Max's face. Max got up in a hurry, got to the closest enclosed cabana, kicked out its occupants, and invited Karen in. Sylvia shook her head in disbelief that Karen would go this far, only because she wanted to help Sylvia find out who Josh's dad was. Sylvia was not even sure what she would do with the information. Would she try to secure child support? He would most likely deny having a child by way of some stripper? If he turned out to be some high powered person, would she open it up to the press? Does she really want to be one of those women sitting across from a news reporter or TV show host telling her sad story. How she fell in love and bore a child that possibly belonged to some celebrity or man of high importance? Her story sounded like a concoction good only for a stomach ache. The real tragedy would be the lost identity of the father to her beloved son. Her story probably wouldn't make prime time or would only last the proverbial fifteen short minutes of fame. Plus, the men she stripped for would fight to keep their names out of the spotlight. No one wants to hear their name along side other such words as stripper, drugs, and rape. The men she took her clothes off for, the ones who specially requested her, would certainly disassociate themselves the moment their names showed up as suspects of a gang rape. *Bunch of hypocrites*, Sylvia thought. In the moment, they'd treated her like a goddess. But threaten their reputation and they'll make her out to be the scum under their shoes.

"Got it," Karen said making her way through the hall.

"I don't know how to thank you," Sylvia said giving her a hug. Karen handed her a key ring with a few keys and a small silver cylinder.

Sylvia approached the door with the keys in hand and she could hear the door unlock automatically. She turned the lock slowly and the door opened. "Let me know if he's coming."

"Okay," Karen affirmed. Karen disappeared as Sylvia closed the door. The room was as beautiful as the rest of the house. There was a desk towards the far wall. On either side were glass windows. There was a large floor to ceiling bookshelf.

"X-Files, where could you be in this really big office," Sylvia asked herself. "If I were a money hungry man with important clients, where would I put your file." Sylvia walked quickly to the desk and pulled the bottom drawer, but there were only a few pieces of paper there. "You must be close," she urged herself to think like Max. To her left was the bookshelf, to her right was a drink cabinet with doors along the bottom. Sylvia started on one side, opening one door after the other. Within each door was a drawer deep enough to house files. She felt as if she was really close. The adrenaline spurred her on. She flipped through file after file and could not find anything related to the X-Files. She pulled the door closet to the window and inside was another drawer. And there it was: X-Files. It was a small folder containing about 25 pages. One of the files was dated to around the time she got pregnant with Josh. "Got it," she texted Karen.

"I'll go get the car," Karen replied. Sylvia looked through a few more sheets and came across some additional photographs attached with paper clips. She thought them to be insignificant at first but read a description from one of the men. Preference: female, 12 - 16 years old, white/Hispanic.

"Oh no," Sylvia said to herself. She picked out another and read. Preference: female, 7 - 10 years old, any race. Sylvia lost her breath as she realized what she was looking at. "He was always quick to cater to the person with the money. But to think, human life meant so little to him. Sylvia was utterly disgusted at what she found. It was as if slime was dripping from the pages. She felt dirty just holding them. Then a sick realization emerged within her mind, I helped him do this to these young girls. Her stomach fell when she saw a little boy, who couldn't have been older than six or seven. That could've been Josh. The thought left her paralyzed in horror. If one of his disgusting clients had a fancy for a little boy, Josh could have very well been the little boy in this picture. Sylvia placed her hand over her mouth to prevent herself from screaming. She remembered seeing the boy's face on posters and t-shirts as the family pleaded for the return of their son on the evening news. The thought materialized indignation so strong that simply finding Josh's father was no longer enough.

She sat down at his computer desk, where there were two screens. The mouse shifted and they came to life. One of the screens requested a password but the other came up with surveillance footage. Sylvia thought the footage looked familiar. The realization hit her like a Mack truck. "This is the living room, bedroom, bathroom, of the apartment. There is even a camera in the fan," Sylvia said to herself in absolute horror and disbelief. "He's been watch me all this time." Sylvia looked out the window facing the pool, making sure to keep Max in her sights. Another frightening realization crept over her. Oh no he's gone, she thought. Max was not at the pool. She had to act quick. She spotted a large drawer in the lower compartment of the computer desk. Sylvia pulled it open and found a stack of DVDs organized in rows. One row was labeled Oceana, another was labeled Broadstone, and another Yacht Club. "How many of these apartments did he have?" Sylvia started to pluck random DVDs from their cases, starting with the one labeled Gerry on the front. It was the most recent in the row for Oceana. She picked up a few from the other rows and shoved them in her coat pocket. She knelt to the ground to get the files. She had to do something about this horrible thing she had found. She gathered the pages, folded them neatly and fitted` them inside the pockets she sewed into her coat. She had only planned for the files and the DVDs were awkwardly placed in her pocket.

A voice came up behind her, "what are you doing in here." It was Max. "First you were in my office at the club and now you're here. What the hell are you doing," his words slurred a bit from having too much to drink. Sylvia knew she would be okay as along as he didn't call for security. Max was not an especially fit man. For minor disagreements with the other girls, he had to call in help from security. Plus Karen was gone, so Sylvia had no choice but to work this out on her own. Seeing what he had done, the skeletons in his closet, Sylvia did not want to run. She wanted to stand up to Max. She wanted to show some teeth and a little grit for once. Most of all, she wanted to wash her hands of the Royal Playhouse and land a swift kick to the balls on her way out.

ᘓ

"Max, I want to know who the guys are that raped me that night fifteen years ago," Sylvia asked nervously. She had avoided this conversation for reasons which went beyond her comprehension.

"Raped you?" Dinero said with a puzzled and almost disgusted look on his face. He looked as if he had just smelled something absolutely repulsive. "You're a whore, you can't rape a whore."

"What," Sylvia was shocked by his remarks. *Don't know why I expected any better*, she thought. "Max please I need to know," Sylvia's voice crackled as she spoke. Shame was definitely the word. It sneaked around her mind, somehow manifesting itself as fear. But the truth of the matter was that she was truly ashamed and deep down she knew Max was right. She was just a whore and this was the life of a whore. But a lot has changed. As a matter of fact, everything has changed.

"I don't have to tell you anything," Max said before turning, with an attempt to walk away.

Sylvia seeing he had no intention to tell her, grabbed his arm. "Max you owe it to me, please," she said with a bogus fortitude she drummed up.

It was obvious though that Max was not falling for it. "I allowed you to go to the best parties. I give you the best gifts. I make sure that even though you don't work nearly as hard as the other girls, you get the VIPs with the money and you come to me with this. Is this the way you show your appreciation? Come up here talking about rape, disrespecting me in my house!" Max's voice in a steady crescendo, rose in its intensity. "Sylvia Velvet Garnet, you were a whore from the beginning and I was the one who gave you a place. If it wasn't for me you wouldn't be living in a nice apartment. If it wasn't for me you wouldn't be driving that nice Benz."

His words didn't cut as deep as they would have only a few months ago. The truth became a lamp unto her feet and a light to her path. She was free of him. "Max Dinero, you seemed to have forgotten that this club was built on my back. Everything you have now is because of me. This club is basically half mine. I let you," shame started to show its ugly head again, causing her stomach to wrench. Her hands and voice shivered like a beggar with hypothermia. "I let you pimp me," angry tears started to roll down her cheeks. The words were hard to say. She had tried so hard to gloss over her own self loathing and it was something she never thought she would have had to face. At least not something she thought she would have faced now. But here it was. "I was only 14 when I sold my virginity to the highest bidder. Only 14 Max; and you were the auctioneer. I gave you my soul and you sold it cheap to build a prison for me and many other girls. Hell, I thought you loved me. I thought you loved me," it was hard for her to believe now that she once felt his love for her. Once upon a time, she yearned deeply for his love. Hell for any love. She would do anything not to disappoint him. She would do anything to make sure he was happy with her. "It must have been easy to manipulate a 14 year old girl, with no dad and low self esteem," her voice swam in her tears. Somehow her tears, the manifestation of her brokenness, made her feel stronger. "There was nothing I wouldn't have done for you." She had felt so fortunate to be hanging with this cute 23 year old college grad.

"I don't have to listen to all your moaning," Max said and pulled his arm from her grasp.

"How much did you make from my virginity Max Dinero. I sold my soul and you reaped the benefits, Max Dinero. I was pulling in seven to eight thousand per night after I lost my virginity. So how much was it," she jeered and prodded his emotions with guilt. "I gave it up all for your dream of owning this club. I've sold my soul for the cement and nails that put this million dollar house of yours together. So I say that I've more than earned that lousy car and the apartment."

"Get out, get out of my house," Max's eyes bulged from his head. The look in his face was murderous. Who knows, he might have killed her if there weren't windows and people right outside dancing. Sylvia picked up her purse containing the contacts, notebook, and pictures and she quickly walked out the door. She left him prowling back and forth like an angry tiger.

She knew his mentality. He had said it himself, "If I allow just one of these whores to get out of line then they will all become rebellious." She knew that her actions now closed the doors to her going back to the Royal Playhouse and any of its parties for good.

Backlash

twenty eight

HIS MIND WAS constantly on her. His focus wandered from one thing to the next leaving him paralyzed, unable to do his work. She had not left the Royal Playhouse and that troubled him. Was some guy's hands roaming the body of the woman he loved and cared for. He just wanted to be near her. To hold her and protect her. His father was right. Making a conscious effort to give yourself to someone also meant that your feelings towards them would grow deeper. The moment he started to actively take part in the process of training Sylvia to climb that rock, he felt different. On the second day when they made it to the top and he gave her that camera, the expression on her face meant the world to him. He could not for the life of him recall an instance where he helped someone without the possibility of getting something in return. The thought troubled him. Was he really that selfish? Was he really that self centered. He would support her over the week that followed, being careful not to trample her out of pride; pride in how educated and knowledgeable he was. At that point he wanted to give her the world, just to see her smile and have her happiness be his joy. The concept was foreign. He wasn't even sure if he was doing it right. But he was willing to try and it seemed as if she wanted to also. Mexico showed him something in himself that he didn't like. Sylvia told him once that she just wants someone to love her and he thought that at the root of it he wanted the same thing too.

Marcus' phone rang, it was Sylvia. "Hey you," Marcus answered, feeling pleasantly surprised that she should call while he dreamed of her. Sylvia's voice over the phone was excited or nervous, Marcus couldn't decide. Without even a hello, she started to unload on Marcus. He could hardly get a word in. In one big long sentence she told him everything she did; from sneaking into Max's office, then his house, and the files she found. She even told him about DVDs. She kept going on and on about a sex trafficking ring or something and that he had it all recorded. "Okay, okay, Sylvia slow down, I can't get what you're saying." Her excitement brought out a Puerto Rican accent Marcus was certainly not used to hearing. "Wait, wait, wait, Sylvia," Marcus attempted holding back the flood water. Attempting to listen to Sylvia this excited was like drinking from a fireman's hose turned on full blast. "You think Max is involved in what? A sex trafficking ring? But how do you know that?" Marcus shouted, surprised at what Sylvia told him. She mentioned something about videos being made and Marcus remembered the video Simon had showed him. Marcus moved to his computer and tried looking for the video Simon had played. There was nothing. *He probably played it directly from his phone*, Marcus thought. Sylvia mentioned some names of people who are in the files she found. Marcus recognized them instantly as CEO and execs of large companies. No wonder Max was trying to find ways to hide his funds, Marcus remembered the conversation he had with Simon. The money he would be making from these guys would certainly get the attention of the IRS if deposited in any US bank. The pieces started to fall in line within Marcus' mind. Men like this would not want their secrets found, Marcus' thoughts became alarming. "Hello, Sylvia, you need to get your findings to the police right away. Sylvia, Hey. Are you there? The line is open, but she's not answering," Marcus said to himself. The tension in his neck tighten ten fold. "Sylvia, can you hear me." He could still hear the idle trotter of her car and swish as other cars passed by. He continued listening, worry running a muck in the depths of his gut. "Sylvia, are you there?" He paced his floor, back and forth, attempting to stay calm. "I've got to go! I've got to go to Miami," he said, his decision spurring his body into action.

ৎর

Marcus found the number for the Miami Dade Police Department, called and filed missing person's report. He was able to get on a flight to Miami and reached Sylvia's apartment in just under 4 hours. By the time he got there, there were a few police officers filing out of Sylvia's apartment. A detective Martinez was standing inside. Marcus told him everything he could about Sylvia. He described the color of her eyes, her soft blushing lips, and flowing black hair which reached down her back. He could just picture Sylvia, the way she looked laying on the bed in Mexico with the morning light shining through the room window. He remembered how he was so upset that morning.

"Mr Warren…Mr Warren…Marcus," Detective Martinez said raising his voice. An ice cold feeling rolled over Marcus. The blood drained from his face and panic rose. "Mr Warren, is there anything else you can tell me? Any known associates who might want to harm her?"

"Yeah," his mind returned muddled but coherent enough. "She said she found out something about her employer, Max Dinero. Something to do with sex trafficking. She didn't finish telling me before she was gone from the line."

"Did you hear anything while you were on the line," Detective Martinez questioned.

"No, one minute she was on the line with me and another minute she was gone." Marcus couldn't help his babbling. A headache began to set in. "I was about to tell her to go to the police with the information she had found."

"Any idea the form of what she found? Was it computer data related, something she saw, or some kind of physical evidence?" the detective asked.

"She mentioned something about files and maybe even DVDs, I'm not sure. She was quite hysterical," Marcus said with his palms to his temple attempting to massage away the impending anguish brewing in his head.

"Okay, thank you Mr Warren," Detective Martinez pulled a card out of his wallet and handed it to Marcus. "Please if you come across any additional information, please let me know. We're going to check in on Max Dinero."

"Were you able to track her phone," Marcus asked.

"Yes, we found her car and cell phone not far from here," Detective Martinez said. He probably saw the increased tension in Marcus' face and attempted to amend, "But don't worry, I'm going to try to get every available resource on this." Detective Martinez stepped out of the apartment and left Marcus standing there alone. Marcus recognized the apartment from the surveillance video he'd seen of Sylvia. It felt a bit abnormal standing in the same place where so much had happened. The furnishing, the style, and view would've been amazing on any other circumstance, but Marcus couldn't bring himself to enjoy it when Sylvia could possibly be in trouble.

A call came over Marcus' phone from a number he didn't recognize, "area code 305, Miami." His heart lurched in his chest. "Hello, Sylvia?" He answered the line quickly, hoping to hear her voice.

"No, it's Karen," the voice over the line said.

"Karen, hey! Have you seen Sylvia? Is she with you," Marcus had forgotten about Karen and that her and Sylvia were best friends.

"No I was calling to find out the same thing," Karen replied. "Marcus, we found something and I think it might tick Max off."

"Yeah I know, I believe she's been abducted because of that very same thing," Marcus replied, his voice sounding angry and hopeless.

"Abducted? Sylvia was kidnapped? You can't be serious! What the hell am I going to do," Karen sounded hysterical.

"What do you mean? Why would you need to do anything," Marcus replied almost offended by the remark.

"I was with her when we went to Maxy D's house. I have the documents she stole. Once they realize she doesn't have the files they are going to come after me," Karen's voice started to crack. "What the hell, man! What the hell!"

"Why didn't you just go to the police," Marcus asked in suspicion.

"Are you kidding. I don't trust the police," Karen replied, sounding shocked that Marcus asked the questioned. "Some of the guys in this file are the police. Plus didn't you hear about that serial killer on the loose. He was a police officer too you know."

"Hey, listen to me," Marcus commanded bringing to a halt Karen's frenzy. Karen was difficult to rein in once she got on a role. "Meet me on the corner of Lincoln and Michigan in front of the Apple store. You know where that is?"

"Of course I know where that is. I'm Miss Miami. I know this city like the back of my hand," she said as though a second ago she wasn't freaking out. "Ok, I'll see you there!"

Mama

twenty nine

"I CAN'T BELIEVE YOU'RE here. Oh mother it's so good to see you again. I know, I should be quiet, daddy is sleeping in the other room, but seeing you here and now, like this. It was so unexpected. I almost didn't believe my eyes when I got the call to come pick you up. To tell you the truth, they want me to take you to the pirates. They want me to take you far away from here, somewhere no one will never find you, but I can't let you go mama. You're too important to me. I really don't know what they do with the others I send them, but who cares right. You are all that matters. Just you and me. See I made everything just the way you like it. We're going to have so much fun, just you, me, and papa; before you burn." James smiled with evil intent written all over his face. He sat on the back seat of his large black SUV smoking another cigarette with the windows up. The head of a very beautiful woman laid in his lap. She was unconscious, put to sleep by a shot of animal tranquilizer. The door on the passenger side opens and a man jumbs into the black SUV.

"Max Dinero," the man said.

"Do you have her yet?" Max asked the driver to the black SUV.

"Yeah, I got her," the man motioned towards the back seat. Max turned and looked, a smile lit up his face.

"Did she have the files?" Max interrogated the driver. He didn't like to be questioned and grew increasingly annoyed.

"You hired me to get a girl and I did, what else do you want?" the driver replied through gritted teeth.

"I told you to retrieve the files with the girl," Max insisted.

"I didn't see any files," the driver, unwilling in his response, not wanting to be held responsible for not finding the files.

"Did you check her apartment?"

"Yeah, I didn't find anything. Plus there were cops filing into the building so I had to make a quick exit," the driver explained.

"Cops?" Max exclaimed, "What happened. Parks I thought you were a professional. How were the police tipped off so quickly," Max demanding in his tone.

"She was talking to someone on her phone. I had a small window of time to get her so I took the chance. They probably got worried about her and called the police," Parks defended his position as best he could.

"I'm going to send you a picture and address of another girl. I want you to pick her up too. And Parks, I want them alive. After we get those files, take them to the pirates. Got that Parks," Max commanded. Does he know of my obsessions, Parks questioned within himself.

"I will call you, when I have her in my possession," Parks replied before Max hopped out the front seat and disappeared into his own car. His phone lit up with the face of another beautiful girl, whose complexion was fairer than the one he had already taken. She had red hair with blue eyes. He was almost sure she had blonde hair before she dyed it. His mind wondered about Jessica, his wife, who he burned alive. He wondered what state she might have been in when the police found her. He remembered when he first saw her as a paramedic, she was a dope head back then. He simply left her in the same state he had found her; doped up with a house burning down all around her. His wonder was a matter of curiosity and not of concern. She served her purpose, he thought. His companion for the last six years had probably been burned to a crisp. No need dwelling on insignificant things, when there is work to be done. "Nana, see what I've done? I've been a good boy Nana," James muttered in prayer to his dead grandmother. He finished his cigarette, like the candles of the saints and opened the window allowing the smoke to bellow out. He dropped the butt adding one more to the four already on the ground. Nana, looking down from heaven, he was sure would be proud of him. He imagined she would be wearing some kind of robe of white or something. She probably still had those terrible glasses, the one that made her look like one of those creepy old cat ladies. But grandma's house did not smell like kitty litter. Nope, grandma's house smelled like bleach; lots and lots of bleach. Oh how much his cheeks would burn after she had pinched them. Why do old women insist on pinching the cheeks of children. It really ought to be outlawed.

"Jesus loves you," she use to say. "He died for you on the cross. He died to take away all your sins."

"What about mama and papa," the young James Parks asked.

"What about your parents sweetie?" Nana questioned in confusion.

"Did Jesus die to take away their sins too," he asked quite eagerly.

"Of course he did baby," Nana said. "He loves your mama and papa so deeply, that if they only ask he will forgive them of their sins."

"Oh, what if they died. What if they died and didn't ask for forgiveness or for Jesus to come into their hearts. What would happen if they died then," James asked again quite eagerly.

"Well honey," Nana always called James by something sweet. For a while, James thought that Nana might have been the witch from the children's story Hansel and Gretel. He could picture her cooking him up and having him for diner, literally. Why else would she call him something like sweetie pie or sugar bumpkin or pumpkin. She clearly saw him as some kind of edible delight and simply wanted to eat him. Even in the face of telling her grandson that something terrible, something horrendous, something absolutely unthinkable will happen if his parents did not repent from their sins, she still found something sweet and delightful to call him. It was really no surprise to James when grandma died of diabetes. At least she died happy he thought. "If they don't repent and come to know Jesus Christ as Lord then they will certainly, most likely go to hell." There was a very pained look on Nana's face when she said it. She probably thought that James was actually worried about the eternal salvation of his parents. She thought that he might actually be battling the justice of God as he must punish those who have turned away from his son who died for the redemption of the human race. But no, James thought it best to help the justice of God to move a bit more swiftly. The morning daddy died, mama knew he was out drinking. She knew he wouldn't have made it home without some kind of help. Though she would not be the one to go and actually try to get him out of the bar. One might suffer terrible blows at the hands of papa if he wasn't ready to leave the bar that night. So she remained in the house and demanded that James go and fetch papa. Because James thought it necessary to eat that day, he made his way to Mickey's Irish pub where he found daddy slumped over the bar counter. He seemed ready, James thought. James attempted to awake him, which resulted in a black eye. When they were finally out and on their way home, James saw the opportunity of a lifetime. The opportunity to help God's justice along. He walked behind daddy, attempting to keep him out of harms way. Then a beautiful black Buick Grand National came rolling down the street. It was brand-new and James always wanted to ride in the Buick. But he knew his daddy wouldn't go for it. If only he could just look inside, that would really be enough to satisfy his curiosity. But how might he see inside of that brand-new black Buick that was rolling down the street, the answer was very easy, Daddy. Hell, he was already stumbling, James would just help him stumble in the right direction. And just at the right time daddy's head came flying off after kissing the right headlight of that Buick Grand National. James got his wish. He was able to see inside of that black Buick. It was everything the magazines said it was. This one had beautiful black suede seats. It must have been only a few weeks old because it still had that new car smell.

"See Mama, everything is perfect. I just need to pick up the red head for the pirates and then I'll have you all for myself," his eyes brightened and mouth curled. He held Sylvia's hair, placed it to his nose and breathed deeply, inhaling the scent of her. He bent over her, stuck out his tongue and licked her forehead, "I really want to have you now." He continued to lick down the side of her face, a warm feeling ran down the entire length of his body. She aroused him, but he held himself, "No, you're right Nana, I have to be a good boy." James left the back seat and got in the driver's seat.

⁃

"There she is," he said to himself. "Mama we've almost got the red head. Just wait a little longer and we'll finally have our time together before you burn in hell. Now Mama, you cannot escape God's judgment. Papa is already waiting for us back at the house and we can't keep him waiting. You know how he gets when you make him wait," James sounding more cheerful, more sadistic as the moment of his ultimate pleasure drew nearer. The woman James associated as mama was stirring on the back seat. Sylvia twisted and turned and was surprised to find both her hands handcuffed to the child seat restraints and her legs bound with zip ties. There was also a gag in her mouth. She started to cough from thick putrid atmosphere inside the Suburban. "See mama, I told you, just like papa use to do. Just brings back memories doesn't it," James was abnormally cheery but then his voice and attitude would transform as quick as flipping a switch. "Memories of the beatings, the black eyes, and bleeding that you allowed me to go through." Then cheery again, "the best childhood any boy could ask for." James turned to see the red head jump into her car and sped off. "Now let's see where this little red head is going?" James noticed that after saying red head, Sylvia's head perked up attempting to see. "Oh, so you know this little red head. I bet you and her did something real naughty didn't you mama. I always knew you were more than just gossiping fools." James pulled out behind Karen's car staying approximately two car lengths behind. She got on the causeway, passing through an area which looked like a shipping yard. They passed by some very beautiful homes, which seemed to require special access, but he could clearly see them as they sat pretty on the waterfront. He passed a sign which said, Welcome to Miami Beach. "Well Mama, doesn't seem like red head is going to make it very easy for me." James lifted his arm rest and pulled out a hand gun. The moment his hand touched metal, he became silent. He followed her to a section in town where there were many people walking. She parked in a somewhat secluded area. He would have to grab her before she got out in the open. He quickly parked and tried jumping out the car before she did, but she seemed to have been in a hurry. He noticed that in her hand she clutched a leather satchel large enough to house the files the Max was so desperately looking for. She was tall and had a long stride. He followed her close, attempting not to lose her quick steps. Because of the crowd he lost sight of her for a moment. He struggled to get clear of a few people who blocked his way then he suddenly came up on her, far closer than he anticipated. He became startled as he met eyes with the man she was speaking to.

James heard the man say, "you were followed." James turned and ducked behind a group of people walking towards him. He scurried into an alley attempting to get out of sight. He heard hurried footsteps coming in his direction. He ran in a crouch and tried to see if he was being followed. He was. The man he met eyes with was hot on his trail. James pulled the gun from his pants waist and held it low in his right hand. The chance of being spotted was far too high, he would have to get to the back of the building where there would be no one watching. James got to the back of the building, found a dark corner, stood in it and waited. He was not a shooter, he had never fired his gun as a police officer. People died too quick from gun shot wounds, he thought. Fire, on the other hand, was far better. There was something beautiful about the flames. The way it danced, the way it consumed the thing it caught in it's clutches. Fire, now that's a good way to send someone to their eternal place of torment.

Pursuit

t h i r t y

THE MAN MARCUS saw, seemed familiar. Actually, it would seem as though quite recently he had seen that face. Police are looking for James Parks who is a major suspect in the kidnapping and murder of over eight individuals, the news reporter's voice was like a distant echo in his mind. The memory sent an instant dread down his entire body. Marcus ran at full blast, just wanting to catch up to him. He felt that if he could just follow the guy, see where he went, he might find information on where Sylvia might be. He hated the thought that this guy might actually have Sylvia in his custody. He finally got to the end of the alley, behind the buildings. There was a dark figure standing in the shadows. Unafraid Marcus shouted, "where is Sylvia? Tell me where she is." The man held up a gun which caused Marcus to freeze like a deer in headlights. His heart raced, attempting to escape its enclosure.

"Give me the files," the man demanded. "Give me the files," he spoke again. Marcus had the satchel in one hand. He's going to shoot me, Marcus thought. He could see the muscles in his biceps tense and the tendons in his forearm strengthened. The adrenaline running through Marcus caused him to quiver, though fear kept him frozen. Fight or flight. This is definitely a moment to take flight. Marcus dropped to a stoop and sprang to his left, hiding behind the large metal blue garbage dumpster. This man came after Karen, so he must know where Sylvia is, Marcus attempted to reassure himself. He knew the risk and he had to remind himself of the reward. He probably has her. She might even be close by. Marcus realized quickly that the dumpster was not a proper cover as the man could easily come around and shoot him there. Marcus quickly ran down another alley and tried taking cover in the shadows just as the man did. He looked back through the alley way to see if he was being pursued. There was no one. The shadows, he thought. He was hiding in the shadows. But would he really stand around expecting me to come after him. "Ahhh, you're over thinking this thing Marcus," he said to himself, attempting to will his body to move. Sylvia moved effortlessly under pressure and here he was frozen in fear. He remembered Mexico again.

He remembered what his father said, "Every step I take, I go higher up that mountain, I defeat my fear and my struggle against the things that scare me the most. Every step I make up that giant rock, I place fear in a headlock and take victory by the horn and make it mine." He was glad he heard those words. He thought nothing of them then, but those words were life to him now.

"I am afraid," he said to himself again. "I guess that makes me human." Marcus turned his sights to the shadows and ran head long to the spot where the man had been hiding. His eyes readjusted to the darkness, but it did not take long for him to realize he was gone. His heart sank and he felt even more ashamed of himself. His hesitation might have very well cost Sylvia her life. But then he could hear it. There were footsteps running away from him. He started after the sound, attempting to follow more cautiously this time. He came upon a cross section in the buildings. He looked in all three directions and saw no one. "Oh come on," he said under his breath. "If I were a killer or kidnapper where would I go. He looked down the alleyways again and saw that one led back to the crowds of Lincoln Ave. "Probably not there," he muttered under his breath. The other alleyway lead to the street, "not there either." He's after the files, Marcus thought. He wants to get at me and the best place to do that is in these alleys, he thought. "Alright then let's go," Marcus started down the third alley which led to a secluded parking lot. It would be easy for this man to hide behind the cars. Plus, the trees created many other shadows to obscure vision. Marcus certainly didn't want to think about how dangerous this was. He stood at the entrance of the parking lot and simply listened. He ignored the sounds of the street and the people walking up and down going to restaurants and making conversations. He ignored the music playing from the varied shops. He singled out the area in front of him. There was a large black SUV parked in the corner. Something told him that might be the vehicle he was looking for. "That was the SUV," Marcus said under his breath, remembering the 'Be On the Look Out' issued by the Police. "On the news," the thoughts came rushing back in. "He's a serial killer. I have to call the detective," Marcus pulled out his cell phone and called Detective Martinez and told him what happened and where he was.

"Mr Warren, please do not approach the vehicle," the detective warned him.

"Ok, you got it," Marcus lied. If there was a chance Sylvia was in that SUV he would have to check. After hanging up with detective Martinez, Marcus started towards the SUV. He tried looking through the windows but the tints were too dark to make out what was going on inside. Marcus got close and could hear someone inside, muffled as though they were gagged. "Sylvia is that you?" Marcus became excited and spoke louder than he intended. He tried opening the doors but they were locked. He tried to elbow the glass but the glass was somehow reinforced. He picked up a rock and tried smashing it into the passenger side window. The glass cracked but did not break all the way through. He kept hitting it but the glass was resilient. He could hear the sounds inside the SUV grow louder as though she was trying to scream at him from the other side. He looked at the darkly tinted windows, "I don't know how to get it," he said in frustration. He looked through the windscreen and could see Sylvia dark figure. She must be tied up in there, he thought. The shriek coming from the SUV sounded more and more alarming. James Parks was right behind him. For a split second Marcus saw his reflection in the dark of the tints and moved just in time avoiding the stab of a syringe.

James Parks' hand slammed against the glass of the SUV, bending the needle. He threw the syringe aside and quickly charged into Marcus with his shoulders. James, using his hands reached behind Marcus' knees, unearthed his legs, and threw him to the ground, which dislodged the satchel from Marcus' grasp. Marcus was no fighter, but he was no stranger to a spar. His physique, after all, came from his frequent trips to a mixed martial arts gym in downtown Atlanta. Marcus was on the ground the large SUV to one side and James Parks the serial killer to the other. Parks lifted, what seemed like a size 13 boot to stomp Marcus' face. Marcus lifted his hands in defense, caught James' boot and twisted his entire body throwing James into the SUV. James' other foot snagged and caused him to loose balance slamming face first into the side of the SUV. Marcus was right beneath him and James came falling like a large timber landing on top of Marcus. James quickly regained his equilibrium, much faster than Marcus expected. Marcus could hear the shrieks coming from the SUV again and could feel a sudden surge of energy. James was attempting to get back to his feet again. Marcus reached for James' leg again, pulling him to the ground again, this time putting him in a leg lock. Marcus could hear Sylvia screaming at the top of her lungs through the gag. He looked up at the SUV and could barely see her figure peering through the window. Marcus' eyes darted back to James who was writhing in pain at the prospect of having his knee dislocated. James seemed to have been reaching for something. It must be the gun, Marcus thought. It had fallen, probably dislodged when James fell. James' hand wrapped around the handle of the gun. Marcus quickly let go of his leg, hopped to his feet, but James was already taking aim. Marcus ran to the other side of the SUV escaping two shots aimed at his legs. James scampered to his feet and Marcus escaped into the shadows attempting to take cover. Marcus' heart fell when he heard the chirp of the alarm system on the SUV unlocking the door to the vehicle. The front passenger door opened and Marcus rushed towards the driver side. He reached for the handle and pulled but it was already locked. He slammed his fist against the window and screamed, more frustration overwhelming his reason, "give her back. Give her back you monster, give her back." Marcus' fist hit the glass over and over again, hoping that the stronghold would give way to his demand. Tears began to run down his face. James' appeared in the driver's side window smiling, blood ran down his face. He lifted into plain sight the satchel Marcus had been carrying. Marcus' anger renewed afresh. Though his fist was bloodied from the repeated blows, he insisted on breaking through. He had seen her. She had pressed her face against the rear driver side window. Marcus reached with his bloodied hands attempting to feel something, anything that connect him to her. The SUV's engine revved and pulled out in a hurry, all the while Marcus attempted to stop the nearly 6 ton battering ram. He tried even though he knew all his efforts would fail. "I'm not dead yet and I'm going to find you," he said out loud.

Gone

t h i r t y   o n e

"YOU'VE BEEN A terrible mother," the kidnapper shouted loud causing Sylvia's ears to ring. "You're a terrible mother and I hope you know that. That's why you're going to burn." He was breathing heavy. How did he know about Josh, she thought. Had he been watching her that long that he'd know all about her? But how did she not notice? Plus, she had only stolen the files a few days ago. Was Max planning to get rid of her all this time? She had so many question and no one to ask. "You and dad, are the worst parents ever. If ever there was a worst parents award you two would win year after year." Sylvia was thrown by his words. He sounded like a child locked in a 35 year old body. Is he mad, she questioned herself? Yes, he might actually be, she answered her own query. He didn't even seem upset about the tussle where Marcus had almost broken his leg. Who is this guy, Sylvia questioned herself but found no recollection to draw any conclusions. At first glance, Sylvia would have never thought someone like this would ever contain the heart to do what he's doing now. If he wasn't so disheveled from the fight, he could have easily competed with Simon in the looks department. "I hate you mother. You hear that. I hate you," James' rants continued. He would peer back at Sylvia every so often as he directed his words towards her. His heart has been battered, Sylvia thought. He hates his mother. Under slightly different circumstances could Josh turn out like this? Sylvia's heart broke as she heard the voice of her son through this obviously crazy maniac.

"I refuse to let you go without at least trying," she spoke softly to Josh and to her own determination. His shouts brought her back and she looked him in the eyes as he peered back at her. His eyes were wild and angry. The gag which was tied to the back of her head finally loosened and Sylvia was able to slip the bridle down from her mouth leaving it hanging around her neck. He picked up a match and swept it across the side of the box. Sylvia saw a small flame kindle and quickly start to burn. The kidnapper lit up a cigarette and started smoking but did not open the windows. Sylvia was somewhat used to others smoking indoors, an occupational hazard of a high end stripper. "I know baby," she said to him, loud enough for him to hear. There were nerves in her voice. He looked back at her. The look on his face was pure rage. She could hardly stop herself from screaming. "Baby, I know, I haven't been a good mother. I've been absolutely the worst. You were such a special boy and I feel like I lost the opportunity to tell you how much I love you," she said as she attempted to read his face. She searched for some sign, any sign. Would he soften, she questioned herself. It was a risk worth taking. She continued, "but I love you baby," speaking softly as though to a child; as thought to Josh. "I love you. I didn't see it before. I was blind. I know, it was all my fault and you were so strong. What your father," Sylvia paused for a moment, her words caught in her throat. "Your father and I did to you is unforgivable, but I want you to know that I love you baby," she said, with a picture of Josh in her mind. He meant so much to her. Sylvia felt the weight of her neglect of Josh. The gravity of it seemed so plain now. How many times had she broken his heart. How many birthdays did she forget to call or take him out for something as simple as an ice cream cone? How many of his games did she miss? How many years did she put the responsibility of his care onto someone else. Too many, far too many, Sylvia thought. He needs his mother. He needs me and no one else will do. Sylvia determined there and then that if she should make it through this she would fight for her son. She would give her life for her son. The kidnapper became silent as he drove on. "I'm going to take good care of you from now on okay Josh," Sylvia continued. But the frightening rage returned to his face.

"Josh?" James screamed at the top of his lungs. "You liar, my name is James. You were only pretending. You don't love me! You never loved me! Grandma, grandma was the only one who loved me. You don't even know what love is."

"James, please," Sylvia pleaded, attempting to recapture his attention.

"I'm going to let you burn like the others," James seethed, spit flying from his clenched teeth.

"James!" Sylvia shouted, the way her mother would shout when attempting to calm her past rages. "You listen to me right now boy. I am your mother and you will not speak to me in that manner." James pulled the car over to the side of the street. His body went ridged as though frozen in time. Then he started to shake his head violently. James pounded the staring wheel with both hands. And as if that wasn't enough, he started banging his head against it cutting his forehead and making it bleed. Sylvia somewhat recognized the behavior. She felt that way sometimes, locked away in her apartment. The times she felt like flying over the balcony. The times she felt like drinking herself into a mind numbing stupor. "But baby, I still love you?" His violent actions against himself continued. Sylvia raised her voice and shouted at the top of her lungs, "James, I still love you!" James froze again, his head solidly against the steering wheel.

"Love," his voice cracked as though about to cry. "What is love?" He reached into his arm rest and picked out what seemed like a cell phone. He pressed two buttons and the phone started to dial.

"I've got one for you," the kidnapper said over the phone.

"One? Did you get the red head," the voice over the phone questioned with much interest. Sylvia could hear the pip squeak male voice through the handset.

"No, but I was able to nab the files," the kidnapper said with calm resolve.

"I'll send a location to your phone. It will be the drop off spot. It will be near the harbor, come tonight," the voice over the phone instructed.

"And I'll be getting her back right," the kidnapper added.

"Parks, you don't tell me what to do. I am the employer. I'm the one with the money," the man over the phone snapped sharply. He looked back at her, the dread apparent on her face, she sat back attempting to obscure her fright in the darkness of the limo tinted SUV. He faced forward again. Maybe he didn't see me, she thought. Or maybe he gets off on people being afraid of him. Either way, she was still alive. Sylvia didn't want to think that her life might end tonight. She had staved off the thoughts but hope was quickly fading. Marcus had tried to rescue her. He fought so hard, Sylvia's heart swelled knowing that he had placed his life on the line for her. She felt unworthy of such a sacrifice and would have hated herself if he was ever hurt because of her. She remembered the look on his face. He was terrified of loosing her. He didn't want to loose me, she thought.

"I don't want to loose you either Marcus," she muttered to herself so Parks could not hear her. The SUV jerked as it exited the causeway and pulled into a shipping yard. There were large shipment containers stacked on each other all around. The SUV drove all the way to the dock where there was a large yacht stationed. It came to a halt and there stood a man at the top of a ramp which led to the entrance to the large yacht. He was dressed in what looked like a bathrobe and fuzzy slippers. There was a cigar hanging from his lips. At the bottom of the ramp were two muscle-bound men in black suits, white shirts, and black ties. Parks looked back at Sylvia and smiled. He reached into the center console again and pulled out a set of keys which he threw to the back seat within Sylvia's reach. Had what she said reached him, she questioned in her mind? Or was this part of the plan all along? He picked up the satchel and hopped out of the SUV. Sylvia loosed the handcuffs and the zip ties from around her legs. She peered through the front windshield. She could hear the muffled bass rumbling voices speaking outside.

"You're getting sloppy Parks," the man dressed in the robe said.

"Don't worry, everything is back to normal," Parks replied.

"Back to normal? I almost thought we'd have to cut you loose Parks. This isn't good for business Parks," the man replied.

"Did he really have to say his name that many times," Sylvia said to herself, knowing that her words would not carry.

"Cut me loose, I'm the best you've got. There is no one in your entire organization who's been around as long as I, who knows how to get things done like I do, whose gotten you the best girls for the best prices. Cut me loose," Parks' face contorted in rage.

"Where are the files," the man in the robe questioned. Parks held up the satchel, indicating the files where inside.

"Where is my money," Parks replied. The man in the robe gave a slight flick of his wrist, something barely noticeable. Both muscle bound guys pulled out their guns. Parks tried to pull his gun also, but they shot first. Sylvia's mouth hit the floor, but there was no sound for a full five seconds. Then suddenly an ear piercing scream pulsed from her which surprised even Sylvia herself. She cupped her mouth with her hands to stop herself.

"You've become far too reckless Parks and you're drawing too much attention to us, we can't have you around anymore Parks," the man in the robe stepped back into the entrance of the yacht. "Bring the girl." Parks stumbled to his knees. One of the men walked up to him and one shot him straight in the head. Parks slumped over. He was dead. The other man rounded the SUV. Sylvia quickly got to the drivers' and locked the doors. The key was still in Parks' pocket. She pressed the brake and pushed the button to start the car. She placed the car in reverse hoping she'd be able to escape their reach before the car shut off. But it wasn't far enough and this time they had the key. They unlocked the doors and Sylvia locked them again. They kept coming closer. Every time they would unlock the doors, Sylvia would lock it again. She looked around for something that could be used as a weapon. To her surprise, Parks had left his cell phone in the car. She wished she had found it sooner. She picked up the cell phone and dialed Marcus' number and hid the phone under the seat. She could hear when the line picked up, "I'm at the Miami Shipping Container Terminal." She repeated to herself a few times hoping that he was listening. The men approached and finally opened the door. As soon as they did she kicked landing a foot to one of the big men's chest. The blow didn't phase him much, he simply stepped back and lunged forward again, that time he grabbed her legs. Sylvia tried to kick free, but it was to no avail. She spotted a hidden pocket in the side of the driver's seat, tugged at it and a syringe flopped out. She grabbed it and stabbed one of the arms that held her legs. She pumped the clear contents of the syringe leaving it completely dry. The man grabbed the syringe and threw it aside and started after Sylvia again. This time his grip was not as tight and she was able to loose her leg and land a kick to the face. The man fell backwards to the ground, unable to shake the drowsy feeling, which Sylvia was sure, was now enveloping his brain and soon his entire body. The other man had gone around to the other side of the vehicle, opened the door and got Sylvia in a head lock and pulled her out of the SUV. "Let go of me. Let go of me," the man's grip was tight and fighting him was making her head hurt. She shoved her hand in his face, but he was unaffected by her efforts. He dragged her through the entrance of the yacht, kicking and screaming, "let go of me. Let go." When he finally did, she was facing a fat old man reclining on a sectional in the belly of the ship.

"She's a feisty one isn't she? She's a little old, but I'm sure that pretty mouth and sexy legs will fetch me top dollar," the old man spat as he spoke.

The man in the robe appeared by the old man's side, "the satchel that Parks brought us is empty." The old man's face went red with anger. "That file has a listing of all our names, if the FBI gets their hands on it," the old man said before getting cut off mid sentence.

"I know, I know, we'll get it," the man in the robe said.

"Set sail now. And take care of this. Even if you have to burn the whole thing down," the old man said. His voice was husky and with an accent, probably Italian, Sylvia was not sure. "Lock her in the cabin with the rest." The muscle bound man firmly held her arm and squeezed it. *That will certainly bruise later*, Sylvia thought. She knew that a bruise would be the least of her worries. It was too late to tell herself not to panic and it was hard keeping it subdued. The muscles in her face twitched and her stomach fell. She was losing the will to fight, not clear how she could do anything except be a prisoner. She stepped into a room where there were four other girls. Right away she could tell that they were all drugged. Tears welled up in her eyes and ran down her cheeks.

Lost

t h i r t y   t w o

MARCUS CALLED DETECTIVE Martinez and told her everything that had just happened; the meeting with Karen, his run in with James Parks, and the documents he retrieved. He's going to have the shock of his life when he realizes I took all the files from the satchel, Marcus thought smiling to himself. His triumph quickly faded when he realized that James could very well hurt Sylvia because of it. "Stupid, stupid," he muttered to himself.

"Marcus, thank you for calling. I think the best thing for you to do now is let us take care of it from here. I want you to stay where you are, I have a unit in the area who can come get those files out of your hands. I'm sure there are also a few people in the FBI who would really like to get their hands on a list like that," Detective Martinez explained and Marcus shook his head, actively listening to every word she said.

"Detective, hold on," Marcus stopped her when he paused. "I have another call coming in. I'm not sure of the number, but it might be important." Marcus placed the detective on hold and picked up the other line. "Hello, hello."

"I am in the Miami Shipping Container Terminal," Sylvia's muffled voice came over the line. "I am in the Miami Shipping Container Terminal." She sounded panicked and afraid, but she was no longer gagged. Maybe she got away, he thought.

"Sylvia is that you. Sylvia," Marcus said attempting to get some response to confirm what he was thinking. He just wanted this night of terror to end. He was tired of the back and forth and always feeling a step behind. He just wanted Sylvia back. The voice faded and there was what sounded like a scuffle. Marcus conferenced in Martinez to listen in on the call. "Detective, it's Sylvia. She said she was at the Miami Container Shipping Terminal." Marcus could hear Martinez's voice calling for all available units in the area to head to the Shipping Terminal.

"Alright Marcus, we're heading there now. Hey, stay put and I'll be in contact," Detective Martinez said before hanging up the phone. Marcus was adverse to sitting still. He pulled up a maps app on his phone and searched for the Miami Shipping Container Terminal. He was close, the traffic in this area was beginning to lighten up. I could get there before Martinez, he thought.

"I'm going," he said with a resolve that placed him into motion. Marcus hurried to the terminal and was surprised to see there were a few police cars there already. By the time he had arrived, Martinez was pulling up with him. Marcus remembered he had the files in his jacket pocket, he pulled them out and took pictures with his phone before tucking them in again. He walked up to Martinez, who gave a slight nob when he saw

Marcus. "I had to come, I was just right down the street. So don't give me that look."

"There is no sign of Sylvia. But the police did find a body," Martinez said. "Come with me." Marcus crossed the yellow tape and walked with Martinez to where the body was found. The man was shot in the head. He was on his knees and slumped over backwards.

"That's him. That's the guy I got in a fight with tonight. I think he's the same guy from the news," Marcus said.

"Yes, he's James Parks. His car is right over there," Martinez pointed out. "I believe the same people who shot James Parks over here, probably have Sylvia now. There doesn't seem to be anymore tracks leading away from here, but we're having the area searched just in case. We also found a prepaid cell phone inside the SUV with a single number in it. The contact says 'The Pirates.' Does that sound familiar. Does it sound like something he might have said?" Martinez asked.

"No," Marcus said and shook his head.

"Well, we're having the number on the phone tracked. Maybe we can find the cell tower it last pinged and narrow down their location from there. Mr Warren, I suggest you find a hotel and get some rest, it's been a long night. And it's almost 2 AM already," Martinez probably spotted the dazed look on his face and realized he couldn't handle anymore excitement tonight.

"Yeah, I'll take you up on that," Marcus said feeling numb. He turned and walked back to his car. The moment he sat down, his phone lit up and started to ring. It was Karen. "Hey," Marcus had little words.

"Hey Marcus, any luck," Karen asked, her concern sounded genuine, though Marcus was in no mood to answer any questions.

"I don't know Karen," he said in frustration. "I don't know where she is! She's gone." Marcus felt a mixture of fear and anger. He could not bare the thought of losing her like this. He wanted her safe in his arms. Nothing else really mattered. Her past, everything she'd been through, everything she'd done paled in comparison to loosing her for good. "I don't want to lose her Karen. But I feel like she's slipping right through my fingers," Marcus' voice cracked. He shook his head, fighting back the tears. This is not the time to mourn.

"Have you spoken to Max?" Karen asked. "I was speaking to the other girls and they haven't seen him."

"Yeah, he must know where she is or where these guys are taking her," Marcus said, finding a new light at the end of the tunnel.

"He's probably held up at his mansion in the Gables," Karen continued.

"Coral Gables? That's not far from here right?"

"I'll text you the address, okay. Keep me update please Marcus," Karen pleaded. Marcus hung up the line. There came a knock on the window of his car.

"Is everything alright," Detective Martinez asked.

"Yeah…just updating my friend on the night. Oh, I almost forgot, here you go," Marcus reached into his jacket pocket, retrieved the documents and handed them to Martinez.

"Hey, get some rest okay?" Martinez said.

"Okay," Marcus lied. He knew there was one more thing he had to do tonight. He rolled up his window, drove a few minutes down the street and parked. Marcus opened the photo app on his phone which contained photos of the files Sylvia risked her life getting. "These are profiles of the type of entertainment, Max's different clients like," Marcus spoke out loud. He was tired and was finding it more difficult keeping his thoughts straight. He came across a photo. It had no address, it just said the Jolly Roger. "That's got to be him. His operations are probably all on a boat or yacht. Who knows, the name is probably the Jolly Roger," Marcus concluded. "What kind of evil egotistical maniac would name his boat the Jolly Roger," Marcus said in disgust. It was mostly his tired, frustrated, brain talking. "The same type who would hunt women like pirates hunt for treasure. Women are objects for him. They don't have a voice or feelings. They don't deserve to be loved or protected. They are simply a means of fattening his Swiss Bank account," Marcus answered his own question.

෫ℭ

The text came in from Karen with the address to Max's house in Coral Gables. Marcus' GPS took him down Alhambra drive and rounding the bend he heard tires screeching and headlights seemed to have appeared out of no where. Marcus swerved to the right and narrowly missed an Audi sports car careening down the center of the street. It took the corner at a breakneck pace. Marcus cursed the reckless Florida drivers and continued on in the direction his GPS indicated. It was apparent from the moment he got to Max's house that something was not right. He stepped out of the car and could smell something burning. He saw lights flickering through the windows. His suspicions were confirmed when he saw one of the curtains go up in flames. Marcus ran up to the house, kicked the door and it flew open. It was already partially open. Marcus' thoughts ran back on the car he just saw. He looked around to see where the flames were concentrated. Max might be in that direction. There was one section of the house which had a more dense concentration of flames than the other. Marcus grabbed one of the curtains which was not on fire, dipped it in the large fish tank and wrapped it around himself. He ran in the direction of the flames and came upon a door which was also partially open. He kicked it fully open and walked into what looked like an office. Max was bleeding on the floor from a gunshot wound to his side and leg. He was completely surrounded by the flames. Marcus looked back and saw his path too was blocked in flames. There were windows in the office and one that led to the pool. Marcus was able to get to Max who was breathing shallow breaths. He placed the wet curtain around him and hoisted him over his shoulder. Marcus charged at the window and kicked. The window bent outward. He faced the windows and turned his back to the roaring flames. The freshly smoldering arm chair caught the back of his jacket. He charged at the window again and kicked. The frame of the window popped out and there was a ring of flames in the opening, reminding Marcus of the years gone when his Dad had taken him to the circus. This felt like a circus act, he thought. Marcus charged again and threw Max through the opening. Max clumsily fell through the ring of fire into a small garden, the soft earth and colorful flowers breaking his fall. Marcus hopped through the opening and suddenly felt the rushing heat on his back. He ran straight for the pool and fell in. Cold water saturated his entire body, but he could still feel the burn on his back. He had sustained at least second degree burns. He would have to get medical attention for that. Time was against him; Max was not in good shape. He climbed out of the pool and rushed over to him. He turned him flat on his back and slapped him in the face a few times. "Max, hey, Max," Marcus panted and slapped his face willing him to stay alive. "Max, where are they taking her. Where are they taking her? For once in your miserable life, do something good before you die. Where are they taking her?" Marcus' voice shouted. Marcus noticed his lips moving, but what he was saying was too low. The sound of his voice was drowned out by the crackling of the fire behind them. Marcus placed his ear close to his mouth and listened closely.

"They...going to sell...Thailand," Max could barely breathe the words audible enough for Marcus to hear.

"Thailand, really," Marcus sounded exasperated and not knowing how to feel about the situation Sylvia was now in. He was angry, he was sad, he just wanted to smash something, he wanted to breakdown and cry.

Redeemed

thirty three

THERE CAME A knock at his room door. *Who's that, I wasn't expecting anyone*, Chad thought as he got up to open the door. Behind it was his brother.

"Hey, are you busy?" Mike asked, still standing outside the door.

"No, come in," Chad replied. His brother had been missing in action, off studying whatever he'd been studying. Come to think of it, he didn't really know what his brother studied in school. Chad, in that short moment, started to feel the separation between he and his brother. Though they were family and there was no animosity between them, they were not real brothers. They had not been to each other what real brothers ought to be.

"We haven't had a chance to talk. And I know it's my fault and I'm sorry," Mike said, looking Chad directly in the eyes. Chad could tell he was being sincere. Mike had such sorrowful eyes where there once was lots of sparkle and life. "I want to change that. I think brothers should be there for each other, do you agree?"

"Yeah," Chad replied, nodding. His eyes found places around the room away from his brother.

"Hey," Mike said, as a bright idea seemed to have emerged. "Let's go out for breakfast. I know this really nice Cuban restaurant. There breakfast is amazing."

"Ah…" Chad couldn't quite find a nice way to say 'no, absolutely not.'

"I know you probably don't eat breakfast, but give it a try, you won't regret it," Mike rebutted before Chad could find an excuse not to go.

"I have a lot of," Chad attempted a semi-coherent, but totally untrue excuse.

"To do, right. You have a lot to do," Mike finished his sentence. "I do too, but see the thing is, you're my brother and this is important. So let's go. Plus, I'm going to pester you all morning if you don't get your butt out of this room and have breakfast with your kin," Mike said and smiled.

"Kin? Of all the words you could've used you decided on kin," Chad poked fun, smiled and nodded. "Alright! Alright! Let's go." Both boys got dressed and jumped into Mike's black Mustang. They talked and poked fun at each other, much like they use to do when they were kids. Chad was reminded of that childish innocence and selfless fun they use to have. He didn't realize how much he missed his brother. High School was a dividing factor in their relationship. When Mike had gone on to higher education, Chad was three years behind him in middle school. They were not only attending separate schools, but Mike was a huge social butterfly, always going out with friends and spending little of his time at home. Chad was too young to go out on his own, though no one would have stopped him if he did disappear for a few hours. Chad remembered spending his whole day on the couch watching TV with no one to disturb him, though he wanted to be disturbed. Loneliness did not feel like a bitter enough word to describe how he felt. Abandoned maybe? *Yes*, he thought, *I felt abandoned.* The thoughts made him more tight lipped and less playful. Mike cruised through the streets of the city to a restaurant at Bayfront Park. The restaurant over looked the bay of Miami. Birds fluttered all around and it was still pretty early, so there weren't many people out on this sunny Saturday morning.

"I heard what happened to your friend. You know, about his mom and everything," Mike said, cautiously tippy toeing around the subject.

"Yeah?" Chad questioned trying not to say too much, attempting to test the depth of his brother's knowledge so he wouldn't divulge too much information. Chad had secrets that he figured he would keep to his dying grave.

"Well I don't know much really. It came out that she was a stripper at the Royal Playhouse, something happened, and she was kidnapped," Mike explained.

"The owner of the club, her former employer died in a house fire, so a lot of the details are lost," Chad said, terminating any notion that he might know something; and though he did, he certainly didn't want to tell.

"How is he doing, Josh I mean?" Mike asked.

"He's doing fine," Chad lied, he had no idea how Josh was doing. He hadn't spoken to Josh in a while now. Even though Chad had been back playing basketball, he kept his distance. Chad would often skip going to the locker room and gym because he simply didn't want to see Josh and Brian. He and Luis had also kept their distance. Their relationship became very uncomfortable after the fight Luis had with Josh and Brian. Even though Chad understood what he was trying to do, he'd gone too far.

"I saw the way you looked at Josh," Luis had said, attempting to explain his actions. "And...I got a little jealous."

"A little jealous? You started a terrible rumor which wasn't even true," Chad was more upset than he'd ever remembered being.

"Chad, I didn't want to lose you," Luis had pleaded, with tears in his eyes. "I love you."

"Love? Don't throw around that word like you know what it means. Would love hurt the object of your affection. No, you were just looking out for yourself," Chad knew that his words had stung Luis. The bitterness in his voice was reinforced by the memory of his mother's parting. She did not love him, though she said she did. He knew that she would not call, though she said she would. Mom loved herself far more than she loved dad or Mike or me, Chad thought.

Mike sat down at the table, their food in hand, "oh man, you're going to love this."

"Have you spoken to mom?" Chad asked in an air of nonchalance. It was a lingering thought, revolving in his mind.

"No she hasn't call," Mike responded with a smile.

"Why are you smiling?" Chad asked, puzzled at his brother's expression.

"Oh am I. I don't know, I must be really happy about this food I guess," Mike said jokingly. Chad wasn't sure if he should believe his brother. He'd brought up a serious concern and Mike was more happy about the food than he was upset about the health of his family.

"Weren't you in the least curious? Didn't you want to find out why she left," Chad questioned in disbelief. He hadn't touched his food.

"I asked dad," Mike replied.

"Yeah and…," Chad drawled.

"And nothing. He didn't want to talk about it," Mike answered, sounding satisfied with his own answer.

"What…that's it! You asked dad, didn't get an answer and just gave up? Don't you care?" Chad questioned, his anger flared at his brother's indifference.

"I do care, but that doesn't mean I'm going to walk around with a sour puss look on my face all day," Mike replied with more of his smug I don't care attitude. Mike impaled another piece of egg with fried yucca and jammed it into his mouth. "You should try your food, especially the Chorizo, it is so good!"

"I can't believe you," Chad said quietly, his eyes flaring. "You just don't understand."

"Chad, I do understand. The thing is I've decided to forgive them and let it go," Mike replied as calmly as before, still smiling. "I'm just happy to be out with my only brother. Chad I see the look on your face when you come in. You're all dark and angry and brooding, but I've realized that life is too short for that. Over the past few months, I've learned so much about what it really means to love. I've learned what it really means to give yourself to the poor and the needy with no strings attached."

"Okay, now you're sounding like one of those religious people. Now you're sounding like one of those Christians," Chad replied with a snarl.

"Why, thank you! As a matter of fact, I am one of those people," Mike said jokingly. He took his last few bites, satisfied he leaned back in his chair. Chad saw Mike's empty plate and looked down at his full one. He'd tasted the sausage and it was good, but hadn't touch anything else. "I know these last few months have been rough for you and for me too. But you don't have to carry around this burden. Life will be full of disappointments. But there is a better way. You can be free of it. Let me tell you, being free is a lot better than trying to face this all on your own."

"Mike, I'm not buying into this religion thing," Chad replied.

"I'm not asking you to buy into anything. Chad, I just want you to think about it and if you want further help, give this number a call," Mike said and pulled a business card out of his pocket. "This is the church I attend. The number here is the cell phone of one of the pastors."

"Grief counselor," Chad read the title under the Pastor's name. "I don't need a…"

"There's one more thing I wanted to tell you. Actually it's the real reason I asked you to breakfast," Mike paused, making sure he had Chad's full attention. "Chad…" Mike paused again, "I only have three, maybe four months to live." There was a silence between the two. Time stopped. The birds halted in mid flight. Everything was so still. It was like the eye of a terrible storm. But soon the destruction would come roaring back.

"What!? Are you kidding, because that's not very funny," Chad said loudly, letting the reins go free, emotions flying everwhere. The other patrons of the restaurant looked around to see where that loud voice was coming from.

"Chad, I'm dying," Mike repeated calmly.

"But you look fine. You look completely healthy," Chad replied, his voice began to crack and tears broke the seams.

"Yeah, goes to show you can look perfectly fine on the outside, but be totally broken on the inside; pancreatic cancer. Unfortunately no cure, short of a miracle, which I'm still open to," Mike said and chuckled.

"But you're so young. You have your whole life ahead of you. You can't die now," Chad's words were swallowed up in tears.

"Mom and dad already know. We've been trying hard to find some kind of solution but nothing has worked. All the doctors and experts have given a negative report. Dad's been very upset, very angry. Probably why he went searching for comfort in the arms of other women. He's had a real hard time. Mom was trying to stay strong, but I told her I haven't been taking the pills. They really don't help. I've lost a lot of weight," Mike said. Chad had recognized his brother was getting a little thin, but he'd simply attributed it to dieting and maybe a little exercise. He even thought that the stress of school seemed like a more viable reason than cancer. Looking at him now, Chad didn't think his brother looked deathly hollow. He looked like a young and in shape version of his slightly overweight teenage brother Mike. "I just want you to know that I am at peace and I'm ready to die when the time comes. I didn't see it before, but I now see how much you struggle and I want you to live in this same light that I have found." Mike's eyes also filled up with tears. He stood up and both brothers hugged tightly, not wanting to let go.

ॐ

Chad stood before the door, hesitated then looked back to the black Mustang parked by the side of the street. His brother sat in the car, looking out the driver side window. One arm stuck out the window and urged Chad to knock. Chad gave the door a few nervous raps of his knuckles then stood back. There was a single car in the drive way, but he'd hoped that Josh was not home. An older man opened the door.

Bernie, if Chad remembered correctly. "Hello sir, is Josh home?"

"Yeah, give me a second," Bernie said, leaving the door open he called for Josh. Josh came to the door and the moment he spotted Chad, the look on his face turned to pure disdain.

Josh stepped outside the house and said, "yeah, what do you want?"

"Hey, I just wanted to say that I'm really sorry for everything that's happened. I know things haven't been so great between us lately, but I was hoping you'd forgive me," Chad said, his eyes burning a hole in the ground.

"You and your boyfriend were responsible for almost ruining the most amazing thing I've ever had," Josh allowed all his emotions to run free. "Please, get off my porch!"

"I know and I'm sorry," Chad looked up and his face was wet with tears. He turned and walked down the steps of the house and towards the car. Though it did not turn out the way he wanted, he felt better.

"Chad wait!" Josh started after him. "I'm sorry too. Things have been a little rough with my mom missing. Everything feels different now and to be honest, I don't know how to handle it."

"I know what you mean," Chad's tears ran freely. He tried to wipe his face in his shirt. "There's a lot of changes for me too. I'll tell you about it sometime."

"Thank you Chad," the boys shook hands then realized it was not sufficient and hugged. "Do you want to come inside."

"No, I'm spending the day with my big bro," Chad said and angled his head towards the Mustang.

"Oh, okay, cool, then I'll see you in school on Monday," Josh said.

"Yeah," Chad agreed. He rejoined his brother in the Mustang.

"How did it go," Mike asked.

"I'm sure you saw, stop acting dumb," Chad replied.

"Just wanted your take on the matter, alright let's go," Mike said, sounding adventurous.

"Where to next?" Chad questioned.

"Let's go see mom!"

Found

t h i r t y   f o u r

THE CLOUDS SHOT by his window. It was a clear day and flight conditions were good. It had been a full three months since Marcus had seen Sylvia. His mind was still on her. Her screams and shrieks haunted his dreams. He was only inches away from reaching her, touching her, saving her from the horrors of the last three months. He wasn't strong enough. He wasn't decisive enough. While the FBI did their investigation, Marcus hid himself in his work; the only thing that could take his mind off Sylvia. He took to the gym every chance he got. If there was ever a moment he had to fight to protect the ones he loved, he would be ready.

Gilford and Martha had been very supportive, checking in on numerous occasions. "Are there any new developments in the investigation?" Gilford asked with Martha attempting to listen in on the same phone. Their presence and support helped Marcus not to go over the edge. "Son keep your head up and never give up. A man who finds a good wife finds a good thing and receives favor from God," he would say. Marcus hung on those words. Her faults were indeed magnified by those who threw stones. Where were the men who found pleasure in the curves and crevices of her body. Where were the men who would pay hundreds and thousands to have her strip naked in front of them; to have their fantasies come to life. Would anyone look for her or was she replaced by some other fantasy with long legs and a big butt.

"She is worth finding," he said to himself as the ocean came and passed. "Sylvia, I told you that I wanted to love you and I want to love you more. I want you to know that I looked after your son as best I could. I checked up on him every chance I got. We've become very good friends Sylvia. He's a really good boy, extremely smart. Your friend Karen has not been the same. She's taken your loss very hard and has been fighting depression. I referred her to a friend of mine, a therapist, who's been working with her. She's doing a lot better. Turns out she had quite a bit of money stashed away. When Max died it forced her to act. She just needed a little push. Her safety net was gone and she opened a very nice hair salon. A few of the girls from the club work there now. Oh and I guess I forgot to mention, Max died. He was in the hospital for a while, but he had burns all over his body. Sylvia, things are a lot different than when you left. I'm a lot different too. I have to be honest. I thought about giving up. I figured there's no telling where you are now. So I went to the theater one night to get lost in someone else's story. It was a spur of the moment thing. In the foyer of the theater I saw this old man. He was hobbling along pushing his wife in a wheel chair. There was something beautiful about the sight. Not just their appearance, because really, the old man looked like a creaky old house. But the act caught my attention. Turns out he was going to the same show I was seeing: Wicked. Sylvia, the entire show passed and I couldn't get my eyes off the man and his wife. He was so careful with her. He straightened her hair, he fixed her dressed, and positioned her to get the best view of the stage. I had to talk to them after the show. I approached him, exchanging pleasantries and the like. I asked him how he enjoyed it and I was surprised to hear that he didn't actually like the show. Yet, he came every time the show was in town. I asked him why?"

"It's her favorite," the old man had replied as though that settled the matter.

"So I turned to ask the woman in the wheelchair," tears began to well up in Marcus' eyes. Marcus was thankful that his first class seat gave him enough space to have some level of privacy. "I was surprised to find the woman unresponsive. I waited a few moments but there was only a blank look on her face."

"She probably won't respond," the old man replied. "My wife has not responded for over 7 years now," he continued. "But I take good care of her. I give her baths, get her dressed, and take her to her favorite shows and to church on Sundays." The old man's voice cracked as a large smile lit up his face, "it has been my pleasure being her husband these many years and until death do us part, I will love her as best as I can."

"Sylvia, I was speechless and thought to myself that this must be what it means to have undying love. I want that. I want that so much. So I'm not giving up yet. I'm coming to get you. Sylvia, I'm coming to get you," Marcus said with conviction. He sent a message through the wind, hoping it would find it's way to her heart. The plane landed in Bangkok, Thailand. The city from the sky was beautiful. The lights reminded Marcus of Las Vegas. A driver waited outside the airport with a sign. He took him to a hotel in the center of town. There were three men and a woman seated inside. One of the men was obviously a tech, the other two carried guns on their sides, and the woman was a Thai translator. "Good evening," Marcus walked into the room solemnly. One person after the next stood up and greeted Marcus with a hand shake.

"Marcus, my name is agent McDonald. I'll update you on our progress so far. Over the last few days we've had a new development which is important for us to consider in this rescue effort. We could go today and literally bust Sylvia out of there. There is protection around her, but this is something we could do right now. But, while scouting yesterday, agent Lindsay here was able to pinpoint the location of a very powerful person. They are high up on the food chain and this is a rare opportunity for us. So unfortunately we won't be able to go for Sylvia right now," Agent McDonald paused, giving Marcus the opportunity to speak. Marcus could tell that everyone in the room was expecting him to go off.

"I don't care what it takes," Marcus spoke softly. "I do not want Sylvia staying in that place longer than she has to. So do what you have to do."

"If we go in right away and take Sylvia out, it will alert the higher ups and we might lose this huge opportunity," McDonald continued. People always seem to put you on the back burner Sylvia, Marcus thought.

"I'll be in my room," Marcus' room was next door to this one and without another word he left the room going to his own room to rest. About fifteen minutes passed and there came a knocking at the door. Marcus opened to the translator. She was clutching a laptop under her arm.

"Can I come in?" she asked. Marcus nodded. She sat at the desk, opened her laptop and pulled up a website, "this picture was posted on this backpage site about two weeks ago. Does this look like the woman you're searching for?" Marcus peered at the pictures which was posted below a title which read: Sexy Latina ready to please you.

Marcus breathed in deeply, "yeah that's her."

"I can take you to her," the translator said.

"Why," Marcus asked.

"I don't think what they are doing to you is right, so I want to help you. But I would suggest you make contact with her first and we can figure out a way to get her free," the translator said.

"Okay, thank you, I'll do it," Marcus replied gratefully.

℣

"I'm looking for a little American flavor," he said to his Thai translator.

"Ok, no problem," Jina said in a heavy Thai accent. "Bring out the girls." Seven girls came out and lined up Marcus took a look and non of them looked anything like Sylvia.

"No, there was one on your website. These girls are too young, I want someone a little more seasoned," Marcus said to his translator.

"These girls are young and tight, very nice body, satisfaction guaranteed," Jina replied. Marcus sighed attempting not to loose his patience.

"I want the girl I saw on your website, she is the only reason I'm here," Marcus said agitation boiling in his voice. His translator spoke, but she went on a bit longer than she should have. "What did you say?"

"I merely told her that you have specific taste in women and these won't do," Xin replied.

"I have girl in back, nothing but trouble since arrive," Jina said before flinging up her hand to the other girls and they all walked away. She signaled for another girl, whispered in her ear and the girl went off at once. "She will bring her. We will see if this the girl you look for." Twenty minutes passed and she was not out yet.

"What is going on? Why is it taking so long?" Marcus asked and the translator relayed the question.

"I told you, this girl trouble maker. She long ahhh," Jina broke off into Thai which the translator was able to finish what she was saying.

"She always fights to get ready, so she takes long," Xin said.

"Then I will go to her," Marcus said.

"Oh, yes, yes you go," Jina quick to have Marcus go in which would mean her making some money off her trouble girl. Marcus walked into a room with a small bed shrouded in a red sheer lace fabric. So this is what a cheap brothel looks like. There was a woman laying on the bed. Marcus sat on a chair in the corner of the room.

"Hello, don't be shy, you can come to the bed," the woman said.

"Sylvia," Marcus said as he heard a very familiar voice he'd been so longing to hear. "Sylvia, I've finally found you."

"Marcus," Sylvia sounded as though she questioned what her ears just heard. The woman quickly scurried off the bed, pushed the sheer fabric aside. She was wearing lace panties you might find at a cheesy sex store.

She saw Marcus and became instantly saddened. No, he thought. She was ashamed. He knew that she didn't want him to see her like this. She covered herself with her arms, sitting there on the side of the bed. He took off his jacket and wrapped it around her.

Her heart fluttered like a thousand little butteries in the bright of spring. "My love," she whispered. She looked in his eyes and became lost in his eternity. No words came, but she knew the ocean of love he had for her. She wrapped her arms around him. He could not escape her grasp and he didn't want to. Tears were running down her face and her ears were pressed against his chest. His warmth was radiating and his heart was racing. Without a thought or effort, without a trace, all her pain was washed away. All the people who used her, in an instant, did not matter. The bitterness of being betrayed and sold off suddenly became sweet when she accepted his love. Who would have thought to rescue a whore. A woman of ill repute. Who would have thought to listen to the heart cry and prayers of a woman broken in spirit. His love was deep. It went beyond how she looked and what she'd been through.

There was no innocence in her. Her virginity was taken long ago. She was unwanted. But when she cried out for someone to love her, he answered her call and came running. Marcus took her in his arms and carried her out of the room. Jina came running over, "what you doing. You cannot take her." The translator was near and came over.

"This woman does not belong to you. She is a US citizen and you cannot keep her enslaved here," Marcus said, the translator translated.

"You not in America. You not take her," she repeated.

"How much," Marcus almost spat at her. "How much do you want for her."

"3 million baht," Jina replied. Marcus looked to his translator who was already calculating the exchange.

"She's asking almost a 100k US dollars," Xin clarified. Marcus placed Sylvia on one of the chairs. Picked out his cell phone and called his European banker.

"Account number?" Marcus demanded. Jina was surprised that he would actually agree to such a price. She spoke the number to Xin who wrote it down and handed it to Marcus. Marcus relayed the number to his banker, "it's done. And if I ever so much as smell your presence anywhere near her, I will burn this place down." The eyes of the translator brightened and she cautiously spoke the words Marcus instructed her to. He picked up Sylvia and walked out of Bangkok Beauties said, "now you belong to me and no one else."

Happy Birthday

t h i r t y   f i v e

"THE LOCAL MEDIA got a hold of the story: Woman Rescued by Boyfriend from Clutches of Sex Trafficking. Sylvia was approached by book publishers and Hollywood execs wanting to do a movie adaptation of her story. Captive: Saved by Love. I was just glad she made it home. I thought I'd lost her forever. After three months, most had given up hope. Even Gilford and Martha, Marcus' mom and dad, flew all the way from Sonoma Valley to see us and offer their support. Gilford hadn't given up though. He said that even if she did pass away, the woman he met was a fighter. She would have given them a run for their money all the way to the end. She had the courage to face her fears and prevail. But to be honest, I did not see that in my mom. I did not see the fighter, the delicate flower, and the woman she is. For many years, I saw the disappointment and the reason for my grief. But now, I am proud to call her my mother." Josh dropped the piece of paper from his face and went back to his seat. The class broke out in a wild applause.

"Thank you Mr Bradley for that amazing piece. I do have to say in addition that sex trafficking is by and large one of the biggest epidemics of our time. Our society seems to always find ways to hurt each other. Will you make difference? I would have never thought that one of my students would be so closely affected by sex trafficking, but here it is, right at our doorstep. Don't you ever feel like there is nothing you can do. If you remain silent, then this epidemic will certain consume us all. Well...I believe Mr Bradley was the last presentation today. So please have a wonderful weekend and see you next week," Ms Anders closed the text book on her desk marking the end of the class period.

What seemed like a routine day at school turned into many congratulatory wishes on getting his mother back and happy birthdays all in one. Josh had taken some time off school to be with his mother who was in rehab. He would be heading there after school. Josh thought it best to celebrate his birthday being with his mother. Having her back meant more than anything else in the world. There were times when he thought that she was gone for good. Having her back was as if she'd been resurrected from the dead.

Rena was amazing during this hard time of his life. She knew just what to say and when to say it. Losing Sylvia brought back horrible memories for Rena and there were moments where they both cried. They both mourned and she was equally as happy that Josh got a second chance with his mom. Rena was so happy when she heard of Sylvia's return. There were more tears and this time those tears were mixed with laughing and joy. Josh couldn't imagine making it through this dark night without Rena.

Marcus picked him up today. "Grandma wants to ride with us to see your mother," Marcus explained. "So I'm just going to pull by to pick her, then we can go see Mom." Marcus pulled up in front of grandma Sophia's house honked the horn waited a few minutes, but she didn't come out. "Hey, go see what's keeping her."

"Okay!" Josh hopped out the car and turned the keys to the front door of the house, opened and...

"Surprise!" A room of friends and family shouted as Josh walked into grandma Sophie's home. Of course, this had to be Marcus' doing. He doesn't know that I hate surprises, Josh thought. He hated it for this exact reason: He was actually surprised. So much so, that his mouth, lurched open like a fly trap awaiting its next victim, would only issue a few inaudible noises. "Ah, ah, ah..," Josh said, standing their speechless. He stood there looking like a complete moron; and Rena with an adorable smile on her face.

"Are you serious," Josh headed towards her. "You spent the whole day with me and you couldn't even give me a clue of what was going down? I am very disappointed Rena!" Josh spouted, attempting to sound upset.

"Happy Birthday Josh," Sylvia was seated in the couch which was somewhat centered in the crowd.

"Mom, you're out of the hospital," Josh said in excitement. Sylvia had been kept drugged to remain docile and when she got home, she wanted to fight. She'd said it herself, she hated the feeling of being controlled by her desires. So instead of merely giving in to the addiction forced on her, she chose to fight it tooth and nail.

"I'll be heading back but I couldn't miss your birthday," Sylvia smiled as Josh came close to her, threw his arms around her and kissed her on the cheek.

"You," he turned his sights to Marcus who came through the door with a goofy smile on his face. "I know this is all you. I know this is all you. I hate surprises and still yet…thank you for everything." Josh hugged him tightly.

"Hey, happy birthday bro," Brian and Chad chimed in together. They both came over and shook Josh's hand giving him a more manly version of the hug he gave Marcus. "I know you dead beats are just here because of the food."

"Hell yeah," they said together as though it was all rehearsed. Rena came after, as beautiful as ever.

"Happy Birthday to you," she sang.

"I didn't know you could sing," Josh said surprised and amused. They hugged and Rena kissed him lightly on the lips. His head swooned. Brian and Chad whooped and hollered. "I hate you guys," Josh looked back at them.

Kling…kling…kling…kling…kling Marcus stood by the kitchen with a champagne glass in hand. "Can I have everyone's attention please," he shouted. The voices calmed and all eyes were on him. He walked over to Sylvia, bent down on one knee, "losing you for those three months has made me realize that I don't want to live the rest of my life without you. I've come to love you deeply and I want to love you more. It would so honor me if you would be mine forever. Sylvia will you marry me." Marcus pulled out a black velvet box from the inside of his leather jacket. He opened it and inside was a beast of a ring. Rena's and Sophia's eyes gleamed as they saw the mammoth of a diamond. It was elegant and glistened as the evening light shined on it. Josh knew for certain that Sylvia didn't even see the ring, because her head was nodding even before he opened the box.

She launched out of the couch, threw her arms around his neck, and shouted "yes, yes, I will." She was laughing and crying all at the same time. The entire room broke out in a bigger and louder applause.

Josh surveyed room and thought, life until now was not easy and he'd become accustomed to the pain. He had no perspective on what it meant to love and be loved. His eyes drifted towards Rena. Loving her, protecting her, drying her tears, had brought him more satisfaction than what he'd felt before. He did not consider himself where she was concerned. He knew that any selfishness might starve this delicate orchid of what she really needs. So he gave to her and the more he gave, the deeper he felt. His love for her was deeper than the oceans.

Seeing the joy of Sylvia and Marcus he thought, the love of his mother and a soon to be father brought completeness to my life. It was a completeness he never thought he needed. Josh felt as though he'd been holding his breath and was now breathing for the first time. There was nothing like the selfless love of his mother and father.

Josh knew that while he lived, there would be more challenges. There would be more reasons to mourn and cry. But he knew that he was stronger now, because love had made him stronger than he'd ever been.

Dear Diary

t h i r t y   s i x

Dear Diary

*D*IARY *DOESN'T REALLY make a very good name. I don't really want to talk to Diary. I'm better off all it Karen or something. But I already have Karen,* Sylvia thought as she sat by herself in one of Sophia's spare rooms. She mulled over a pretty pink book with purple and gold bows strung with lace. The book seemed more appropriate for a teenage girl than a grown woman, but Marcus had gotten it for her and so she would show her gratitude by actually writing something in it. Sylvia had been seeing a psychologist who'd recommended a diary.

"Whenever you're feeling overwhelmed by the memories of your past, write it down," Dr Nancy Ekland had said.

"What good would that do," Sylvia had asked. Not in rebellion, but curious as to the reason behind the method.

"Writing it down will hopefully help you accept that these things happened to you. And what happened to you was terrible. There's no sense living in denial or an illusion. You were kidnapped. You were enslaved. You were sexually abused. On the other hand, realize that what was done to you and the things you were forced to do, does not have to define who you are. Writing it down will help to reduce the power and enormity those events have in your mind. It is unfortunate that the atrocities of the past few months is now apart of you. It is now part of your history and has left a mark on you. But it doesn't have to have power over you." Dr Ekland smiled a big beautiful smile. "Sylvia, you have something a lot of women only dream about. You have someone who loves you." Sylvia's eyes had brimmed with tears, just as they did at the memory of this consultation. "True and real love heals many pains and many hurts. Allow yourself to love as you are loved."

"Thank you doctor," was all Sylvia could reply without bursting.

Sylvia marked a line through the words 'Dear Diary.' She sat and thought for a moment. She could hear Bernie, Sophia, and Karen bustling through the living room. She thought of Josh and Marcus. She was not able to find who his father was and come to think of it she didn't really have a very good relationship with her own father either. On a day like today, she thought, she would want her father by her side; arm in arm. And so she began writing again:

Hi Papa,

It's me, Sylvia. I know we haven't spoken for a while and I'm not even sure you know my name. But here I am, your daughter. Dr Ekland told me that if I'm feeling overwhelmed I should write it down. Well, I'm feeling a little

overwhelmed today. Not overwhelmed with sadness or grief. And even though I

could be depressed, I'm not. I am overwhelmed with joy Papa. I am truly

overwhelmed with joy. Papa, if you can hear me, I want you to know that I am

loved. I know I don't deserve to be loved. I've made mistakes which most people

end up paying a dear price for. But I am so blessed that I should be loved.

    The thing is papa, I was lost. My world came tumbling down all around

me. I ended up in a place where I couldn't find myself. I was kidnapped and sold

like a piece meat or someone's merchandise. And while in that place, I was forced

to give myself to numerous men. It wasn't long before I started to believe that I

was no longer worthy of love. I started to believe that I was no longer worthy of

care or protection or worthy of life. Papa I felt so useless. And what good would it

do for someone so useless to go on living? Who would miss me? So I decided that

this world would be better without me. I had decided that today, I would break

the glass vase and cut my wrist. I would hide in the corner of the room so no one

would find me until it was too late. But then he walked in. Marcus walked in.

Papa, he saved me from myself.

Tears began to wet the page. "Girl you in there," Karen's voice boomed through the room door.

"Yeah," Sylvia said, wiping the tears from her eyes.

"Hurry up, we got to get going soon," Karen replied. What a slave driver, Sylvia thought.

"Alright, I'm almost done," Sylvia assured her.

So you see Papa why I'm overwhelmed. I hated myself but he loved me. I despised what I'd become but he wanted me. I thought money was all I ever needed, but I realize now that money can go up in flames but love lasts forever.

It's my wedding day today Papa, so I have to call it quits; or else the fiery red head outside might blast me into oblivion. The dress is beautiful and I know you would like it. Anyway, I have to go, but don't you worry, when my heart becomes overwhelmed again you'll hear about it; which I imagine might be really soon.

ttyl :) Sylvia G.

"Alright, I'm here," Sylvia said exiting the room. Karen came rushing over.

"The limo is waiting outside, let's get going," Karen handily picked up the train to Sylvia's dress and they hurried to the Rolls Royce parked in front Sophia's house. "Let's not keep Babyface waiting." Sylvia stopped suddenly, Karen almost ramming into her. "Girl, what the hell!"

"I just remember something!"

"Oh no, what?" Karen exclaimed.

"I love you Karen. I really do," Sylvia said softly.

"What!?" Karen confused at Sylvia's sudden confession.

"I love you very much. Marcus told me what you did to help and there are no words to…" Sylvia's words failed.

"You need to stop, makeup artists are not cheap and we can't have your makeup running before first drinks at the reception," Karen said, attempting to keep a serious demeanor. She stood and both girls embraced. "Okay, let's Go! Go! Go!"

"Alright…" Sylvia said, giddy with excitement.

The white Rolls Royce stopped, its chrome glistening in the bright Florida sunshine. Sylvia couldn't have asked for better weather. It was a cool fall evening. The driver, very cordially opened the door where a hand reached down to take hers. It was Joshua. *He looked so handsome*, Sylvia thought. He was dressed in a standard black tuxedo with a bow tie. *A bow tie, really Marcus, a bow tie?* As she stepped out of the car, her eyes met his shoes, which were brand new Chuck Taylor All Star Black Leather Converse. *Nice touch, alright you've redeemed yourself Marcus.* She allowed Josh to help her out of the car. Their arms interlocked and beautiful music played from the live band. Sylvia basked in the beauty of every note played by the pianist. An accompaniment of double bass, acoustic guitar, and the light beat of a drum changed the entire atmosphere. Sylvia could not remember fantasizing about the day she would be married and what that would look like. The planning of this wedding was done mostly by Sophia. Sylvia felt utterly unworthy to be celebrated with such beauty. The wedding was held in an outdoor garden. In the center was a beautiful white gazebo where Marcus stood with the minister, bridesmaids and groomsmen. The outer perimeter of the garden was flanked by thick palm fronds blocking the outside world and locking Sylvia and her guests in a world of elegance. The greens of the garden were complimented by white roses, white lilies, white orchids and white petunias. White wisteria's were hung from a very large and very old oak tree. The wisteria's drenched the entire garden in an intoxicating fragrance.

All their guests, which for Sylvia were mostly strippers she new from the Royal Playhouse, looked back from their seats. She took in their smiling faces and almost lost her nerves. That feeling of worthlessness was still there; still clawing at her insides. It still tried to gain some kind of foot hold. But Josh stood next to her. He started to walk, urging her forward. *It's not too late, you could turn back now*, another other voice surfaced in Sylvia's mind. If he ever finds out about all you've done he'll leave you. Joshua held her and he kept walking, so she kept walking. *Does he really love you?* All men are the same. They cannot be trusted. They were half way to the gazebo now. Marcus' features became more clear from beneath the veil. Seated on the front row was Gilford and Martha, Marcus' parents. Next to them was Sophia who beamed. She clutched a handkerchief which she used to dab her eyes. Sylvia's feet became more hesitant with each step. She was almost at the front row and she felt Josh pull against her rigid body. She froze and their eyes met. But there came another hand, it was Gilford. Sylvia was breathing hard, but she locked arms with the man who seemed to be always smiling. He urged her on. A still small voice spoke in her. The sound made it's way through the clamor and confusion of the fear which tried to dominate her. The small voice resounded, "you are surrounded by good men who will bear witness this day to your union with Marcus. Allow their love for you to guard over the union you'll have with Marcus. These men, Joshua and Gilford, will not allow your heart to break like days before. If you fall, they will pick you up."

Gilford released her and Marcus took his place. They stood before the minister. She remembered the look on Marcus' face the first time she saw him at the club. She remembered when he stood up to his best friend for her, just because she stood up for someone else. She remembered the look on his face when she saw him in that bedroom in Thailand. She remembered when he paid a price no one else would've paid. She was not worthless. She was loved.

Their wedding was by far the best day of Sylvia's life. After the ceremony, they all danced well into the evening. After the sunset, fireworks display stunned all the guests. Sylvia and Marcus would spend the night at the Mandarin Oriental Hotel on Miami Beach before flying out to Italy in the morning. "I want you now," Sylvia whispered in Marcus' ear. His face brightened. The two bid their family and friends goodbye and they hurried to the Rolls Royce who awaited their instructions. Marcus had the keys to the room and wasted no time in the lobby. The doors to the elevator opened on the 10th floor and an elderly couple were greeted by the newly weds locked in passionate embrace and kissing. They allowed the elevator to pass. The newly weds got to the room and Marcus lifted his bride and carried her across the threshold.

Now that they were alone, he would take his time. There was no rush. There was no other place for them to be in this moment than to be with each other. His hands tenderly peeled away the layers of her ceremonial garment. The touch of their skin communicated far deeper than words could explain. He teased her with his tongue until she begged for him. He gave himself to her. The rush of all that he was filled her entire being. Being with him was far different than what she'd experienced. It was as if she was having sex for the first time. He was not imposing. He did not try to take from her. He gave to her, catering to her every desire. Every thrust was for her pleasure; every kiss for her delight. She in turn gave to him. All that she was was for him to enjoy. Their bodies became one, both giving and receiving in perfect unity.

Italy was beautiful. At least the little they saw from the window of their quaint master suite. They did not venture out much, but spent more and more time with each other. Sylvia was probably more to blame. "She is like a ravenous sex starved beast," Marcus joked. Sylvia had never been this intimate with anyone before. Her memory of sex paled in comparison to the intimacy she shared with Marcus. Intimacy, a culmination of deep love and passionate sex. She wrote this as another overwhelming experience in her letters to Papa.

Acknowledgement

This book was inspired by a very interesting conversation between a young woman who stripped for a living and myself. I worked at a hotel and she came in late one night and requested a room. She'd then asked me the question, "do you think your mother would like me?" In all my life, I'd never heard a pickup line like this. I could smell the liquor on her breath, so I didn't take her seriously. I decided to play the little game, knowing that there was another guy waiting out in the car for her.

"I'm sure you're a nice person on the inside," I said. It was pretty obvious from the way she was dressed that no proud mother would ever want a woman like this on their son's arm.

But then she shocked me with her next statement, "I just want somebody to love me." Those words left me speechless. I've never encountered such blatant vulnerability even among friends. It has now been eight years later and I still remember her words. That woman and others like her, was the real reason I wrote this book. I admit that this genre of writing was not my first choice, but for my first published novel I thought it essential to writer a story based on this woman's desire to be loved.

I would also like to thank my most amazing wife for helping stay on target. When my creativity threatened to change the entire story and write to satisfy the market, she pulled me back in line, helping me focus on the vision. She has also listened to my constant bickering and was the first to read my work, chapter by chapter with constructive critiques and detailed corrections. I am a better write because of you.

Last but not least, thank you to my awesome editor Fran Lebowitz. Though she has many years of experience working with big name authors, she took the time to read my work, helped me cut the fat, and now I have a lean and sexy piece novel for all to read.

Thank you for reading, I hope this work was as pleasurable to read as it was to write. You can find more information on upcoming books on my website: anovelescape.com

www.ingramcontent.com/pod-product-compliance
Lightning Source LLC
Chambersburg PA
CBHW030016180626
46810CB00001B/72